Giselle V. Steele

RJ BLACKSTONE

New York   Blackstone   London

Rivers Never Fill The Sea

A NOVEL

RJ BLACKSTONE LTD
A Division of S&W Publishing
New York, NY 10020

Copyright ©2018 by Giselle V. Steele
Poem: *Days Gone By,* by Giselle V. Steele copyright ©2008 by Giselle V. Steele

FIRST EDITION RJ Blackstone January 2018

RJ Blackstone Ltd and design are trademarks of S&W Publishing used under license by the publisher of this book.

DESIGNED BY LIAM PRESCOTT

Manufactured in the United States of America

Library of Congress Cataloging-In-Publication Data is on file with the Library of Congress.

ISBN: 0-9769949-9-2
ISBN: 0-9769949-8-4 (ebook)

For my family, friends, and readers who have joined me on this complex maze called life, where there is only one entrance and one exit. Remember, part of the fun is solving the puzzle! Are we having fun yet?

Gratitude goes especially to my sister and friend, Joanne. You have always been supportive of my work and my cynical jokes, and you're a die-hard romantic! Well, you asked for it, so here it is.

Special dedication goes to my son, Damian, who shares my love of creating worlds.

What does a person gain from all his hard work
at which he toils under the sun?
A generation is going, and a generation is coming,
but the earth remains forever.
The sun rises, and the sun sets;
Then it hurries back to the place where it rises again.
The wind goes south and circles around to the north;
Round and round it continuously circles;
The wind keeps making its rounds.
All the streams flow into the sea,
yet the sea is not full.
To the place from which the streams flow,
there they return so as to flow again...
...I saw all the works that were done under the sun,
And look! Everything was futile, a chasing after the wind.

-Book of Ecclesiastes

"Some lives are not lived, they are endured."

-Giselle V. Steele

CHAPTER 1
WOODROSE BY THE SEA

A town takes a long, drawn-out breath when it is first born. It bristles, and yawns, stretches, and glows as it develops over time. Each passing era buries its secrets deep in its furrows and locks its mysteries within its boundaries. The land bears the scars of wounds of time past and its people. In the late 1800s, the coastal town of Woodrose was not yet born.

It was uninhabited for the most part, at least by humans. Day after day, the sea lay profoundly calm and dark-green. The abysmal waters clutched within its depths innumerable fish and the magnificent marine monsters that lurked in the coolness of its caverns.

There were times when the roar of the ocean grew intense. The rain fell sideways like long silver thorns pushed by the wind. The vast sea would swell and become agitated, angrily flinging its waves up and then plunging them down forcefully into its depths.

Then, after rivaling a Beethoven concerto in intensity, a quiet stillness swept over the hills. The sun was done burnishing the shore and retreated into the sea with its face flushed in a crimson glow. From among the rocky tidal areas, spotted sandpipers emerged, pecking at oysters, mussels, and limpets from the rocks.

Once again, the soft wind of the morning murmured, and the golden evenings buzzed with life flitting among the coastal sage scrubs that covered the small sand hills and serpentine slopes. Vibrant blooms of lilac, soft pinks, and orange appeared as sprinklings along the landscape.

It's a curious thing about territory and land, but it seems to follow the same pattern time and again. The first pioneers of a town are the first to leave. Being quickly replaced once the harshness of the virgin soil has been smoothed over. By businessmen, doctors, and lawyers who come in to assist with the further development of it.

One such capitalist was Mike Mason, a rich and smart land developer. Mike and his wife, Helena, both emanated from an affluent background of English and Scottish descent. They had only one child, and they named her Katherine, though she opted early on for the more casual name of Kate.

It was around 1942 when the Mason's moved into the town of Woodrose. The city grew in population almost overnight, and it came to be the town that the family called their home, and in time, it came to be the town the Masons owned.

When Kate was small, the sandy hills of Woodrose were dotted with just a few little wooden summer cottages. Mike Mason felt uneasy in what he considered primitive surroundings, and so did his wife. Kate, however, was not so quick to assess the area and deem it unfit. She felt happy and at home.

During the early years of the coastal town, it experienced a slow-growing industrial period. Water was channeled in from wells, and service was left to the town's youths. Two of the youngsters, Flynn and Gavyn Brennan, eagerly delivered water by the bucket to customers for pocket money. They certainly didn't become rich, but at twelve and eleven years old respectively, they didn't need to.

They did, however, grow into bona fide residents of the community. When an approaching storm was set to move through the town, they helped by planting shrubbery to hold down blowing sand. The boys quickly became used to the chump change. After noticing an increase in earnings with each job, they took on the work of helping in any way they could, assisting in paving the principal streets, and constructing a city pier.

On December 16, 1943, the wooden pier was completed, and the whole town celebrated with a grand display of fireworks that sparkled luminously across the black canvas of the night sky and shimmered on the darkened ocean. At around 7:00 p.m., there was the ceremonial cutting of a four-foot tiered cake on the recently constructed boardwalk by the staff at the newly opened Makayla's Bakery.

Everyone was there: the Woodrose police department, local fishermen, and dockworkers, the operators of the Woodrose Trolley, Maximo's Pyrotechnics Company, and all of the local families, rich and poor.

Then, real progress came barreling down the tracks in 1944 when cast-iron, ornamental electric lights were installed along the ocean strand, and a streamlined diesel railway station popped up. But the progress came with a price, and the sleepy town of Woodrose would never be the same again.

CHAPTER 2
THE STRONGBOX

BLACKWATER CANYON: 1979

Those time-weathered moments of Woodrose perpetually played in Kate's mind like a movie projected onto her brain. Not all of the memories were heartwarmingly good, though. And at first, she desperately sought a way to keep the reel-to-reel from running those that she found were too fresh and painful to relive.

Eventually, she did find a way; she stored them in a strongbox and kept them securely locked inside her mind. There they would be safely put away, but never forgotten, ready for the day she might suddenly feel a longing to view them.

It was late on a Friday when the sun had filtered its last rays of gold in through the clouds, that the time had come unexpectedly. Earlier that day, Kate had received a handful of mail which she had put away until evening. Then she remembered them on the kitchen table and began to go through them one by one.

Within the stack of letters, there was an envelope bearing the name of someone whose memory she had put away in the strongbox long ago. Kate lifted the envelope slowly from the pile of letters and analyzed the outside, then quickly opened it and read its contents. The handwriting she recognized, but the request expressed within the letter hit like a ton of bricks.

That day, after reading the note, Kate found the courage, and for the first time, the need to view the movie of memories conserved in her mind. She began to relive the romance and the tragedies of life in her coastal town long ago.

The recollections were much fresher than she had anticipated, and they streamed into her mind as if it all had just happened. But the hurt from the memories streamed in just as quickly, and she felt the familiar pain in her throat once again.

She peered out at the large glowing moon from her bedroom window, and the tears began collecting. Kate thought to herself, this night was going to bring something different, and she could feel a change was about to happen. The wind, the mist, and the night all spoke to her with nebulous words as she watched the billows of dark gray clouds roaming in search of star-filled skies as they intermittently shrouded the moon's light.

Inside, nightfall had created long shadows that gloomed upwards from the corners of the small room. The light grew fainter with each inch of the wall it would scale up. The bed and nightstand struggled to keep their presence, but as the darkness grew, they began to lose their distinction to gray. The room, along with Kate, was swallowed up by the blackness.

The pale light of the moon broke through the shadows on the window and made her hands appear luminous as Kate made an effort at opening it. The skin on the back of her hands resembled porcelain with its white vitrified translucency, and the fingers were slender and long.

Kate had just turned fifty years old, but she appeared older in her frailty. Thin veins peeked out from beneath a veil of skin as she struggled to loosen the window, and it suddenly became unstuck as she pulled it upwards. A radiant streak of platinum light streamed in, and a wisp of wet night air blew back the sheer white curtains.

A strong smell of dried roses clung to the air of the room. Kate had gathered about a dozen red ones from her garden weeks ago as she did every spring, but unlike the other times, this time, she would not tend to snipping the rotting leaves and changing the water in the vase.

A cream-colored cat named Ella was curled in the corner of the living room by the stone fireplace, indifferent to the events unfolding around her but visibly jittery at the impending weather change. Kate kept an eye on her cat. She knew she would be uneasy with the flashes of light and crackle of thunder in the skies.

Ella always appeared to be dressed for an elegant masquerade ball. Her pale luxurious fur had chic black accents on her paws and the end of her tail, and a black mask around her tanzanite-blue eyes that twinkled cleverly. Kate had always loved cats, particularly Siamese ones. She thought of them as mysterious and mystifying, and as a little girl, she was sure they were. There were ancient sailor stories that claimed cats caused storms through magic stored in their tails. She was inclined to believe that the yarns might be true, so whenever a storm was near, she would hide under her bed with her cat and stroke its fur, hoping it would calm the rainstorm.

One day, when she was around ten years old, the winter season came bristling in with heavy wind and rain. Kate attentively watched the odd ways of her Siamese cat while in her bedroom. It was at this time that she decided there was no magic collected in feline tails. Her cat was just…Siamese. Later on, in the years as an adult, she read how cats were able to perceive shifts in barometric pressure before a storm. That made the whole peculiar thing even more interesting.

Kate peered out of the window after the first clap of thunder threatened the peaceful night sky. The paleness of her face was highlighted by moonlit shadows, and the finely formed features were accentuated with a frost of light on her cheekbones, eyelids, and lips.

She glanced back at her cat. The thought of leaving Ella brought a momentary pain deep inside her stomach. Her cat was much more delicate and sensitive to things around her than her dog, Bear. Bear hadn't even looked back when he was dropped off at her mother's earlier that day. He didn't appear to mind at all. His motto seemed to be, just feed me, and we'll get along just fine.

But Ella was more complicated than that. In truth, she was a lot like Kate. The sharp pain of absence was familiar to Kate; she had felt it many years ago, albeit much stronger.

"You'll be staying here, Ella. You'll be okay, I promise," she said, gently smoothing back her fur.

Kate had arranged for her neighbor next door, the one with two eager kids, to pick Ella up in the morning. And tend to her while she was away, a kind of impromptu temporary adoption.

The cat watched Kate steadily, and only her eyes moved as she followed her owner's movements around the room. Kate zipped up the luggage on her bed and turned back to the window to peek out; it had begun to collect raindrops at a steady pace.

She breathed out as she watched them falling gently on the glass, and her mind fell deep into thought. This night, she wouldn't be giving Ella her last bowl of milk before bed or caressing her fur in the morning light. Tonight was different.

CHAPTER 3
A CAB DRIVE THROUGH CHANGE

The brassy sound of a car horn startled Kate, and she looked out to see a car pull up in front of her home. It was turquoise blue with a yellow hood and top. The words were hard to distinguish through the now steady rain, but through squinted eyes, she could make out Checker Cab Company written on its side.

Gathering her two small pieces of luggage and a large, brown paper bag, she bent down. With shaky hands, she stroked Ella under the chin and smoothed the fur on her back, running her fingers down slowly as Ella shut her eyes contentedly.

"I'll miss you, dear friend. Be good," she whispered.

A loud thumping came from the door; it was the cab driver knocking. "Hello?" A man's voice boomed from outside.

Kate spoke softly to Ella, "he seems very impatient, doesn't he?"

The cat replied with a soft meow, but her eyes stayed fixed on the entrance, anticipating some sort of movement. When nothing happened, she lowered her head, wrapped her furry tail around her body, and closed her eyes.

Kate hurried to the door and opened it wide. The rain fell noisily outside. "Yes, I'm ready," she said to the lanky, dark-haired man standing at the entrance.

"Oh...ok, I was just wondering cuz there was no lights on and...," he said, loosely motioning to the window of the house.

Kate didn't take much notice of the man. Instead, she distractedly asked, "Could you help me with the luggage?"

"Oh, yeah, of course." He quickly reached into the doorway and grabbed both bags. He lifted them more easily than he had anticipated, and his lips formed a crooked smile. "Whoa!" You travel light!" He said. He pumped the arm, holding the luggage up and down to demonstrate its weightlessness.

"Yep," she replied curtly but made an effort to smile a little as she threw a tan trench coat around her shoulders. She didn't feel like talking much right now.

Kate stepped out on the porch of her home and looked around. The rain was falling sideways and looked like silver pine needles as it pummeled the ground hard. The water gleamed where the lamplight caught the drops. In the wet darkness, it was hard to make out the handcrafted stone and woodwork on the front of the home. It had been her castle and place of refuge for many years, ever since that day.

The driver didn't appear to be bothered at all by the heavy rain, as he placed the luggage in the trunk. When he finished, he dropped his arms at his side and turned to look at Kate. She was standing under the leaden raindrops, staring dismally and absently at the house. Her auburn hair, speckled with a few silver streaks, glistened under the moon. Each strand was so sodden that the long curls fell limp and coiled loosely like the arms of an octopus as they clung to the back of her coat.

The driver approached her guardedly as if he were afraid of waking her up from a catatonic state.

"Miss," he spoke softly, bending slightly at the knees to peer at her downcast face. "You ready?"

Kate's surroundings slowly emerged back into view. "Ah, yes, I am," she said, but her eyes still seemed vacant.

"You ok?" he asked.

"Yeah," she nodded, breaking out of her introspection.

Kate looked down at the asphalt as the driver opened the car door. The rain was washing away the gold and red leaves that had fallen days before, and they floated helplessly down into the gutter. She felt like one of them, but there was not only helplessness but also a feeling of release from captivity of some sort, something she couldn't yet define.

The cab driver stood in the rain with his hand out to aid her in the car. When she finally noticed, she smiled apologetically, to which he tipped his head and helped her inside.

Taking a quick glance, the driver checked for traffic in the side view mirror, then pulled onto the street. They reached a stop sign, and he glanced at her in the rearview mirror. "Uh," he started to say in a cautious tone. "I'm just wondering..." he glanced at his watch, "if you need some kind of assistance? You look kinda ...well, you know...distracted or something." He analyzed her face for a moment with concern. A warmth grew in his eyes, and he broke into a smile. "I'm a cab driver, but I can also be a good listener." His voice trailed off as he looked back to the road, "very good one," he added. He waited for a car to cross in front of them, and they continued down the street.

Kate was looking out the window and, at first, said nothing. About a minute of uncomfortable silence passed with the driver glancing at the road and inquisitively back at her.

"It's hard to explain," she finally said, dryly.

He nodded emphatically. "Oh, yeah, sure, I get that. And if you don't want to talk about it, that's fine too. I know...I mean... if I'm coming across as nosey, I apologize for that. I just like my customers to feel welcomed in my cab. I don't know, does that make sense?"

"Yes," Kate replied.

Her eyes met his in the mirror for a moment. Then she turned her face to look out of the window again.

"My name is Stan, by the way. Sorry, I should have introduced myself earlier." He spoke loudly over the noise of the car.

"I'm Kate," she replied softly, with her eyes set on the trees quickly passing on the highway.

She intrigued Stan. He was used to picking up people who were loaded at that time of night and with no money! Those passengers were far from quiet and distant; they were loud and obnoxious. "Sure is lonely out tonight," Stan said, to break the silence.

"Yes, it is."

"I was just thinking to myself how it is that I usually pick up folks around town that are smashed, you know? They couldn't even walk a straight path home, much less drive."

Kate smiled a little. "I can imagine," she said quietly.

The rain had lessened its drumming, but the thick dark clouds directly above signaled that it was just a pause in the action. There were tall leafy trees that stood guard overhead, shielding the roadway from the light of the street lamps and making the dark, wet street appear desolate.

After a few minutes, the driver turned onto Highway 101 going west.

"Traffic should be light at this time. Roads are slick," he said, throwing his voice to the backseat.

Kate did not reply. She was immersed in her thoughts. The night looked darker from inside the car, and the street lamps cast an almost suffocating amber glow on the freeway. It glistened off the wet asphalt.

"We got a storm moving in. It's quieted down somewhat, but the best is yet to come, as they say," he said, chuckling to himself, "Imagine that! A storm with wind gusts of 75 miles per hour!" He glanced back in time to see Kate's eyebrows come together slightly.

"Sounds pretty menacing," she said.

"Yeah, they said it's gonna be a big storm!" The driver's head was tilted slightly, so his left ear was toward his shoulder, and he put his head back slightly while letting out a short chuckle, "Ha! Big storm. Yeah, right," he retorted. "It's Cali! You know? Maybe back East in Buffalo, but Cali, I don't think so, you know? " He laughed and looked casually around the streets.

Stan's easy-going nature made Kate feel better, and she relaxed a little. "Yes, it always feels like summer here!" she said and smiled a little. Her eyes were fixed directly out of the window, but on nothing in particular.

"I remember one time there was a large tropical storm predicted to move in overnight," she started, "and it did. Taking part of the pier and damaging a lot of sea vessels." Both her voice and eyes seemed to be far away.

Stan smiled, glancing back at her. He was pleased that at least she was speaking a little and coming out of her shell. "Wow, sounds bad. I mean to take out some of the pier," he replied, surveying the street before him. "Where was this?"

"Woodrose."

"Woodrose? Yeah, I think I've heard about that happening there. I never thought it was that bad, though, wow. Thought it was hype. Long time ago, right?"

Kate's eyes grew distant. "It was the month of November, about 30 years ago," she said. "Sounds long ago, but to me, it's as if it happened yesterday." She looked down at her hands folded on her lap. "It was a terrible tragedy. It caused heavy flooding, destruction, and even deaths."

"Wuao!" Stan's mouth formed a circle and stayed that way for a few seconds as he kept driving.

Kate continued to speak as if someone had pushed the play button on the recorded memories in her mind. "There were two other ones that I can remember, too, but that one was the largest. It was unfortunate for the people who rode the trolley from inland cities to catch fish on the pier because after that one big storm, it was completely destroyed." She paused a moment, and her voice dropped. "A lot of things were destroyed during that time," she said with a soft, dismal tone.

The driver's eyebrows were together in the middle, and his eyes shifted back at her. "I hadn't heard about all of that before," he said watchfully, being careful not to tread on what already seemed like a painful memory. He paused a moment, then quietly asked, "Back in the late 40s, eh?"

Kate nodded and looked up through the window at the gathering dark clouds. "Yes, a long time ago," she said gently. Then she dropped her head back on the seat's headrest. It suddenly felt as heavy as a bowling ball.

They drove on through the dark, half-empty freeway. Every now and then, a shiny Lamborghini or a dark-windowed Bentley would whiz by. Many things had changed since the years Kate knew. Not that time or change made any difference to her. Tucked away in Blackwater Canyon, she hadn't even noticed that the cities around her had grown expeditiously, and society had grown with them.

Folks no longer seemed to enjoy lazy afternoons riding trolleys. The communities no longer had the time or maybe the interest in coming together for a feast or celebration of some sort. They had become the movers and shakers of the world, always out driving its freeways, walking its streets, and hanging around upscale bars and clubs. Kate was oblivious to these changes and knew nothing of the nightlife or day-life of the current downtown. Her home in the canyon had become her safe haven for many years. After those eventful and tragic days, and the many years that followed.

"Stop here, please, "she said, as the driver approached the beach pier. He pulled into a parking space and turned around in his seat to look at her.

"I'll be right back," she told him as she opened the cab door.

"What? You serious?" The driver followed her out with his eyes. He looked as shocked as if she had just handed him a $500 bill for cab fare.

"Yes, I'll be just a minute," she said, stepping out of the cab.

"But..." He glanced at his watch and stuck his head out through the cab window. "Hey, it's pretty vacant right now. It's kind of dangerous to be walking around out there in the middle of all this rain. I mean, it's *really* late at night!"

Kate was just a few feet from the cab, and she turned around and ducked down a little to peer inside the window. "Or really *early* in the morning," she said with a half-smile and turned back toward the pier. The driver smiled at her. She was quiet but with a daring side to her, and he liked that. He got out quickly to join her as she walked briskly toward the pier.

"Well, I guess I could use some fresh rain air," he said. But what he really meant was you might need some company. He wasn't sure why, but this woman seemed fragile to him, but she seemed to need a friend.

"Hope it's alright that I join you," he said

"Of course, it's okay," she responded. She stopped, leaned on the railing, and looked up. Scattered raindrops felt fresh against Kate's skin. The wind had picked up and was wreaking havoc, whipping her hair around and splattering drops on her raincoat. An ominous dark outer ring appeared around the pale moon, making it look mysterious. At times, it would take refuge behind the storm clouds, and its glow would become barely visible until a gap formed. Then you could see the platinum edges as they gradually changed from deep gray to a silvery blue radiance in preparation for dawn.

Kate began to walk the length of the pier but stopped midway. She seemed to be looking for something on the horizon, then her eyes locked in on a certain point in the hills, and they took on a different gaze, distant and forlorn.

Stan watched her as he leaned his elbows on the structure, and he studied her face. Her delicate features were beautiful.

Her eyes were expansive and slightly drawn out toward the outside. They reminded him of the ones on the cat he had seen at her home, and their color was a deep gold like a Topaz stone with a childlike twinkle within. Her face was oval with cheekbones set high, and her mouth was small and perfectly shaped. The skin on her face had a few lines that barely scratched the surface. Around the outer corners of her eyes and between her brows.

After a few moments of silence, Kate glanced down at her watch, though she took no notice of the time; instead, she suddenly seemed to realize that he was braving the storm right beside her.

"You don't have to do this," she said.

"What? You mean, accompany you?"

"Yes, get soaking wet in this storm! I'm just getting my thoughts together before I take my trip."

"No problem. I don't think it would be safe to drop off anyone here at this time, much less a very kind girl such as yourself."

Kate smiled thankfully. "I appreciate your company," she said, and a corner of her mouth turned up a little, "And I appreciate you calling me a *girl* at my age!"

Stan let out a subdued chuckle. "Whadda you mean? I had you pinned at about 20 years old! Right?" he replied and smiled broadly.

"Nowhere near close!" she said, shaking her head and laughing.

Kate looked back out at the ocean. The shuffling of the waves had increased, and it was now wild, gusty, and loud. "I guess I'd better get going if I'm going to catch my plane," she said. This time, she made a point of looking at the time. A sudden jolt came to her, "I think I'm already late! Must have been reminiscing way too long!" she said frantically. Her voice strained over the ocean's roar, "Do you think we can make it if my flight leaves in half an hour?"

"To the airport in under half an hour? I guarantee it!" He smirked proudly.

CHAPTER 4
THE QUIET ZONE

MANHATTAN, NEW YORK

The morning was formed of fog when she stepped out of the cab. The city was washed in monochromatic tones; the tall silvery buildings, the sidewalks, even the trees were casting their steel-gray shadows on the streets. The air was icy-cool and brittle.

The four-story hospital was square with a red brick exterior. From the walkway leading to it, you could see a few of the rooms with a faint yellow glow in the windows, and a sign that read *Hospital Zone--Quiet*.

Inside the lobby, it was bright and shiny, with a few nurses quietly flitting around the polished floors. The first thing she saw was a chest-high, long, dark oak counter centered in the middle of the wall that faced the entry, and behind it was a dark-paneled oak door.

One nurse, a middle-aged, matronly-looking woman, was impeccably dressed in a white uniform. Kate noticed how many things had changed since the

1940s. The younger nurses now wore dresses with much shorter knee-length uniforms. They wore a black sweater on top of their unstarched outfits and white stockings without a seam in the back.

A nurse who appeared to be in her twenties stood by a counter. Her face was an artwork of flawless makeup and perfectly styled hair. She was busy examining papers that were attached to a clipboard.

Sitting behind the large reception desk was a chubby nurse who wore a friendly, smiling face as she jotted something down and sipped from a cup full of steaming coffee. There was virtually no noise, no ringing phones, no chatter. The nurses spoke in whisper-like voices to each other when needed.

Kate walked past a large waiting room where dark oak wooden armchairs were neatly lined up against the walls in rows of four. There were a few people seated scattered about the place. The walls were a freshly painted mint-green color.

Kate looked down at the floor as she walked; it was buffed to a shine. She could see her reflection in the green and white tiles, which had little black veins running through them.

The long corridor leading to the rooms was dim and still. Each of the doors had small square lights hanging above, directly in the middle of the white doors. Kate stepped by each room, cautiously and stealthily. She had a nervous feeling in the pit of her stomach. The time had come to find out what the mysterious note was all about, and her mind was flooded with thoughts and fears as her hand retrieved the folded letter from her coat pocket.

The note had been a shock when she first read it. She had never expected to hear from or receive anything from the sender after so many years. The letter was brief, and it read, in part:

Immensely important:
Go to Kings Hospital in Manhattan, New York.
Look for room 145.
Gavyn

A TIME INTERVAL is a pause, an interruption in something. For Kate, since that day in Woodrose, her existence had become a life with sporadic irregular patterns - a life interrupted. Hearing from Gavyn had ended that time interval in her life, although what would happen next upon seeing him, she didn't know.

The fifth door on the right had the numbers 145 above it. Kate looked back down the corridor as she placed her hand on the steel knob and turned it. She stepped inside into a depersonalized, blackened room, cold, shadowy, and deathly quiet. The only illumination was a stream of soft beige sunlight from a window near the bed.

Her eyes jetted around the room nervously as she prepared herself for what she was about to see, then they landed on the figure lying in bed.

"Gavyn?" she called out softly. But there was no response or movement from the figure on the bed. "Gavyn, it's me, Kate. I came as soon as I got your letter."

The figure lay still, but she could hear what sounded like shallow breathing. She approached hesitantly, taking small, quiet steps. The shadowed light reflected on the man's body in slants across his face and hands, and it made his features hard to make out in the dark. The fingers were interlaced and resting on his stomach. The ring finger of his hand twitched lightly, and a flash emitted from it. Slowly, she moved closer to see what it was.

It was a sterling silver championship boxing ring. She only knew one person who had that ring. Kate felt her body numb. Mustering courage, she swiveled a small lamp that hung on the wall behind the bed with a shaky hand and aimed it at the man's face. What she saw shocked her.

Her mind began to dissolve into another world of long ago. Slowly, the sounds of shuffling feet and whispering nurses dissipated, and the room seemed to liquefy around her.

CHAPTER 5
JOURNEY BACK IN TIME

L ike the sun, when it slowly emerges from sleep, first softly, then in bursts over the mountains, as it filters between the trees. The recollections sifted through her mind, ultimately surrendering to a steady stream of memories.

She remembered how the sunlight shone like glistening gold then. The sea lay deep and green. And she remembered the sounds of the harbor. Every morning would bring the tolling of metallic tones, the clanging of irons, bells, and boat whistles jangling along the boardwalk. And the thumping of thick rope that would beat against the wood of the ships and startle the seagulls, sending them squawking into flight. Even now, they invaded her mind, sharp and clear.

If time travel were possible, in her mind, Kate had just realized that feat. Suddenly, it was 1947.

Kate Mason and Flynn Brennan were both 18 years old. Standing on the beach pier, they could feel the hot sun's long, fiery nails, digging into their skin as the soft ocean breeze played around them.

"Oh, wait..." Flynn said, "There's something in my pocket." He smiled a devious and visibly nervous smile.

Kate shielded her eyes from the glare by pressing down on the top of her wide-brimmed hat and looked up at his face.

"What is it?" she asked, softly giggling. She was caught up in a feeling, watching Flynn's skittish expression.

Flynn smiled as he dug into his pocket, purposely taking his time. And Kate wrung her hands in front of her. She was excited about receiving something from him because anything that came from Flynn was a treasure. "What is it, Flynn? Show me already!" she playfully demanded to know.

Flynn looked out to the vast sea, and his eyes squinted with unbridled excitement. His hand wrapped around the package, still in his pocket. "I'm not sure...of what it could be..." he grinned, "let's see..." Suddenly, his face took on a hesitant look; he took out a small box and opened it for her to look inside. She saw a multicolored flash emit from the white box, and Kate drew in a breath.

"Remember the moonstones I found last month diving in the ocean?" he asked, smiling at her. The white velvet box displayed a ring with a glowing moonstone in the middle. If it were a flower, the ring would be a rosebud with the moonstone at its center and small sapphires dotting the encircling leaves.

"The most gorgeous ring I've ever seen! It looks like a rose," she said, beaming.

Flynn brought her to him and, bending down a little, buried his smiling face in her auburn hair. He whispered into her hair as he wrapped his arms around her waist. "Guess the jeweler really did her job well because this isn't just any old moonstone ring, you know."

"Oh, no?" She smiled at him.

"Nope. It's a promise ring...in fact, it's a promise, promise."

"What on earth is a *promise, promise*?" Kate laughed gleefully.

"A promise to the second power means you're getting double the guarantee of happiness. Rosebuds are always little reminders that something beautiful, like a wedding, is going to happen soon."

Kate placed her cheek next to his chest. "I can't wait for that to happen!" she replied.

Flynn took her face in his hands, and her eyes shone as luminous and golden as honey, half-hidden behind her lashes. To Flynn, looking into the intense gold of her eyes was like looking into the deepest part of a topaz.

"This moonstone represents a promise that one day very soon, we'll set out to discover the entire world. Did you know that Alexander Island is really an island?" he asked.

"Yes, I read something about snow. So, you have plans to take me on a sled ride to Antarctica?" Kate laughed warmly.

"If you're willing."

"I am," she replied softly.

Kate looked down the long pier toward the ocean; it looked like a protracted wooden ladder someone had extended over the blue waters. She didn't glance at Flynn, but could feel his eyes on her face. His look lingered on her for a moment. Then shifted to the sea and straight down at the churning waves. He leaned his elbows on the wood railing, and as if mapping out a course in his mind, he watched the water pound the pylons of the pier.

"That is my promise," he said, turning his face a little toward her. "I promise you I will do everything in my power…one day…just you and me."

His eyes showed determination, and the shine of youth burned within them, but there was also concern. He thought of his dad, his brother, Kate's family, and their enormously different backgrounds.

Kate put her arms around him, and with her face resting on his chest, she could feel his heartbeat beneath her cheek. It beat strongly and as resolutely as Flynn himself. She smiled, and he felt her lips move. He looked down and tapped a kiss on top of her girlish head.

At that moment, he became aware of footsteps approaching. He knew that familiar sound of those heavy boots. They were unmistakable to him, the way they shuffled with slow, goading steps. Flynn stiffened, and Kate sensed it immediately and stepped back to look up at his face. Her eyes shifted when she noticed the man standing near them.

"Flynn!" The man's dry voice boomed above the squeaking seagulls and waves.

Flynn was visibly bothered by the interruption and by who it was. It was his father, Tyson Brennan.

"Yeah?" he asked. He rolled his eyes a little and let out a short breath, but he didn't look at him; instead, he hung his head over the pier again to watch the waves.

"*Yeah*? What kind of response is that?" Ty's mouth was in a sideways slant, and the lips were stretched out in a small, tight smile. He moved a little from side to side, shifting his weight from one foot to the other as a bull does when he's getting irritated.

"Did you need something, Dad?" he asked through tightened lips, and his voice sounded restrained. Flynn looked out to the blue horizon.

Kate couldn't tell if he was gathering patience or nerve. He always seemed to be on the defensive with his dad. They spoke to each other as if using their words and tone in a boxing ring.

Flynn glanced fleetingly at Kate, then back out to sea. "By the way, aren't you going to say hello to Kate, at least?" he asked. He felt indifferent to his father's acknowledgment but was bothered when it involved Kate.

Ty smiled, and his mouth looked like a crocodile's. He breathed out long and dug his hands into his pockets, jiggling the coins that were inside. "Uh-huh, of course… how are you, Kate?" he finally asked, offhandedly.

Kate quickly shifted her eyes to the water, then back to him. She felt very uncomfortable around him. "I'm fine, thanks," she said curtly.

Ty's smile was frozen on his face, and his eyes were harsh and severe. Life was a constant frustration that brewed inside him, like percolating coffee; it would simmer and sometimes get to the point of boiling over.

The Mason family was the flame that made the coffeepot boil and a constant aggravation to him. He would often say that knowing the Masons felt the same as walking around with a jagged rock in his shoe all day.

Kate's father, Mike Mason, the wealthy land developer, had run the Brennan's out of house and home, choosing big money over the soul of a human. At least that was what Ty had concluded. In this case, their home was all that the Brennans had after Flynn's mother died. Ty had to scramble when given notice of the impending destruction of his home. His house was one in a row of ten set for demolition under the orders of Mike Mason. Luckily, he found a smaller beach home that had been spared, at least for now.

Though Kate had been an innocent observer of the whole thing, it didn't matter to Ty, and he still held it against her. It was, after all, her family, and she came from that line of no goods. The whole thing was sad to see. Kate, as a young girl, had been oblivious to the inner workings of her father's business and had no clue of anything that was transpiring. As it sometimes is being an only child, she had been pampered by her parents and kept in the dark about most things.

But as much as Ty held those things against the Masons, Kate held things against Ty. His often-brutal self-centered way made her dislike him, and at times she felt repulsed by his harsh belittling of Flynn and Gavyn. Kate's dad, she thought, was the exact opposite. He was kind and generous, even using some of the lands he obtained for the construction of large parks for children. He was a land developer, but far from the callous personification that Ty sought to pin on him. That was her opinion of her dad.

CHAPTER 6
DEMOLITION NOTICE

The feuding had begun some years back on one sun-filled southern California day, a day that would become a turning point in their lives. The same day that Ty wished to forget and Kate wished always to remember. The first day she met Flynn. Fifteen-year-old Kate had accompanied her father on the visit that resulted in the subsequent demolition of the Brennan home.

Flynn was fifteen years old but had the natural physique of a bodybuilder, something Ty took full advantage of. He would save money by assigning his son to do everything from plumbing to construction around the home. On that day, Flynn had been repairing the roof of the house, which was leaking from a past storm. It was nearing noon when, under the beams of sweltering sun, Flynn looked down, searching for Gavyn.

"Hey, get me something to drink, Gav!" he yelled, probing the yard and wiping his forehead with his arm.

But Gavyn couldn't hear his brother yelling from the hammock he was swaying in, yards from his house. When there was no response, Flynn jumped down from the highest point on the roof, landing swiftly to a rolling stop.

His younger brother was by then on his way back to the house when he saw the flip from the roof. Being fourteen years old, Gavyn was infinitely amused and shook his head from side to side, grinning. "You're gonna break something, and dad's gonna be real upset with you when you have to miss workouts!" he said.

"Good, it'll give me an excuse to not see his face!" he replied scornfully. Flynn stood up and dusted himself off. "Hey, where were you?" He started to ask, then became aware of someone standing a few feet away. He realized it was the pretty girl who lived on the hill. Unfortunately, she had seen his not-so-pretty fall, and his face flushed red. He didn't know her, but he had seen her with her family on the pier on several occasions.

Kate was standing around, waiting for her father to carry out some sort of business with Tyson Brennan. She had giggled when he landed awkwardly and rolled, but it had been a soft giggle, and Flynn had not heard it. When he stood up and began to shake off the dust, she was taken by the handsome and rugged Flynn. He was tall and tanned, and blonde streaks ran throughout his light brown hair. His eyes were the color of a sea wave with varying hues of blue.

Kate smiled at him and tilted her chin down a little. "Are you hurt?" she asked. Her youthful eyes sparkled with vivacity.

"No," he half-smiled at her. "Just embarrassed, I guess. Feel like a clown."

"Oh, that's good." Her words tumbled out distractedly, and when she realized what she had said, she quickly added, "I mean that you're not hurt!" They both laughed at her quick salvage.

Gavyn had walked over to the two. "You're one of the Masons, aren't you?" he inquired curiously. "We saw you before on the pier."

Flynn's mouth tightened, embarrassed at his brother's illiteracy around a girl as refined as Kate. *"We've*, numbskull. Not, *we seen*," he said to him from the corner of his mouth, hoping Kate hadn't caught his brother's bad English.

It wasn't that Gavyn was dumber than Flynn, but he just didn't find an interest in anything outside of girls and boxing. He didn't understand the big deal with it anyway.

"That's what I just said, Flynn!" he said and smiled at Kate as someone relaxed after a couple of drinks.

Kate giggled a little. She had never been around people as laidback as the two of them, and she liked the feeling. "Yes, I'm Mike Mason's daughter. My name is Kate," she replied, and her eyes had a glint of light in them as they quickly darted back to Flynn's face. She smiled warmly, and Flynn sheepishly returned the smile.

Kate Mason was not your ordinary girl, rich, yes, but ordinary, not in the least. One of the things that made her different was that she never felt the need to distinguish between the haves and have-nots. 'We're all just people,' she would often tell her close circle of friends. Her friends had never known anyone who could accept the common folk as just people.

But to Kate, there was no dissimilarity. We're all people living on the same earth was her philosophy. Pain and love, they were all functions of the soul. Money could buy new cars and houses, but money couldn't buy you the mind of a writer or the heart of a poet. That was free, and it lived in the soul of a person. There's nothing that paper bills or gold bars have that makes any difference in those things. Therefore, she contended, she valued more that which was innate rather than obtained.

For Kate, it was the warmth of a person that drew them to her, not how full their pockets were. But Kate's mother disagreed with her philosophy, worried a lot about it, and frowned upon it.

Kate was childlike and beautiful. She was slender and had a glow to her skin as if gold poured from her pores. Her shoulder-length auburn hair was usually brushed in the style of Veronica Lake. She had a fragile but self-reliant look to her, which made her an instant attraction to most guys her age. In fact, everyone seemed to be drawn to her, everyone but Ty Brennan.

"Flynn!" His father appeared at the front door, and his expression was strangely serious.

"Yeah?" asked Flynn, turning to look at him.

His father tossed keys in his direction, and Flynn caught them in the air and looked at his dad's face. "What's this for?"

"Need you to start up the truck and figure out what's wrong with the start-up, it cranks but fizzles," Ty said to him.

Flynn tossed the keys up and caught them. "Ok, if I start it, can I take it for a spin? I mean to check things out, make sure it's running good?" he asked, hopeful.

Meanwhile, Gavyn, keen on the situation, moved in front of Kate, hiding her small frame from view. Had Ty noticed the Mason girl there, they wouldn't have been allowed to take the truck for a spin.

Kate was eyeing the truck and didn't notice Gavyn's move, and Ty didn't notice Kate. Ty's head went back a little, and he studied Flynn's face a moment as if he were looking through bifocals. "Yeah, ok," he said, and walked back inside.

Flynn turned to Kate and Gavyn and smiled sneakily. "Wanna go for a ride down Seaside Drive?" he asked.

Kate smiled, a little unsure. "Uh, ok. But we have to go and come back before my dad comes out and notices we are gone."

"Yeah! I feel like a nice frosty malt! Let's go to Jensens!" Gavyn said. He had already hopped in the back of the red Ford pickup, and Kate and Flynn joined him.

The engine complained at first. It whined a little, and with the first turn of the key, it made a clicking sound, then another click and two more clicks until it burst into a roar from under the hood. "I think it's the battery!" Flynn yelled over the acceleration of the motor. "Let's go over to Dan's Auto Shop and pick one up. Dad's got a running tab with Dan," he said.

The three teens drove down Seaside Drive like it was a racecourse, and Kate felt exhilarated and free. Her hair came loose in the wind, and her pinned waves fell down over her shoulders, and the ocean breeze ran through it. Then suddenly, the accelerator seemed to stiffen under Flynn's foot, and the truck began to cough.

"Aww, Flynn! The danged thing is dying! Think we'll make it to Jensens?" Gavyn asked, with all the excitement drained from him like a popped balloon.

Flynn pumped the accelerator, and the truck lurched forward, then sputtered and lost its speed. "I don't know, first the battery, and now I think we have no gas," said Flynn.

The red truck coughed again loudly as if it had sticky phlegm to expel, and the engine died. Flynn was able to coast the truck to the side of the road, and he got out, slamming the door behind him. "Figures… this piece of junk!" he yelled, slamming his hand on the hood.

Gavyn got out too and echoed the sentiment, kicking one of the tires. He put his hands in his pockets and looked around, "What are we going to do now, Flynn?" he asked him.

Flynn pursed his lips, looked down the road, and breathed out slowly. "We'll have to walk to the pump," he said.

Gavyn glanced in the back window at Kate, who had turned around in the front seat and was looking back at them. "Um, what about her?" he asked. When he looked at Flynn, the sunlight shone directly into his eyes, and he squinted with one eye nearly closed.

Flynn's expression changed and softened. He stepped over to the truck and leaned his head in through the open side window. "Uh, I'm sorry, Kate," he said, genuinely apologetic. He watched her as she turned back around to face the frontwards, and she tipped her chin down and repinned her hair. His expression was more of a hypnotic gaze than a mere look as he watched her.

"Oh, that's alright," Kate said. She tilted her head a little and smiled at him. "What are you two going to do? I have to find a way back and soon," she said.

"Yeah, don't worry, I'll have it running in no time! I'm really sorry about this. Hope you're not upset," he said. Gavyn shook his head and smiled at Flynn's apparent cringe-worthy gush.

The car had stalled on a downward curve in the road. Kate could see the ocean below to the left of them. She looked at the water, then back at Flynn. He wasn't one to show it, but he was waiting anxiously for her response to his apology.

Kate smiled kindly at him. "It's ok. No one knew this would happen," she said, and his eyes glittered at her response.

Flynn stood motionless, staring at Kate's face, and he suddenly felt a jab to the side of his stomach. His reflex made him slightly bend at the waist, and he simpered, aware that Gavyn was waking him up from his trance. "Ok, well," Flynn started and lightly tapped Gavyn, "we'll walk over to the gas station. You stay here cuz it's hot, and you probably don't want to walk in the heat..." he said to Kate.

"What?" Kate protested. "No siree, I'm going with you!" She giggled a little and hopped out of the truck.

Flynn smiled big and looked adoringly at her, and Gavyn nudged him. "Come on, we'll never get back!" he said, and they began to walk down the steep hill to the Shell gas station.

The heat didn't feel too bad for Kate. She had made a good decision that morning to wear light blue linen shorts and a white shirt tucked into them. She gathered her hair into a ponytail, and it fell long and shiny down her back.

The air was fresh, and the sunlight rose up from the asphalt in transparent squiggly waves as they made their way down. Every so often, a soft waft of salty sea breeze would refresh their sun-imbued faces. The three talked about things they liked, and of course, the subject landed on boxing. Gavyn displayed his approval of it, while Flynn assumed the opposite stance.

"What do you like about it, Gavyn?" Kate asked. "It's so violent."

"I don't see it that way. I see it like a sport," said Gavyn.

"A sport?" she asked.

"A blood sport," Flynn said.

"No, no…you just don't like it, that's all. You don't understand the *finesse* involved, as dad would say," Gavyn replied.

"Oh, you gonna quote dad now? He's a great one to quote! End of the conversation, then," Flynn responded, annoyed.

Gavyn looked down and away toward the ocean. He knew he had stepped on some toes mentioning his dad, so he stayed quiet after that.

Kate was silent and thinking. Every now and then, she'd sneak a look at Flynn's face.

There was so much more to him than even he realized, she thought. He was different and profound. She feared the feeling she was beginning to have for him; she feared the changes it might bring. If she opened him up and looked inside, what would she find? She was afraid of that, too.

They got the gas and the battery for the truck, and although the trip was cut short, it was quite eventful. When the three returned, Kate's father's business with Ty had finished, and he was leaning back on his car with his hands in his pockets. He stood up and smoothed his tie when he noticed them coming up the way.

"Oops," she said under her breath at the sight of him. "Looks like they finished."

The truck clambered past him and into the carport of the beach house. Ty leaned out of the screen door, then went back in when he noticed it was the truck. "Is your dad going to be mad at you?" asked Flynn.

"No, he'll get over it," she said.

"You sure? I could talk to him and explain the gasoline thing."

"No, I'm sure. It's okay," Kate said and hopped out of the truck.

"Hey, do you think I could...ah, maybe have your phone number?" Flynn asked.

Gavyn waited anxiously to see how the request would play out. A girl like Kate, well, not just anybody could get that phone number. But apparently, Flynn wasn't just anybody because the next thing Gavyn's eager eyes witnessed was Kate writing her number down for Flynn. Flynn quickly and surreptitiously stashed it in his pants pocket. "Thanks," he said, with the same googly eyes as before.

"You're welcome!" said Kate, and she waved and walked to her dad.

Mike Mason looked at her and grimaced at the red pickup, but he didn't say anything. They boarded his brand-new, blue Buick convertible and sped off.

Mike always rode with the tan top down, and that day it allowed Kate a good view of Flynn and Gavyn as they drove by, and she turned around in her seat and looked back once they had passed them. They got smaller and smaller as they stood in the middle of the road, eyeing the blue sedan hurrying down the street.

"Turn around, sweetheart," her father called to her. "We're about to take some hairpin curves," he warned.

Kate twisted back around and settled into the blue leather seat. Her dad changed gears on the three-speed manual, and the car hummed and lurched forward a little.

Kate turned down the AM radio with Ella Fitzgerald singing *Sentimental Journey* and looked for her father's face. It was reddish in color. He took a sharp curve and briefly glanced at her with his eyes. "You just turned down your favorite tune," he said.

"I know. Papa, are you alright?"

"Yes, of course, Kate." He gripped the steering wheel uneasily. He looked straight ahead and shook his head slightly. "Those Brennans," he said, glancing around, but his eyes didn't rest on anything in particular. "I think we're going to have some trouble with them."

"Why, what do you mean?" she asked, "What kind of trouble?"

Mike suddenly realized he had spoken aloud. "Oh, don't worry about it, hon." He smiled, patted her hand resting on her lap, and nodded reassuringly. "I was just thinking about business out loud." He smiled lovingly at her. "Nothing to worry about, though. Turn up that music, eh?"

Kate obliged and asked no further questions. She turned the radio back up a little. But her dad's face stayed flushed, and his eyebrows were furrowed, and she wondered why.

When they arrived home, Kate walked straight to her room without acknowledging her mom, and her mother took notice, as did Stella, the Masons' live-in maid, but she didn't say a word. Kate walked past her, and she quietly set aside her meal.

"Where did you go with Kate?" she asked her husband.

"I had some business to do," he said.

"You took your daughter on business?"

"Yeah, is that against the law?" he said sarcastically.

"Don't get smart with me, Michael!"

"Ok, well, do you prefer I play dumb? You hate that too, remember?" he said with a sneer.

Helena let out a short, heavy breath. "You're so exasperating!"

"Uh-huh," he responded, lazily taking off his tie and unbuttoning his shirt. "Is dinner ready?" he asked.

"I don't know. You'll have to ask Stella," she responded irritably.

The phone rang, but neither one took notice, being deep into their conversation. Kate picked it up on the first ring. It was Flynn. She was pleased, though surprised, that he had called just moments after seeing her. And they talked for hours, shared just about everything, and got closer in doing so, while her parents fought only some rooms away about precisely that.

Later, the conversation continued in the kitchen. Something didn't feel right to Helena. The way Kate looked. When she walked in, she didn't stop to say hello to her.

"So, where did you go for business earlier?" she asked, trying to sound nice to get information from him.

Mike tilted his chair back so that it balanced on the two back legs and looked at her. "Why?" he asked, shifting his head to the side. "Is this going to be another one of those jealous inquiries?"

Helena feigned meekness and looked down at her lap. She seemed almost apologetic. "No, Mike. It's not. I'm just wondering who Kate saw today?"

He seemed to relax at the reason for the questioning. "Oh, well, let's see, we went to old man Jake's farm."

"Old man Jake?" she asked.

"Yeah, just a loner, he lives by himself. But he wasn't home anyhow. By the way, I'm buying his property along with the canal that runs through it. But as I said, he wasn't home. So we headed to the Brennans' home."

Helena's face took on a look of unease, and she twisted her wedding ring absentmindedly. "The Brennans?" she said, almost under her breath.

Mike noticed her apparent concern, and he asked, "Yeah, why?"

"I don't know. I don't like Kate around that family. I've seen those two boys of his watching us while walking on the pier a lot."

Mike Mason looked out into space, envisioning the picture she was painting. "Well," he started talking in a low voice, "I did see them talking a little while."

What?" Helena asked loudly in disbelief, and Mike shushed her, flagging his hand. "You want her to hear us?" he asked.

She brought her voice down. "Mike...I don't like this. I'm uneasy about that family."

Mike nodded in agreement. Then he thought of something he was sure would help. "I know what we can do about this. Kate's only fifteen, and she is just right for Prep school. The one in France, maybe?" he said.

Helena's eyes moved to his face, and she smiled. "You've got a great idea there, Mike! A year, she can spend just a year there, and maybe meet someone else or just plain forget about those boys."

"Yeah, and if that doesn't work, I'm sure I can come up with another plan," he said reassuringly.

CHAPTER 7
THE PHONE CALL

Next day, the ride to the airport was silent and tense. The sea wind had picked up. It blew through the cream-colored flowers of the California Sagebrush and the Black Sage. Kate could see the pale blue flowers as they swayed, yielding to the wet air out of the car window. Helena did most of the talking, trying to convince Kate that this was just part of preparing her for the world out there. But Kate didn't care why she had to go; she only cared that she had to, and it made her angry.

A year isn't a long time, but it can seem like an eternity in the prime of one's youth. Flynn wondered what had happened to the girl he had fallen for and why the sudden disappearance? His mind raced, repeatedly retracing things he had said to her, and sometimes he would cringe at what he had divulged.

Maybe that's why she left, he would often gripe to Gavyn. "Maybe I said too much too soon," he would say.

"You mean about our weirdo family?" Gavyn would reply.

"Yeah, about our dysfunctional family with a weirdo for a dad," said Flynn.

And there were times Gavyn would hit deeper and more meaningfully, and those times he would weigh in in unsubtle ways. "Well, maybe you have absolutely nothing in common with her and her parents," he would say. "Maybe she didn't like you because of the differences between the Masons and us, like dad always says."

If there was one particular thing that would infuriate Flynn, it was anyone quoting his dad. "No, I don't think so," he replied. "And stop quoting, dad!"

But after months of silence and no word from Kate, there came a time when even Flynn, the one who always believed nothing could impede or compete with love, found himself saying, "Yeah, you might be right."

There was much silence during that year. But not because of forgetfulness or lack of caring. Kate's mother had secretly set a rule with the school preventing her from using the phone while there. It wasn't until some months later that Kate was allowed to use the telephone, and only strictly to call home.

Of course, by then, she had made a good friend in a young girl who worked in the Admissions office. And the girl confided in her what she had seen in her files about the restriction. Once Kate was keen on the covert situation, she called home, but instead of heading back to her dorm afterward, she snuck in one other call.

This time, she dared to ring the Brennans' number. However, be it as life sometimes is, the one time she called was the one time a girl answered.

"Hello?" Kate said, a little unsure.

"Who is this?" the female voice answered.

"Excuse me, but who are you?" asked Kate, curious to know but not giving her name. "I'm wondering if I have the right number," she said.

"Who are you looking for?"

"Flynn Brennan."

Lila was furious. Too furious for what it was, just a call, but she was very smitten with Flynn and very possessive.

"This is Lila Redmond...Yes, this is the right number for Flynn," she said, and even through the receiver, she sounded like she was wearing a smirk on her lips.

Kate was silent, thinking. She remembered that name from somewhere, but couldn't recall it. Then she heard Gavyn's voice.

"Hey, Lila! Come on, we're leaving! Who are you talking to?" he asked. "My dad wouldn't want you picking up our phone."

"It's some girl," she answered Gavyn.

"Who?"

"I don't know."

Gavyn grabbed the phone. "Gimme it...hello?" Silence. "Hello? Anyone there?" he spoke loudly into the phone.

Kate stayed silent and, in doing so, heard more than she wanted to.

"Just hang up, Gavyn," she heard Lila say, giggling. "Flynn's waiting for us, and you know I don't want to keep him waiting!"

Gavyn heard a dial tone on the other end of the line, and he hooked the phone back on the cradle. The person had hung up without saying who they were. He shrugged. "They hung up," he said, "wrong number, I guess."

Kate was crushed. The thought of Flynn with another girl burned a deeper scar than she ever thought possible.

Lila suspected the girl on the phone was Kate Mason. Flynn had spoken of the pretty girl on the hill nonstop to friends for some time now. And she had witnessed the exchange of looks between the two of them when on the pier. But presently, she wasn't too concerned since hearing Kate was away at Prep school.

This was the time for Lila to show Flynn how she felt about him, and she wasted no time. She took full advantage of his interest in ocean biology. It consisted of involving her dad and nightly dinners at her house, where they would talk about their mutual interests in oceanography. The truth was, it bored her to death, but she wasn't about to show that to either one, stifling yawns and replacing them with smiles on several occasions.

A year had passed, the sky was a glassy blue and billowy, white clouds with golden-pink borders glided on southerly winds. Flynn stood on the shore, contemplating the year's passing with sadness, and he thought of Kate and everything she still meant to him.

The roar of the ocean had slowed to a soothing susurration. Flynn closed his eyes and listened to the resounding echo of the sea. Then, in it swept, as if born from the ocean itself…it was Kate's voice.

"Flynn!" The call sounded from afar. "Flynn!" The second time was clearer, closer, and louder. Startled from a deep reverie, he flung his eyes open, and Kate was standing before him. It took a moment for his thoughts to catch up to his reverie, and he slowly reached out to touch her face.

"Am I dreaming this?" he asked as he examined the face before him.

"You aren't dreaming," she said softly. "I'm back."

Some believe that deep emotions are stored in the stomach. When someone is nervous, they feel butterflies, and love can produce a churning deep inside. Kate felt these feelings deep inside as if they were in the pit of her stomach. And when the passion traveled to her lips, Kate smiled in just that way, and her eyes grew wet. At that moment, they set the pain behind them. The phone call, the trip abroad, and the distance between them became a blur to them.

"Will you stay?"

"Yes!"

But the bliss was short-lived when another voice rang out from the shoreline, and it was Ty's.

"There you are! Been looking all over for you!" he said, and then he glanced at Kate. "Oh, so you're back?" he appeared underwhelmed.

Kate was stunned back into reality, and she just nodded. "Maybe I'll see you around," she said bitterly.

"You can count on it," Flynn answered, and his eyes followed her.

"No, she can't," his father said.

And that was when Flynn knew the time had come to have that long talk with his dad. Kate was back, and she looked like she felt the same for him. Like time had stood still for the two of them. That was the only sign he needed.

The next day was a warm one again, and Kate decided to head out to the ocean and walk along the shore. At least that's what she had told her mother she was going to do, but the truth was Kate couldn't get Flynn off her mind. So she made a plan to see if she could casually run into him. As things would go, funny enough, Flynn was thinking the same thing as he left his small beach home in search of her early that morning.

He walked up and down the pier a couple of times inconspicuously, or at least thinking he was being so. He was eyeing the hills where she lived for any sign of her walking down the path. He had just about given up the search and stood looking out to the ocean when he felt a tug on his sleeve from behind. He tried to contain the elation and keep his cool when he turned and saw Kate standing there, but unbeknownst to him, he glowed like a lightbulb.

"Hello, Flynn," she said coyly.

"Hi, Kate. Surprised to see you here." He instantly recoiled inside with embarrassment at the mundane statement, but outwardly, he just smiled.

"Oh, yes, I was just taking a walk."

"Yeah, me too." He looked back out to the ocean as he searched desperately for something else to say.

"I decided to stay in Woodrose for summer break," she said.

Flynn smiled and looked down at the wooden boards of the pier. "Where do you usually go?" he asked.

"Europe, usually. To my parents' summer home in France. I spend time with my friend Monique."

Flynn nodded, still looking down. He could feel Kate's eyes on him.

"How about you, Flynn? How do you usually spend your summers?" she asked.

Flynn smiled crookedly. "I don't really have time off," he said. "I just stay around town and do boxing."

"It's not something you like, though, right? Boxing, I mean?"

Flynn shrugged. "It's okay, I guess. Takes too much time from school, I think. But Gavyn doesn't mind that part at all!" He laughed, and Kate joined him.

They were silent for a while, and Kate looked out to the horizon, following the line of water to the hills where it stopped. "You wanna go up to Lavender Hill? I love the view from there," she said.

"Yeah, sure. I'm not that familiar with the hills here. I'm usually exploring stuff under the water."

They walked down the stretch of sand to where the trail started and climbed up the side slope. Then sat on some rocks at the very top.

CHAPTER 8
LAVENDER HILL

One of Kate's favorite reading spots was the flowery knolls near her home. She would sometimes go to watch the sunrise and read. Lavender Hills was home to the Silver Blue butterfly, a rare species, and the best time to spot them was sunrise.

It was then, before the fog barely lifted, that the wind-swept bluffs teemed with dazzling lazuline wings. Kate would often break from her reading and watch as they would flit from one sunflower bush to the next. They would uncurl their long proboscis and use it as a drinking straw and sip deep from the nectar of the yellow blossoms.

Now it was early afternoon, and Kate and Flynn watched the sea's emerald and turquoise-colored waters swirl by the inlet under the blue skies. Pelican Cove was visible directly below them, and they could see on the rocky shore a Great White Egret. It stepped gingerly among the shells and rocks, looking for food. Kate had observed the ocean birds' feeding events many times, but she was usually alone. This time, it felt good to be in his company. The two of them watched as every now and then, the egret's head would jerk up to look out to the ocean. Its eyes watched a brown-feathered Crested Cormorant dive into the water and pluck out a fish. Then the white bird soon lost interest, and he looked back down at its feet and resumed his search. Meanwhile, the Cormorant climbed on a rock and stood for several minutes working the plucked fish in its mouth. After swallowing the fish, it relaxed and stretched its wings out to dry.

Kate reached out and snapped off a berry from a nearby bush. That particular berry bush was a unique shrub. It would rise from among the others with leaves that were bright green and waxy, and it had pale pink flowers that gave red seeds the size and shape of corn kernels. The uniqueness came in the seed itself with its pale coating as sour as a lemon.

"Know what these are?" she asked, turning the berry over in her hand.

"No, I've never even noticed those before," said Flynn

"These are berries from the Lemonade Berry bush. The Native Indians brewed the seeds into a tea. When the neighborhood kids discovered the seeds, we began to use them in lemonade drinks, hence their name."

"And how did you come about discovering that it could be used for that?" he asked, as he squashed the berry between his forefinger and thumb.

"It wasn't scientific or anything like that. Little Freddy, the stocky kid that lives in the yellow house on the strand…"

"Oh yeah, I know Freddy," Flynn added. "He's not little anymore!"

Kate laughed, "Well, when we were about 10 years old, a group of us went on an excursion around these hills, and Freddy tagged along. When he got hungry, he popped one of the berries in his mouth. His lips contorted into some strange puckered shape as he yelled loudly about how sour they were! So, of course, we all had to sample them. I wanted to try it from the safety of my own home, so my friend and I took some and mixed it with water…actually made a pretty good lemonade! Even Stella thought so."

"Stella?"

"Yeah, that's our maid."

"Maid?" Flynn's voice and expression dropped a little. He was far from being able to offer Kate that kind of lifestyle, and that thought would hound him with worry.

Kate stared down at the berries in her hand, recounting the tale. "They are all-purpose berries. Or so Stella says."

"Hmm…what else can you do with them? Can you turn an annoying teen brother, if you had one, blue, for instance, if he ate a lot of them?"

Kate laughed. "No, silly!" Then she stopped and thought a moment. "At least I think not…but we could try!"

Flynn laughed from his gut. "Put it on the calendar! What else can you do with these?" he asked.

"Well, candle making, for one, they use the oil for it. Stella said that all of these coastal scrubs were used as medicinal teas, dyes, and in candle making by the Indians."

Flynn was intrigued. "Killer diller stuff!" he said. But how sour can they be? And he popped one in his mouth.

Kate smiled sneakily while watching and waiting for his reaction. He immediately drew in his mouth, and his eyes scrunched shut. "Oh, man! I won't be able to ever use my mouth again...forevermore!" he said, tightening his lips and trying to prevent them from stretching into a smile.

Kate laughed. "Yep! Sorry, should have warned you!" she said slyly.

After a few moments, the uncomfortable sensation dissipated, and Flynn reclined with his elbows on the grass. Kate leaned back on a tree and gazed out again at the ocean.

"Kate?"

"Yes?"

"I ah, I guess you probably noticed by now that I'm not a real good talker."

Kate turned her head toward him and shielded her eyes with her hand to look at his face. "I think you're the best!" she said, and quickly turned back to the ocean before he could see her blush.

Flynn smiled sheepishly. "Thanks. But…you know, I just wish I were more, you know…I mean," he got nervous, "I don't think I'm good enough to even sit here next to you."

"What?" Kate sat up and turned her body to him. "Flynn Brennan, you are everything good! In my opinion. Would everything good be good enough?"

Flynn smiled and leaned down and kissed her. "I hope you will always feel that way." His face stayed close to hers.

The kiss came to Kate as if on a sea breeze, and her mind and soul felt exhilarated. "I will…always. You can depend on that!"

Flynn felt the invigoration too, and he renewed his efforts at winning her. "I'm not a drinker. I mean, not in excess anyway. I always tell my dad my courage doesn't come out of a bottle. But I've got plenty of moxie to keep what I care about safe," he said, adding to the list of good things.

Kate smiled. "Drinker? Yeah, I know some of those. Aren't you too young anyway?"

Flynn smiled sneakily. "Yeah, guess so. My dad doesn't care what Gav and I do anyway, though. So long as we box. He even encourages us to drink! No sense in waiting some years to be 21, he always says. He says it makes more of a man more quickly, or something stupid like that anyway. But like I said... If I do and when I do, it's not in excess."

"I don't know about your dad, but as I said, you are perfect…to me!"

Flynn sat closer to her and put his arms around her. He thought about what he had just said. "Does it bother you that I'm a fighter?" he asked. Kate paused a moment, carefully weighing her answer and its effect on him. Flynn continued, "I mean, just be truthful. You won't hurt my feelings or anything."

"Okay then…yes, it does."

"Yeah, that's what I thought. It's not really something I like to do either.
It's more my dad's kind of thing."

"Then why do you do it?"

Flynn chucked a small rock he had in his grasp out down over the hill. "My dad… It's hard to explain. I just feel like I have to. But what I want is something else," he said. "Now, with the war ending and all, I wanna do something with my life besides boxing. My dad was dreading having to send us off, not because of the danger, of course. But because of the pause in our boxing career…mine and Gavyn's. I got called for a year, and then the war was over."

"Your dad…he's kind of rough around the edges," Kate said, carefully choosing her words.

"Around the edges? Nah, he's rough all over the place! He's not like your dad. He seems like he cares about you and what happens to you."

"Yes, he does. Both of my parents do, but my mom has a hard time with her own problems, and sometimes she gets caught up in them."

Flynn nodded.

"What is *your* dream, not your dad's, but what would you like to do with your life?" Kate asked, looking up at his face.

His mood changed in an instant, and he felt grateful that she even cared to know. "*My dream* …that is a good way to put it," he said to her, "because that's probably where it will stay, just a dream," he stated glumly.

Kate's eyebrows came together. "Why does it have to?"

"Well, I got this big mountain blocking them, and it's my dad's boxing matches. All he thinks about is boxing. When he was a little older than me, he was forced to let it go," he said, "and now he expects my brother and me to take up where he left off. But what I really want to do is explore beneath the ocean and discover things. I don't know, that probably sounds stupid, but the very first time I went out with Jack, he was like an older brother and the best diver around. I followed him like a guppy follows a big fish. And I learned a lot, and I got keen on it!" Flynn looked down, smiling, then he shook his head slowly from side to side. "Oh, man…wonder why I'm calling myself a guppy in front of a girl I'm trying to impress?" The two burst out laughing.

Intrigued by each other's interests, they took no notice when the day bowed to the night, and they stayed out on the hill until the sun melted like liquid gold into the sea.

CHAPTER 9
THE ANGER RISES

That evening, Gavyn caught up to Flynn as he headed back home.

"Well? Whadda ya think?" Gavyn asked.

"What do you mean? About what?" Flynn asked, but he knew where Gavyn was going with the question.

"About her... that girl. The girl I saw you talking with just now on the hill. She sure is a knock-out!"

"Listen, knucklehead, just forget about her. Do yourself a favor, ok?" Flynn was all of a sudden uneasy about talking with Gavyn about Kate.

"Why? Is she too good for the likes of us?" Gavyn smirked. "I think so anyway, but anyone who gets to marry her will be getting pennies from heaven!"

"Shut up, Gavyn! Stop talking stupid like that! You're just a kid anyway." Flynn snapped at him. "Maybe I plan ahead! Chasing her would be real good fun!" Gavyn grinned.

"Yeah, but you wouldn't know what to do with her if you caught her, now, would you?" Flynn laughed.

"Oh Yeah?" Gavyn began to taunt jovially. He took small steps in an imagined rhythm and circled in front of Flynn while singing obnoxiously, "Brylcreem — A Little Dab'll Do Ya! Brylcreem — You'll look so debonaire. Brylcreem — The gals' they'll pursue ya; they'll love to run their fingers through your hair!"

The tune was from a television commercial for hair cream that would also play on the radio. Flynn ignored him at first, then impulsively stuck out his hand and ran his fingers through Gavyn's hair, making it stick straight up. "There! Maybe that'll help!" he said. They laughed and joked noisily, that is, until they hit a block wall going up the porch steps. It was their dad.

"You two got nothing better to do?" He barked like a sergeant.

They fell quiet instantly, and Flynn disdainfully tightened his lips. He didn't say anything back; he just walked past him and went inside. The screen door slammed behind him, and a couple of grasshoppers singing in the balmy California evening suddenly fell silent.

"Cuz I can find something for you two real quick!" His dad propelled his voice back angrily at Flynn.

Flynn walked into the kitchen and searched the drawers for a box of Junior Mints. He could hear Gavyn trying to excuse the time they spent ditching work as he popped the candy in his mouth. He leaned back on the counter, chewing and listening.

"We weren't fooling around, Dad. Flynn had already finished the roof!" said Gavyn.

Flynn stepped over to the screen door and peeked out at them. Though only in his early teens, he was tall enough to reach the top of the doorframe with his hands extended, and he placed both palms on the framework and lowered his chin to look outside. His dad was in the worst mood either one of them had ever seen him in!

Gavyn was trying to persuade him out of the mood with excuses, but he did not sway. Instead, he stood silently, looking at Gavyn with a menacing stare. Flynn retreated to get a glass of water, but strange sounds from the front yard made him stop and turn around to look out to the yard again. He felt his blood boil up to his head in an instant when he saw his dad holding Gavyn in a headlock.

"I'll teach you boys..." he grunted out the words. "I'll teach you to behave like real men!"

It came from nowhere for Ty; one minute, he was holding Gavyn around the neck, and the next, he had his back pinned up against a nearby tree, looking into the fire in Flynn's eyes. Ty felt a chill come over him. There was a fear that lived inside him, something he would never show within his eyes or in his words. That fear rested on Flynn because, although he wouldn't admit it to himself, he knew he'd been playing with fire for some time now and that maybe he had pushed Flynn too far, for too long.

Ty had scrutinized Flynn carefully from the safety of the outer bounds of the ring, and he knew well what pushing him far could do. He feared what he delighted in, Flynn's unpredictability. That's what made him a star in boxing circles, and Ty wouldn't dream of veering it away from him when he was young. Instead, he chose to fan and scratch at the fire with him, but at times, he was frightened of it.

"Flynn... now... son..." he grunted while attempting to draw in air.

"Flynn!" Ty clenched his teeth, "You're...going...to...be..." He struggled to calm himself because he knew what Flynn could do and probably wanted to do. But Flynn wouldn't ease his grip, and he yelled, "Flynn, you'd better let me go!"

Flynn's rage was beyond reason, and he began to put pressure with his left hand on Ty's throat; he didn't wrap around it with his fingers, just pushed on the cartilage in the front of his neck with his open hand. His eyes were intent and looked foreign to Gavyn. Ty's body was lifted inches from the ground, suspended only by Flynn's hand on his throat.

"Hey, Flynn!" Gavyn tried calling out to him, but he seemed deaf to all sounds. "Flynn!" He grabbed his arm and yanked on it. He scrambled to ease him down and thought of one thing that might do it. "Think about that girl you were with today."

Flynn's eyes seemed to relax a little, but the pressure was still on Ty's throat. Gavyn desperately continued, "You don't want her to hear about you doing something like this, do you?" Gavyn searched his brother's face. Something seemed to trigger, and his grip relaxed, and he placed his hand on his arm, hoping to lessen the hold. Gavyn spoke calmly to him. "That girl from the hill. What was her name?" Then he suddenly remembered. "Kate!" he said. "Kate, remember?"

Flynn lessened his grip on Ty, and he let him drop to the ground in the same way he would drop a dumbbell after a workout. Then he turned and walked past the two. He didn't look at Gavyn or back at his dad; he walked into the house, staring straight ahead.

Ty was on the ground, rubbing his neck and grimacing. "Did you see that?" he asked a perturbed Gavyn. "That boy's practically still a kid," his dad said, coughing and trying to catch his breath. "He's going to be... the best ...prized fighter the world has ever known!" His dad's eyes bugged, and they glistened.

Gavyn didn't know what the new feeling was that came over him; it was a kind of half-pity, half-perturbed sentiment as he watched his dad. What he did come to understand was his own bitterness and disappointment in himself, and he didn't offer to help him up but instead walked back to the house. He was too young to understand his father and the mechanics of greed and selfishness, but in a few years, he would.

Flynn was by no means an uncontrollable monster; in fact, the only time Gavyn had seen him like that was with their dad. When he boxed, it was all business, and it never looked personal. But it was different with Ty; he resented his dad in every way. Those early memories of Flynn finding his way through his dreams as a young man, which meant so much to Kate, meant absolutely nothing to Ty. He was never interested enough to know his sons as people. He didn't care to know about their aspirations, opinions, or feelings. As far as Ty was concerned, boxing and winning were the only things that mattered.

Ty's attitude toward the Masons and vice versa was what prompted young Kate and Flynn to sneak away. Whenever they could and spend their summers at a nearby river, once following it all the way to the sea. Gavyn, being fond of his own neck, had thereby sworn to secrecy whenever they had shared those moments together.

CHAPTER 10
A CHANGE HAS COME

A change had come to the seaside town. It had grown from infancy to a fully-grown village, and its dwellers had grown along with it. Kate and Flynn were two of those residents who were no longer adolescents. They stood on the pier before Ty, resolute in his presence. Even then, after the years that had passed, Ty realized that he still felt trepidation over Flynn's unpredictability and the deep-rooted hatred for Kate's family. His disdain for the Masons, he would surely carry to his death.

The words were few, and Kate began to feel as uneasy as a small fish squirming at the end of a pole. "Think I'd better go now," she said and planted a quick kiss on Flynn's mouth. She moved so quickly that he hardly had time to return the kiss. Kate mumbled goodbye to Ty and walked back down the pier to the parking area.

Flynn turned to his dad with deadpan eyes. "I know what you're doing, Dad," he said tersely. "It's not going to work." He stared at his face, emotionlessly.

His father chuckled. "Really? And just what is it you think I'm doing, son?"

Flynn looked away with eyes. "Don't call me that."

"What...*son*? Well, that's what you are!" Ty's smile was short and faded quickly as he turned to maneuver the conversation and spin it into persuasion. "You know, you say, *don't call me dad*, but who taught you everything you know? You are one of the most sought-after fighters I know! It's in your blood! And guess who taught you to fight like that? Me!" He hit his chest with his fist. "And you're unappreciative of that."

Flynn's eyes burned hot, "You're damn right, I'm unappreciative! Like a guy that gets his arm torn off by a crocodile is unappreciative too! And I'm what? The best fighter in town? Oh yeah, sure, suppose now you'll say the same heartwarming stuff you always say about me *being like my dear old dad*. Especially whenever there's an important fight in town, right?"

Ty downplayed the confrontation a little, "Don't be such a wimpy whiner!" His lips formed a harsh frown, and he looked away from Flynn.

Flynn's voice lowered, "Just remember... I'm no longer sixteen, Dad. You can't call the shots with me anymore." He cautioned him.

"Setting up a good fight isn't calling the shots," said Ty.

"A good fight? The last guy you put me up to fight was my *brother*, Dad!" he scowled back at him.

"So?"

"So I'm not fighting or training Gavyn! You got that? It's over."

"We'll see," Ty responded indifferently.

Flynn stood still, his voice dropped to a low sound from the gut. "I'm nothing...like...you," he emphasized, slowly. So much anger rose up in him that no further words came, and he stared at him bitterly. Flynn turned his body away from him in disgust. He placed his palms on the railing of the pier and looked down at the waves.

"Aaanyway," Ty said, and smiled contentedly. He took pleasure in showing no emotion or response to Flynn's appraisal of him. Ty sauntered down the pier, stopping a few feet away and turning back to him. "You don't have to worry about Gavyn," he said.

Flynn straightened up and looked at his dad, tentatively. "Why?" he asked, wondering what he had up his sleeve. Ty didn't answer, turned around, and continued his stroll down the pier. Flynn stood with his eyes locked on him as he walked away.

A gray-bearded old man was sitting with his legs dangling off the pier, and his fishing rod curved downward into the ocean.

Ty noticed him. "Is that bonito you got there?" he asked in a loud, sociable voice, and he pointed to a bucket of fish near the man.

The old man's eyes dropped to the bucket placed next to him. "Yep, bonito," he responded, in a low, groggy voice. Then he reached back and flipped back the lid on a large cooler. "I got some halibut, Pacific mackerel, sardines, and of course bonito," he went on to say.

Ty stood over the cooler, staring down at its contents. He smiled and nodded approvingly. "Wow! That's quite a catch…quite a catch, he repeated."

Flynn tucked his hands into his pants pockets and eyed his dad from steps away. He would never figure him out, but he didn't really want to anyway. His dad was nothing like him; he was pushy, rude, and he thought he had life all figured out.

He walked back to the round part of the pier, where it stopped in the ocean.

The sea looked unfathomably deep and green. Flynn squinted as he looked out at the faraway horizon.

Flynn was a fighter, and he was one of the best, but that was not where his heart was. He was an adventurer and a discoverer with dreams to realize, and the only thing he knew was that Kate was a part of them.

Ty looked back but could no longer see Flynn standing where he had been. The old man was still talking some nonsense, mostly about fish. "Here's the one I just caught minutes ago," he said, with his gravelly voice, and he moved some smaller fish aside to show a large one at the bottom of the cooler.

"Damn, that's a big fish!" Ty called out aloud and picked up the bonito by its tail. "It's gotta be the biggest bonito I've seen off the pier."

The old man nodded, smiling proudly. "Yeah, well, I've been fishing along this very pier and harbor breakwater rocks since I was eight, so that's gotta account for some kind of skill, huh? I mean by way of experience anyhow," he growled through the wiry hair on his face. His mouth seemed invisible since the coarse beard covered it all. "But there's always a bigger fish, right?" he said, and the bushy mustache moved up and down as he spoke. The old man appeared to be happy to be talking to someone. "What's your name, by the way? I'm Bo Smith," he said, squinting one eye up at Ty, who was looking about the pier, wondering where Flynn had gone. "Oh, uh..." He turned his attention back to the old man. "My name's Ty."

"Nice to meet ya, Ty. Is that short for somethin'? Tyrone, maybe or Tyler?" The old man didn't wait for an answer, and Ty didn't give it. So he went fishing. "Anyway, like I was saying...some guy just caught a 28-pound jackpot yellow onboard the Pacific boat. And the next day, a 40 white seabass! Now that's a good catch!" the old man said, nodding approvingly as he looked out at the ocean. He had a misty look in his eyes and a big smile on his face.

Ty drew in a breath, expanding his chest. He took out a cigar from his shirt pocket and bit off the end, then spat it out as film stars do in tough-guy roles. He made a sound like a balloon deflating quickly as he released his breath and promptly stuck the cigar into the corner of his smirking mouth. "Well, Bo. I'm gonna go get some bourbon," he muttered to the old man. Then, unsure of its feasibility, he thought he'd ask, "You wouldn't happen to like watching boxing matches, would you?" The old man didn't look back up at him and kept fishing.

CHAPTER 11
THE DROP-IN

The next day, ribbons of white fog wrapped long, ephemeral arms around the seaside town. The docks were quiet, and the sea looked like molten silver. All of the oceanfront shops were still closed, and the cobblestones were still wet from the overnight mist.

It was 6:00 in the morning when Ty stepped out, headed for the Drop-In bar. He moved swiftly and silently through the streets, rounding the corners rigidly like a soldier on patrol with his thoughts set only on reaching the establishment and nothing else.

A large Wells Fargo bank straddled the corner, and rows of establishments stood side by side on either side of the street, snuggled together all the way down to the pier. Joanne's Fine Art Studio stood alongside Wendy's Bookstore, with the Wellness pharmacy adjacent to it. You could find Taylor's Theatre On The Strand and Rose's Inn, across the street from Lisa's French Ice Cream shop. Hi-Time Liquor store was next to Art's Barbershop.

Up the narrow street at the top of the hill was a large warehouse once used as a lumber storehouse.

Later in the years, it was repurposed as a pyrotechnics plant where Flynn worked part-time since his early teens and now supervised to finance his oceanic studies. The company specialized in staging outdoor fireworks displays for large civic celebrations such as those held on the day of the christening of the newly built pier.

The Drop-In was the last structure on the street, and it was steps from the pier. Inside, it was dim with dark panels, colorful drinking décor, and a small boxing ring toward the right side of the bar. It was corded off and accessible only from within the bar. The ring was open to the public, but only after noon. It had its own training area with lockers for anyone willing to go for a few rounds of boxing after a few shots of drinks.

The drinking bar had been really just an afterthought for Ty. He figured it would go well with the ring and offer good refreshment and courage to those who wanted to try out boxing for the first time. But the Drop-In was by no means a fully stocked bar such as McNully's down the strand.

The gym was dilapidated with some peeling paint and exposed pipes, but it served its purpose for Ty since he used it before and after hours for training. It was an unfulfilled wish, or an unfulfilled life perhaps, that made him turn to train after a defeat that left him almost dead at the age of twenty. Now at fifty-nine, he searched for his lost past in the eyes and heart of the young ones he trained, and once his own boys were no longer small, he searched in their hearts too.

That morning, Gavyn was jumping rope in the ring when he stopped abruptly. He was drenched in sweat as he grabbed for a towel. He felt frustrated at his own progress, or lack thereof. Sweat and try as he might, he still had a lot of catching up to do before reaching Flynn's status in the ring.

"Whacha doing, Gavyn?" Ty's voice rang out and echoed in the empty room. He ambled around the ring, then stooped under the rope to get inside.

Gavyn breathed out long. "Just taking a minute to cool down, Dad."

"Cool down?" Half a chuckle broke through his tight lips. "You haven't even started here, boy!" Ty walked to the side and leaned back slightly on the ropes. "You know how I feel about laggards..."

"I said I was taking a break!" Gavyn spewed out the words through a tight mouth, but just as quickly, he looked down at the floor.

Ty's eyes went from apathetic and round to flat and narrow in a matter of seconds. He kept calm and quiet as he paced the floor. Gavyn quickly snuck a glance with the corner of his eye at his father. The outburst he had just done made him nervous. It wasn't that he didn't want to please his dad; in fact, that was the problem from the start, he wanted to so much more than Flynn ever did. But his dad didn't think much of that; he only thought of Flynn and his gift for boxing.

Gavyn had learned to duck and sway, not punches but words, whenever his dad was around, spewing out criticism. Ever since childhood, he never quite knew what to expect from his dad. Sometimes it was a slap upside the head, other times worse, but usually when he drank too much.

Flynn had gotten it the nastiest since he was older and tended to be more rebellious. Yet, there was his dad. Day in and day out, trying to convince Flynn to fight and show his loyalty to Ty and the sport. To Gavyn's surprise, it seemed that his outburst hadn't fazed his dad, and this time Ty kept his cool, who knows why, but he did, as he circled the ring, walking slowly and methodically.

He began to speak with a warning tone. "I'm going to tell you something, and I'm only going to tell you once," he said, finally breaking his silence. He stopped dead in his tracks and locked eyes with Gavyn. "I didn't raise no loser. And you and your brother are gonna live my dream, *my* dream!" He pounded his fist on his chest one time. "Do you understand? Cuz I say so!" His face was tense, and Gavyn could see his heartbeat in the bulging veins on his temples. Ty paused a moment to compose himself, but it didn't work, and he began to pace again; his face was flushed red. "Now I don't care if you got something else you want to do, you owe me! When your mother left us, who took you? Your aunt? Your uncle? No! And they certainly could have. Cuz, after she passed, I coulda been gallivanting around. But instead, I put aside my needs for the two of you!" His nostrils flared as he pointed a rigid forefinger at him.

Gavyn remained quiet. He had heard that violin story several times. And he had a hard time believing things precisely as he painted them, but the fact was that the only person who had ever looked after them since that day had been his dad.

Ty stopped pacing, his breathing became slow and steady, and he appeared calmer. After a moment, he asked, "Have you seen Flynn anywhere?" He mumbled the question quickly.

"No," Gavyn said flatly.

Ty nodded short and stiff, and he moved his mouth to the side in a tight crooked line. "Last I saw him, he was with that Mason girl on the pier. You know, I don't like her hanging around so much. Next thing you know, she's got her claws in him. Dames want just one thing, to get their claws in ya."

Gavyn let his chin drop, and he wiped the sweat from the back of his neck with a towel. He eyed his dad as he walked around the ring from beneath his brow.

"So? Who cares, Dad? Anyone in our family could only wish!" Gavyn said brusquely. He straightened up and threw the damp towel down; it landed by his feet on the floor.

Ty stopped all movement and stared at Gavyn. "Who cares? Who cares, Gavyn?" The pitch of his voice went up a notch. "If you're asking that question, then you're a little low on thinking gas. Flynn's got the stuff you need for fightin'! He doesn't need any kind of girly distractions around to mess things up."

Gavyn frowned and turned back to face the ropes. He grasped the thick cord, wrapping his fingers around it, and hung his head low, staring at the floor. "You just don't get it, Dad. She's not what you think," he said.

"I know exactly what she is," Ty said. "They're all girly distractions, whether rich or poor. And I got big plans for Flynn!"

Ty looked straight out in front of him into space. The whole room suddenly disappeared, and he began to admire his fabricated vision of Flynn. There was a slight smile on his lips when Ty started to talk about ten-round, non-title fights, and crown challengers, and throwing out names to the air of the empty room like Louis and Schmeling. His eyes roamed the room as he spoke. But they didn't focus on anything since the vision was all in his head.

"I mean, what more could you want, eh?" he said. "Flynn...he's big and can get really mean." His eyes twinkled. "Especially when you can get his blood to boil...eh, Gavyn?" he quipped, giving a short, quick glance aslant at him. "And most of all, he's quick and tough!" he said, grinning, and his chest broadened.

Gavyn was silent, listening. "Well, he's not the only good fighter around here," Gavyn mumbled. His mouth curled downward, and he dropped his eyes and snuck a look back at his dad like a jockey does when he measures the distance of the horses behind him. "What about me, Dad? I fight with everything I have! I surrender to the sport!"

"You?" Ty's voice boomed. He sauntered over to him, and Gavyn looked down again. Ty searched for his face, and when he found it, his expression took on a pitiful look, and his voice got low. "Well, you're not as quick… not as mean… not as big. You see?" he said, derisively, as he patted Gavyn's ear with his hand. "Keep trying, son, maybe one day. Who knows?" he chuckled.

Gavyn's anger rose, and he pushed his dad's chest. Ty stumbled back. "And you, Dad? What are *you*?" he yelled at him, and there was a red ring around the white of his eyes. "I'll tell you what you are...you're unhinged, yeah, you're nuts!" Gavyn flung a clean towel over his shoulder and quickly ducked under the ropes to leave.

Ty smiled approvingly. He liked it when his sons showed some emotion. But as usual, it was disappointing to him that Gavyn would retreat. He stood and shook his head slowly, thinking and looking at the floor, weighing in on Gavyn's worthlessness. Then he looked up suddenly and called out to him as Gavyn reached the exit door. "Hey!" He stuck out his chin and yelled. "Just remember… you think you got heart, Gavyn, but I've yet to see you bleed!" he shouted after him. "I mean, really bleed," he said, and a grin ran across his face.

Gavyn paused at the exit long enough to acknowledge his dad's words, and a look of disgust washed over his face. Then he pushed the door open without turning around or saying a word and walked out.

CHAPTER 12
SWINGING ON A STAR

It was around noon when the sun dispersed the lacy fog. The rays streamed in and had woken up the seagulls, and it reenergized the seabirds along the shore. There was a soft wind, and a flight of water birds caught an updraft and stayed with it, floating on the air currents while searching the sea for small fish. Upon spotting food, they would swoop down and snatch a mouthful. Then land on the shore squawking and pecking at each other, battling for bits of seaweed and fish snatched up from the sea.

The sun was intense that day, and the effects of its rays could be seen rising up in transparent waves on anything metal: trash cans, light poles, and the steel of the train tracks. The trash had not been picked up yet, and it was beginning to take on a repugnantly sweet smell that permeated the air around it. Anyone walking near it would quickly pick up their pace. However, the gulls took great pleasure in that smell. They liked to scavenge the dump and docks for tidbits, and they took particular pleasure in what the heat brought up from the trash. Tiny flies breeding in and hovering over the warmth of the refuse were a kind of treat for gulls. They had a foraging strategy for catching these alkali flies as they buzzed along the strand. The birds would start at one end of a vast swarm of flies that happened to be loitering on the beach, they would run through a line of them, head down, and bills open, snapping up as much as they could in one sweep.

Gavyn's mind was still spinning, and he didn't notice the seabirds as they cavorted in the sky overhead. He walked past the docks to the trolley tracks, and he looked down the double rails. At that moment, they were empty, but soon the red cars would come rumbling down the way, eating up the tracks that lay alongside the ocean.

The railway was to be shut down soon to make way for newer transportation, and that thought made Gavyn irritable. He didn't know precisely why; he just knew that change, any change, would tend to make him irritable nowadays.

The seaside village, *his* village where he was born and raised, was being transformed. *Change isn't always good*, he remembered saying to Flynn, but he didn't agree. Flynn was all about change and progress. The two brothers didn't have a lot in common. They were opposite in looks, had opposite tastes in women, and even in their choice of music. Gavyn was keen on the sound of Bing Crosby's, *Swinging On A Star*, while Flynn favored Glenn Miller and Benny Goodman.

In fact, the only thing they did have in common was that they would always agree to disagree on just about everything. One of those things was Flynn's friendship with Kate Mason.

It's not that Gavyn didn't like Kate; he just couldn't figure out what she liked about Flynn. What made Kate even look at one of the Brennans? On the rare occasion that they would discuss it, Flynn would put an end to the discussion before it even started. He would say things like, "It was meant to be, so don't worry about it." But the only thing Gavyn thought was *meant to be* was a heartache, and it was just waiting to happen.

He remembered the first time he came to that conclusion. He would see Kate every day, taking a stroll by the shoreline. While every man was sure to look at her, the only ones who would maintain a straight posture and undeviating eye contact were the rich ones.

Gavyn couldn't figure out why someone like her would glance at one of them and how Flynn could have the guts to glance back. As far as influence, power, and riches went, they were way on the other side of the fence. And the fence on her side was made of richly ornate wrought iron, while theirs was cheap wood! Yeah, it was very apparent to Gavyn; she was too good for the likes of a family such as his.

The trolley was right on time, and the hands on the clock hanging on the ticket booth fell on exactly twelve when the noontime trolley came barreling down the tracks. It often looked like it was going to overshoot its stop, startling some of the waiting passengers, but then the train would halt suddenly on a dime.

However, this time, the conductor must have been running late because the brakes' screeching sound was loud and long. A big waft of air pushed back Gavyn's brown hair, making it look almost as if it stood on end. He smoothed it back down with his fingers, and with the help of hair cream, it settled back into place again. It had grown a little over the summer, and he thought of getting a haircut soon, a buzz maybe, and do away with the hair cream altogether.

The train came to a complete stop, and the dry soil whirled up in large lucent curls around the steel wheels. Gavyn could feel the gritty dirt settle on his face and sting his eyes. He blinked and rubbed them a little, then eyed the train's passengers as they disembarked. Since he was standing there and had nowhere, in particular, he had to be, he observed them not suspiciously but curiously.

The first passenger was an older man with a stopwatch hanging from his pocket and a cigar hanging from his mouth; he tipped his chin at him as he walked by. The next one to disembark was a young woman with elegantly curled honey-colored hair and plump, rose-tinted lips. She smiled sheepishly at him as she tried to balance herself unsteadily, wearing black high heels over the tracks.

Gavyn reached out and took her hand to help steady her walk over the rocky pavement. He gazed at her, charmed by her wide-eyed look. "Thank you so much," she said in a soft voice.

At that moment, with no warning, the three-way communication between Gavyn's brain, heart, and lips went numb. He suffered a sudden shortage of words; he stood there in a daze watching her walk past him. His eyes followed her as she walked beyond the tracks toward the fishing permits building, and she disappeared into the office.

He was in a trance. So much so that he didn't realize when someone walked by and carefully closed his gaping mouth for him. The woman who had captured him in a split second with her angelic appearance was a stranger to him, and he had to find out who she was.

Gavyn was amid this museful, inattentive thinking when Kate arrived at the train station. In fact, he might not have noticed Kate was there at all if it weren't for a couple of guys nudging each other and making a loud ruckus. That forced him out of his stupor.

"Well, hi-de-ho!" One of the guys inched forward toward Kate with a big smile.

Kate smiled slightly but kept walking. She moved her auburn hair a little away from her eyes.

"Hey sweetheart," a deep voice tried his luck from the crowd. "Are you rationed?"

Kate nodded her head, yes, emphatically.

"What? Was that a yes?" He nudged the guys, grinning.

"I don't think it was a yes, I think she said she wasn't," one of them said.

"Wasn't taken?" another joined in.

"Yep, that's what she said, she is not rationed! Right doll?"

Kate became uncomfortable and picked up her walking pace.

"Wait now…hold on there!" one of the men yelled after her.

Gavyn, having witnessed the situation, stepped up to walk alongside Kate and threw a glance back at the men.

"Hello, Gavyn!" she said, and she sounded relieved at his presence.

"Those guys bothering you, Kate?" he asked, concerned, and looked back at them again with a stern warning.

The two men were joined by three more, and they were now whistling loudly.

Gavyn became irate at them. "Hey! You doll dizzy or something? This girl is taken! Find something else to do!" he yelled at them.

From the crowd came a chorus of oohs, and a couple of them yelled, "*Sooo*?"

"Who has she taken by? Huh?" one of them hollered and chuckled.

Gavyn laughed at their stupidity. "Wanna know by who? Cuz, it's not me, in case that's what you're thinking."

The guy with the deep voice walked closer to them. "I don't care who it is," he said, challenging him.

"You're not from here, are you?" Gavyn asked.

"Nope, me and my buddies are from clear away from here."

"Yeah, I could tell right away."

"How's that?" The man turned back to his friends. "Hey guys, did you hear that? He could tell right away that we weren't from around here!" They laughed in unison, and the man looked back at Gavyn smugly.

"Let's just walk faster," Kate said, getting nervous at the encounter.

"No, there's no need for that," Gavyn answered, and suddenly he heard a brash, familiar voice.

"What's going on here?" His dad appeared from down the tracks. His look was bold and stern, with his chest out and eyebrows together. "You boys looking for trouble here?" he asked the group of men.

"Who are you, old man? And what business is it of yours?" the burly one asked.

Ty walked over to him and studied his face. "I know you," he said, sounding like he was thinking aloud and shaking his finger at him. "You're Frankie, aren't you?" he asked inquisitively.

"Yeah, that's me," the man answered. "So, how do I know you?"

"Vegas…one of your guys went two rounds with one of my boys," Ty said.

The man seemed to remember, and it suddenly brought some sort of good memory to him. "Oh, yeah, you're Brennan, right? Your kid, he's a *real* good fighter… Flynn, right?" he asked.

Ty stood up straight again and slipped his fingers under the straps of his suspenders. "Yeah, that's him," he smiled. "Listen, don't waste your time here with these two. Whadda ya say we go over to my place and have a couple of beers? Talk a little about setting up something between you and Flynn."

The man faltered a little, unsure. "Between Flynn and me? Ah, well, I don't think…" He looked over at his buddies sitting on some rocks nearby. They all had big grins and eager eyes looking at him.

Frankie felt the pressure, and he broke under it. "Well, ok, sure. I can handle that."

Ty erupted with a belly laugh, slapped the man's back, and then put his arm around his shoulders, and they walked off toward the Drop-In.

Kate felt relieved when the crowd followed Ty, and she turned back to Gavyn.

"Are you going to tell Flynn about what your dad is setting up? He's not going to like it," she said, frowning.

Gavyn kicked some small rocks out of the way. "Yeah, guess I'd better," he said.

Kate's hair shone a deep golden auburn under the sunlight. She squinted toward the pier. "Sometimes…I hate your dad," she said, staring at the shoreline.

Gavyn nodded slowly. "Me too, Kate, me too," he said.

"Have you seen Flynn?" she asked, her eyes narrowed in the bright sunlight as they roved about the shoreline.

"No, not today," he said, glancing around the dock area.

Kate shielded her eyes with her hand from the glare and peered down the tracks in the opposite direction. "You don't suppose he took the train downtown?"

"I don't think so, but I really don't know where he is. Guess you could check…" Gavyn became distracted midsentence when he noticed the same blonde girl –the angel- he had seen earlier emerging from the office. He knew he had to move quickly to catch her. "Don't mean to be rude, Kate, but I really haven't seen or heard from him!" he yelled back to her and smiled nervously as he jetted toward the girl.

"But…" Kate's lips parted a little as she stared at his figure, moving quickly down the pathway. She smiled and let out a breath. A few days before, she had noticed the pretty blonde on the trolley and thought then that the two of them would make a good pair. There was a goofy side to Gavyn that amused Kate, and she giggled as she watched him, with his buck-like, agile sprinting, catch up with the young lady.

CHAPTER 13
THE DECISION

The afternoon bell of the Wayan ship rang eight times offshore. It was an almost mystical, hollow sound, like someone striking a huge empty metal can. The strikes echoed, summoning Kate like the smoke from a genie's bottle.

The ship was mysterious to her, and the fact that she had never been on board added to the mystery. One day, she would venture on board to see what the fuss was all about and solve the mystery.

Gavyn was out of breath but trying to hold back the gasp for air when he approached the blonde woman. "Uh, hello again!" Gavyn stepped up next to her and began to walk in unison with her pace.

She glanced at him by veering her large blue eyes a little to the left, and then she looked straight ahead, brought her chin down, and smiled.

"Ah…what's ah…what's your name? Um…If you don't mind my asking?" The words tumbled out of his mouth without first checking in with his brain. Anxiety would sometimes do that to him. As a kid, his tongue would sometimes tie up so severely that his dad thought he might have had a speech impediment.

The woman didn't seem to mind the stutter, and she asked softly, "What's yours?" Her lips moved in a smile to the side, and she walked on without looking at him.

He couldn't tell if it was shyness or an overabundance of security. "Mine's Gavyn." He took a long step in front of her and blocked her path.

The woman stopped cold in her tracks and looked directly at him. Now that he had forcibly gotten her attention, he bowed exaggeratedly low and made a gesture with his hand as if tipping his hat. She yielded to spontaneous laughter.

"My name is Eva," she said, still giggling. And her eyes stayed on his face.

"Eva...Eva...like Eve! The name of the most beautiful woman that ever existed!"

"How do you know?" she asked, smiling at him.

"Know what?"

"That she was the most beautiful ever?"

"Oh, it's in the history books!"

Eva laughed as if she were being tickled. "It's not in history books, sugar," she responded, with a twinkle in her eyes. "You'd best pick up that dusty old book that's probably lying around your house called the Bible."

Gavyn gazed at her face with a look of sheer fascination. Her skin was light golden beige, and her eyes were large and a glistening sky-blue, and within them, he saw the glow of a tiny radiant sun.

"Oh, ah, yes, of course, the Bible…" he started to say, but his head was in a haze. Then it occurred to him that she might be a church-going girl, the kind he usually had nothing in common with.

"You, ah, you read the Bible much?" he tried asking, inconspicuously.

She smiled a little and looked down. "You have a very amusing way about you, mister! You know that?"

Amusing? What did that mean? He didn't know, but he didn't care for once, and he threw all caution out the window. "Well, Eva, do you, um…" he cleared his throat a little, "do you think you'd like to go out sometime…soon?" His mouth was merely asking, but his eyes were pleading.

"Well, I don't know." She looked down at the cement walkway and watched the sea mist collecting on it. "I mean, I don't know you very well, and my dad, well, he's not the most understanding or trusting kind of guy." She smiled a little hesitantly.

Gavyn was confused. He thought she was receptive to him, but now he wasn't sure. "Your dad? Oh, well, maybe I can talk to him? Who's your dad?"

"My dad is Edward McNully."

"Edward McNully??" He squinted and grinned as if he were waiting for the punchline. But there was no punchline. There's no way an angel like this could come from a brute like McNully, so where was the joke?

"Yes, he owns the bar on Prospect," she said.

Gavyn's expression dropped. "Ohhh...yeah, McNully!" he said. His brain scrambled to make sense of that one. "My brother and I go there sometimes." He stood before her with a grim expression. "So, he's your dad, huh? How come I've never seen you before today?"

"Kind of a long story, my mom and dad are divorced, and my mom is remarried, living in England. She dragged me all over Europe until I turned 18, and that's when I thought it was time I lived with my father for a change," said Eva.

Gavyn looked away and nodded in thought. "So... what do you think he'll flip his wig if he sees us together?" he asked.

Eva giggled; her laughter was like music from heaven to him, and his eyes crinkled at the corners, watching her.

"How did you know he wears one?" she asked, moving her lips a little to the side again in an almost bashful smile. They both broke out in laughter.

"Just a lucky guess," Gavyn said.

"Don't tell anyone, he's sensitive about it," said Eva.

"Oh, I wouldn't dream of it."

They continued to walk and arrived at a small wooden house with a picket fence in the front yard. The fence was in disrepair, and the home seemed unkempt and had grass growing unevenly up the three steps leading to the front door. Gavyn had no idea where McNully lived, but he would never have imagined it like this.

Eva turned around suddenly to him. "Thank you for walking me home," she said, lowering her chin, and her large eyes danced with light.

"You're welcome, Eva," Gavyn said kindly. Then he brought his eyebrows together like he was about to say something of utmost importance, and asked, "When can I see you again?"

"How about tonight?" she answered quickly.

"Tonight?" he asked, surprised, delighted, and a little confused. What about McNully? He wasn't about to ask, though. "Ok, wanna go see Notorious or The Postman Always Rings Twice? I think one of them is playing at Taylor's," he asked excitedly.

"Oh no, I can't go to the movies with you. My dad would kill me!"

Gavyn's face showed confusion. "He doesn't like movies?" he asked dumbly.

"Yeah, he does, but..." said Eva.

Gavyn knew it had been too good to be true.

Then she suddenly said, "I'll sneak out around midnight and meet you at the docks." Her eyes shone brightly.

"The docks? Oh, all right...I mean...Yeah! That's a great idea," he said, and analyzed her face for a moment.

"Gavyn, I don't want you to think I'm a khaki wacky kind of girl, meeting with you at midnight and all. I just… I really like you," Eva added.

He casually brought his hand up to his chest and patted his heart. He was sure it might burst through any minute. "Nope, I would never think you were boy crazy. I can tell that by just looking at you," he said. He took her hand and kissed it gently and long. He kept his lips on her skin and then looked up at her face with his eyes. The gesture was something he had seen in movies and always cringed at it, but now he knew why they did it. "I'll see you then," he said.

Night fell quickly, and the hands of the clock rolled close to midnight, but it hadn't been soon enough for Gavyn, who had been pacing the room for hours trying to keep his mind off his nerves. He had gotten home, eaten dinner, and at about 9:00 pm, he turned off the small television.

The black and white picture faded into the darkness with a muffled thud as he turned the knob on the front. Counting the hours and minutes before midnight hadn't been easy. He had watched a new program called The Ed Sullivan Show. Then he tried reading, and even writing a little to pass the time, but once the hands of the clock hit the long-awaited midnight hour, Gavyn hit the road.

He tiptoed through the house, through the long dark hallway, past his snoring dad, and past the empty room belonging to Flynn. He stopped outside of it for a second, wondering where he might be at that time of night, but then continued on and out the door.

He got to the fog-laced docks quickly and parked his red pickup. He waited inside the car and then got out when he didn't see anyone coming up the way. The pier looked cold and lonely and stood out like a bony, white skeleton stretching out to the darkened sea.

He walked on the boards looking down, and he could see a glimpse of the surf below him between the small gaps in the wooden slabs. The silence was broken by a voice that made him feel a slight tremble in his gut.

"Hello, Gavyn," Eva called to him softly.

He turned to see her standing in front of him in a long black overcoat. Gavyn swallowed quickly and then again unexpectedly. He hoped she wouldn't be able to tell just how nervous she made him.

"Hello, doll." He smiled, and his eyes reflected the moon's glow. The music from the Wayan ship could be heard over the churn of the ocean, and it was currently on a low simmer. Notes from the song *How Deep Is The Ocean* by Ethel Merman seemed to slip right out through the portholes onto the pier where they stood. A woman's silky voice hovered buoyantly above the lights strung on the ship.

Gavyn took Eva's hands and brought her closer, placing her hand on his heart. He held her close as they swayed with the music, and Eva closed her eyes.

The lyrics and the woman's velvet voice descended from the sky like honey. The evening stars sprinkled magic on Gavyn and Eva that night, and after that day, they met at midnight on the pier without fail.

They talked, sipped on wine, and talked some more. The two arrived at the same conclusion one night; for better or worse, they had fallen deeply in love. The better being the deep love they had fallen into, the worse being their circumstances.

But that night, they both ignored their troubling situation. Eva brought along an Oak Weave Picnic Basket filled with a bottle of Monmousseau, red grapes, and cheese. She didn't forget Gavyn's favorite chocolate chip cookies.

Gavyn was a fighter, a boxer by trade, and this unnerved Eva. She didn't want either one of them to be a part of that dark, bloody world of bruises, cuts, and death. And although she didn't know much more than the gruesomeness of boxing, she knew all she needed to know…the heartache.

She had experienced it one day when she was five years old. That day, she had seen her father's eyes swollen as big as the ones she had seen once on a dragonfly's face in a pond near her home. His eyes were red where the white had been and black where the skin had been. Her mother had always shielded her from seeing such things, but that night, he had come home drunk and menacing, like a monster that had stumbled into their quiet home.

As a young girl, days spent at her grandfather's deli were days spent hearing her father cheering on the bloodier of the two monsters and yelling obscenities at the loser of the fights. Just a year later, her grandfather would die, along with her parents' marriage. The deli was inherited by her father, who subsequently breathed new life into it, as he would put it, and it became McNully's Bar.

All of these things ran through Eva's mind as she set out a large blanket on the darkened sand by the pier, and that night Eva voiced her concerns as Gavyn uncorked the wine.

"You don't act or look like a boxer. I mean, they're pretty brutal, aren't they?" Eva had asked.

Gavyn knew she didn't understand that there were boxers, and then, there were boxers. Not all fighters were ragged, brutal, or low down as some thought. It was also a sport of endurance, talent, and strength. In Gavyn's mind, that's what made him a man, and he tried to explain it to her, but to no avail. Eva sat, staring out at the ocean with a blank sort of look.

"I almost couldn't make it," Eva admitted to him.

"Why, what happened?"

"My dad, he's always suspicious. He's afraid I'll do the same as my mom."

"What?"

"Leave him. My mother just up and left my dad, probably because he seemed to love boxing more than her. Anyway, he always has a million questions for me before I leave the house…where are you going? Who are you going to see?"

Gavyn nodded, a little worried. What will he think or do when Eva gets married?

She picked up her empty wine glass and held it in front of her, and Gavyn poured wine into it. Eva spoke as he filled the glass, "It was his obsession with the fights that had taken him down the awful, violent road. That did a lot to undo his marriage to my mother."

Gavyn stopped pouring the wine into her glass and looked into her eyes. "You never have to worry about that with me, Eva. I'll always treat you right."

"I know, love, but I just wish you weren't a part of that world," she said.

Gavyn's eyebrows raised in the middle. "You know I would do anything for you, doll, but I just don't think I could leave boxing right now," he said. He watched as Eva pouted, and she looked to the side and down at the ground. Her expression melted him faster than an ice cube hitting the hot pavement, and he gently touched her face. "I'll see what I can do," he said. Her face brightened instantly, but then he added, "Now it won't be something immediate. I have a contract, there's money, and my dad is involved. But I'll find something else to do, promise you."

Eva was happy with the promise, and she went along with the plan. Much to his own disbelief, Gavyn had found something more potent than his love for boxing, and in no time, he was doing fewer fights while looking for a new job.

The owner of Gavyn's contract, Matt Mazoli, wasn't as difficult as he anticipated. When Gavyn explained the situation, he helped him to get out of it. The money was quickly resolved with some penny pinching and doing without, but the hardest thing was his dad. Gavyn could not think of how to tell him, so he played it cool and avoided him at all costs until he could think of how to break it to him.

The rest of the time, he spent exclusively with Eva, ignoring his dad's yelling at what he perceived as laziness when he didn't show up at the ring. Eventually, Ty found out about the dissolution of the boxing contract, and he was so furious that he ran Gavyn out of the house. Of course, that only helped his cause, and he was more than happy to move in with a friend while he looked for a new job.

Ty was beginning to feel the loss of control and power he had over his sons. Flynn would spend his time with Jack diving, and now Gavyn, whom he could always count on for a fight, had dissolved his contract. After many sleepless nights and drunken days, he decided he had to do some sort of manipulation or scheme to get back his rulership.

CHAPTER 14
BRICKLAYER WANTED

G avyn ran into Flynn at the lunch counter in Rosie's Soda Fountain Shop on a Saturday. The shop's interior had sunny yellow walls and a large mirror behind the marble counter with gooseneck soda spouts. The spinning stools were white, and there were round marble-topped tables and wireframe sweetheart chairs throughout the room that had yellow and white striped cushions.

Flynn snuck up behind Gavyn, who was sitting on one of the yellow stools, about to take a second bite into a sandwich, and he slapped him on the back hard. "Wow, so where have *you* been?" Flynn asked, surprised.

Gavyn spat out some of the bread. "I could ask the same about you!" Gavyn grinned, coughing a little.

"Hmm…something seems different. Did you buy new teeth?" Flynn asked.

Gavyn laughed. "No, you're just seeing more of the ones I already got."

Flynn straddled the seat next to him. "Yeah, I see that. Hey, Kate told me something about you chasing after a nice-looking blonde?"

"Yep, her name is Eva... isn't that the most wonderful name? Nice looking?—that's putting it mildly-- nice acting…Oh yeah! Flynn, I'm going to marry this one!" said Gavyn, excitedly.

"What? Wait now…hold on, there's no rush." Flynn was surprised to hear the word *marry*. He analyzed his face. "You're really bonkers about her, huh?"

"Yeah," he nodded, smiling, and he looked down, "that I am," Gavyn gushed.

"How does she feel about your boxing?"

Gavyn's expression fell. "Not too good. She hates it. But I fixed that already…"

"You fixed that? How?" Flynn grabbed the Coke sitting in front of Gavyn, took a sip, and then gave it back.

"I got out of my contract, that's how!"

"How were you able to do that?"

"Mike Mazoli, he's an ok guy. He helped me to get out."

Flynn nodded slowly. "So, now what are you going to do, for money, I mean?"

Gavyn leaned over his food and shrugged. "I don't know yet. I'm looking for a job." Hey, you know who Eva's dad is?"

"No, who?"

"McNully," Gavyn said.

"The guy who owns that bar on Bayshore Street? You mean *that*, McNully?"

"Yep."

Flynn was quiet as his mind ran through the McNully files in his brain. He didn't know much about him other than he was a bar owner, where he would sometimes go. And he remembered him as a past boxing foe of his dad's.

Gavyn turned a little in his seat and looked at his face. "What have you been up to? Dad says you're hardly home at all, and he's… oh, did he mention to you something about a fight in Vegas?" Gavyn asked, he suddenly looked like the old young Gavyn with his eyes wide and ingenuous.

Flynn looked straight ahead at the large mirror behind the counter, and his voice got monotone. "Yeah, dad told me about some guy named Frankie or something." He looked down and noticed a pack of matches placed in front of him. He took them and absentmindedly fiddled with them. Then he tossed them aside and looked up. "Can I get a Boston Cooler?" he asked the woman behind the counter.

"A *BC*? Sure," she replied, grabbed an ice cream scooper, and held it up in the air while she asked, "whipped cream or not?"

"No cream," he replied, grabbed a French fry from Gavyn's plate, and chewed on it hungrily.

"Well, the thing is, with Kate, I mean, she hasn't been seeing a lot of me lately and…been diving a lot…" Flynn's face was troubled. "Anyway, I'll talk to you about it when we have more time," he said, and disquietude washed over his words.

"Ok," Said Gavyn. "She's a real nice girl. I've gotten to know Kate a little more, you know."

"Yeah, I know. Listen, I don't want to talk about it right now, though, ok?" Flynn asked in a hushed and slow manner.

"Oh yeah, sure, buddy!" said Gavyn.

Flynn watched the server combine the dry ginger ale and a scoop of vanilla ice cream and blend them together. She set it down in front of him. "Thanks," he said.

"Oh, you're so welcome!" she answered and winked, holding her smile a little too long.

Flynn noticed her smitten expression and looked down at his drink.

"So, Frankie, he's the guy you mercifully went three rounds with last year, remember?" Gavyn asked.

"Yeah, sure, I remember. So what does Dad want with that match-up? It wasn't balanced before. Why would it be now?" Flynn asked.

Gavyn swallowed his last piece of sandwich. "Maybe he's looking for a sure win," he said.

Flynn nodded slowly. "Yeah, must be. I'm too busy for that."

Gavyn sat up in his seat, and his eyes brightened. He was always very interested in what Flynn was up to. He was the more adventurous of the two, and Gavyn sort of lived adventures through him.

"I've been diving with Jack, you know?" said Flynn, and his face brightened.

"Yeah, and?" asked Gavyn.

"Well, I want to make that my full-time profession."

"You mean a cave diver like him?"

"Any kind of diver. I think that's much more stable for Kate and respectable for me."

"Not to mention more fun, right?" Gavyn grinned.

Flynn laughed. "Yeah, much more!"

"Oh, hey, I almost forgot, and you would have killed me!" he said, digging into his pants pocket. "You're looking for a job, right? Well, here it is. I almost threw it away. Some guy handed it to me today." He presented a piece of paper.

Gavyn took it and read the flier; *Bricklayer Wanted: Apply at 14604 Hunt St.* "This is in downtown, right?" he asked, interested.

"Yeah. I hear it pays real good too." Flynn drank the last of his soda and set the glass down. "Well, Jack's waiting on me to go diving." He stood up and patted his back. "Let me know how it goes with the job," he said.

"I will! Thanks, Flynn, this is perfect! Hey, if you need me, I'm staying at Ernie's for right now," Gavyn yelled to him.

"Ernie's? Wow, you must have a lot of patience," he smirked.

Ernie had been nicknamed sloth for a good reason. He was a good guy, but he was infamous for his slowness from talking to working to thinking; he did all things slowly.

Gavyn laughed and watched his brother walk out, then turned back to the girl behind the counter. "You got a phone booth here?" he asked.

"Yeah, it's over there by the back wall."

"Thanks."

"Sure, um, hey, your friend is cute!" she said, pouring a drink for another customer.

"Uh, yeah, I'll be sure to tell him you said that!" he said. Gavyn wanted to call the office at the job site first, then Eva.

CHAPTER 15
VEGAS BOUND

B reaking free from the arms of thick fog, the red trolley meandered down the stretch of beach until it crossed over the street lanes into the highway and made its way into downtown the next morning. Eva was balancing a set of cards on her lap, trying to write on them.

They were announcement cards used to reveal an engagement or small wedding, but Eva wasn't using them for either. Gavyn had already proposed marriage with a simple but sparkling two-carat round diamond, and she had accepted. Still, there would be no wedding to invite people to. They had decided that the best thing to do would be to elope to Las Vegas and marry quietly. The cards would instead be used to announce the official engagement of the two of them, a kind of FYI notice.

The trolley slowed down at the corner of Maple and Bond Street. Eva stuffed the cards in her purse before disembarking on Adams St. It was a dreary Monday, and the sun looked gray in the sky. Downtown was surprisingly void of people that day, and Eva was able to shop peacefully for a unique dress she had in mind. Her eyes immediately fell on a fancy dress displayed in the window of Jeanette's Bridal Boutique, and she stepped inside the shop through the French double glass doors.

Underneath gilded chandeliers, Eva picked through the long rows of lace, satin, and beaded gowns. The dress hangers slid noisily as she dragged them one by one on the metal bar. But none of them were what she had in mind for the civil ceremony in Vegas.

Then she caught sight of a formal dress at the end of the row. An elegant wool crepe tailored dress that hugged the waist and fell just below the knee. The color was French beige, and it had a demure bridal hat of the same color to be worn aslant on the head. She tried on the hat. It was sophisticatedly ornamented with a few silk feathers, small flowers, and netting that fell over her forehead, mysteriously veiling Eva's glasslike, large blue eyes.

In the late 1940s, the Las Vegas strip was something straight out of the Wild West frontier, combined with glamour and excitement. The town looked like a gleaming pearl in the middle of vast sand. Hotels seemed to pop up overnight. The Flamingo Hotel was the third to open and the first to break from the old west traditional style, followed by others.

The view driving in from California was a barren desert. The first thing seen was the 120-foot neon Fremont sign on Fremont Street lined with budding casinos. The strip was being transformed from its original one-horse town origin to rebirth with entertainment venues and wedding chapels. Las Vegas was quickly becoming the romance capital of the world, and it became famous for its quickie weddings and just as quickie divorces.

It was on an inspiringly beautiful weekday in Nevada when Gavyn and Eva stood before each other with their hands coiled together, listening to the court clerk officiate the wedding. An hour later, they were married and happy.

They walked the streets and dined at El Rancho, where Nick Collins and his orchestra headlined the evening's entertainment.

Gavyn noticed the sax player on stage and nudged Eva to look up from the menu. "Doesn't that guy look familiar?"

Eva analyzed his face. "Yeah, I've seen him before. He works on the Wayan ship. I've seen him boarding the water taxi in Woodrose," she said.

"Yeah, that's what I thought." Gavyn shrugged. "Pff! Must have a lot of dough to be doing both joints," he said and looked back down at his menu.

The waiter came to their table, and they both ordered steaks and drinks. And they made plans; first, they would live in Woodrose, of course, they both agreed. Then, how many kids and how soon, two, and not for a couple of years, they decided.

That evening on the long road back to Woodrose, they excitedly made more plans and decisions. Their first hurdle would be Eva's dad, and that was going to be a big one. He had made her promise that she wouldn't leave him as her mother did. He was going to be furious with her.

"How should I tell him?" she asked, on the way back home.

Gavyn weighed his words. "I think you should just lay it on him."

"Really? But that seems so…I don't know…harsh," she replied.

"Believe me, it's best to just get it all out there, honey. Better your father finds out from you than from someone else."

"Yeah, guess you're right. I'll have to wait until dad gets back."

"Where did he go?"

"He had some business or something in Chicago. I didn't ask what it was about. So he left the bar to Freddie."

Gavyn nodded, and they drove on through the night.

Eva had decided to tell her father the first thing when he arrived home in a couple of days. Her mother would be informed as soon as she found the first public telephone at a turnout on the desert highway. A while later, the phone was found, and Eva's mother was notified of her daughter's marriage. Of course, she insisted on at least meeting her new son-in-law. She preferred the two fly to London, but Eva and Gavyn wanted to set up roots first at home.

Five hours into their drive, the sun had set slowly and with a deeply quiet hush of red. When they arrived home, the town of Woodrose was soundless and tranquil. The sea was still, and the pier was empty. Gavyn had gotten Ernie to move out of the apartment they shared so that he could set up house with Eva. And after a few beers and promises of a blind date with one of Eva's friends, Ernie had complied with the agreement at a slow, steady pace.

The yellow lights of the pier flickered warmly on the strand, and a soft block of light could be seen from the small square windows of the houses that faced the beach. It was the perfect night for Gavyn and Eva, one they would never forget.

CHAPTER 16
MAC'S FURY

A few days later, Gavyn walked alone by the pier. He had taken a week off before beginning his new job for his honeymoon. After spending the long morning and even longer afternoon shopping with Eva, he dropped her off at the Beauty Salon to get her hair done, then took her home.

He had some time to think about everything from the last week, and he wondered what Eva's dad, Mac, would say about their marriage. And of course, his dad hadn't even told him where he had been lately. He guessed this was as good a time as any to talk, and he walked over to the Drop-In. It was early evening, but it was dark, and the sea shimmered like a silver necklace in a black velvet sachet under the moonlight.

His dad was outside sweeping, and he looked up and narrowed his eyes when he saw Gavyn walking up to him. "Where have you been?" he asked, lowered his head, and began sweeping the concrete wet with ocean mist again.

"I uh, I went to Vegas," said Gavyn.

His father stopped and leaned on the broom for a moment, and he analyzed Gavyn's face, then tapped the concrete with the brush to shake off the dust. "Vegas, huh?" he said.

Gavyn could almost see the inner workings of his father's brain revolving just by the peculiar expression on his face and short use of words. He was planning something, and nothing was going to get in the way of his plan.

"Yeah, I..." began Gavyn.

"What about that fight I'm working on?" he asked, with his eyes focused on Gavyn's face. "I don't know what you were doing in Vegas, and I don't care, Gavyn, you know why?" The small veins in his broadened eyes showed red and protruding, and his expression seemed strangely enlivened.

Gavyn looked down and shook his head no. He didn't really want to know why. In fact, the last thing he was interested in knowing was what his dad was up to while he was gone.

His father didn't wait for an answer from him. "Well, because...you ready for this?" he asked, excitedly.

"Yeah, ready as I'll ever be," Gavyn replied through semi-closed lips.

Ty tapped Gavyn's chest with the back of his hand lightly. "I've got you down to fight The Fox!" he said, smiling big. "Can you believe it? I finally got to set it up." Ty shifted his weight and spread his legs as if he was about to toss a pizza. "*Abe The Fox and Gavyn*

Brennan," he said, looking up at the sky and passing his hand over imaginary words written there. "Huh? Whaddya think?" he said. But his smile soon faded, and his eyes grew serious when he noticed Gavyn's expression.

"I'm not fighting anymore, Dad," Gavyn said.

"Ha! I'll bet! I know it's all you ever wanted, and now with stupid Flynn out of the way, with his little diving expeditions and other time-wasting stuff, it's your turn for the limelight! I know you won't pass that up!"

"Well, I am going to pass it up, Dad. I have something new in my life. Something to tell you about."

Ty sensed the type of news coming his way as keenly as a bear senses the smell of an animal carcass from a distance of twenty miles away. He stood silently, just waiting for Gavyn's words to come out.

Gavyn drew in a breath. "I got married in Vegas," he said, looking down, then up at this face.

Ty walked around a few steps, and he scanned the pier. His lips were in a tight line, and he nodded emphatically. "I see…well, it doesn't matter. I set up a contract already," he said in a tired voice. "Marriage doesn't interfere with that, none. We'll talk about this later." He waved him off, then stopped and looked back. "You can't just back outta this, Gavyn!" Ty warned, pointing a finger in Gavyn's face. Then he walked away.

Gavyn stood, thinking. He turned his head toward the pounding surf, and he buried his hands in his pockets, and started walking the shoreline up to the trolley. He angrily kicked some of the gravel stones out of the way as he crossed the steel rails.

"Hey, Gavyn!"

He heard a voice call to him from down the empty tracks. But he ignored it and didn't look up. He wasn't in the mood to talk with anyone.

"Hey, you! Goofball!"

That time Gavyn glanced up and saw a familiar face running toward him in the hazy late of night.

The man was dressed in a US Army Khaki tunic and trousers with a peaked visor cap pulled low over his forehead. On his face was a wide grin, and his cheeks were sunburned.

Gavyn instantly recognized the face. "Bennie! When did you arrive? Just now?" He caught up to him and gave him a brief but firm hug. "I thought you had a year left to go or something."

Bennie laughed, but his eyes were a little tense. There seemed to be a small light of joy trying to emerge from inside him, but some sort of tension kept it trapped. "No, I had two years left, but then I just had to go another four years." His mouth stretched in a stiff smile as he scanned the ground.

Gavyn's smile locked a little, and his eyes showed concern. "So you're staying there?" he asked.

"Yep!" replied Bennie, "and not just one..." he said, holding up his forefinger and exaggerating his voice and movements, "...not two... but four!" Bennie's smile dropped, and his eyes wandered over to Gavyn's face. His voice softened. "You know, every time I called home to talk to my dad, he would say..." Bennie stuck out his chest and mimicked a grand voice...*Son, why don't you go for another round? We're right proud of you! There's not much for you to do around here anyways!*" Bennie laughed weakly and shook his head. "That old dad of mine," he said, and his eyes flicked at Gavyn as he kicked an empty beer can down the curb. "Folks don't want me around so much anymore. Too many kids, I guess. So I thought, hey! Why not go where they do want ya?"

Gavyn listened and stared at his friend's face for a moment. He decided to approach him optimistically. "Well, who needs them! Right?" he said.

Bennie nodded, "Yep."

"And, things ain't so bad... you're on leave, and we can paint the town, right? Turned twenty-one a few weeks ago!" Gavyn cheered him on. He felt lousy for his friend. If anyone knew about deadbeat dads, it was Gavyn.

Bennie's smile was wide as he dug his jittery hand into his pocket and pulled up a crinkled dollar bill. "Yep! You're soooo right, my friend! Hey! Wowza, so you're officially twenty-one already? Hey, come on, let's go on a bender," he said, and the corners of his mouth twitched a little.

Maybe it was the sunburn, but Bennie already looked like he had had too much to drink. His eyes were pink and glossy, and his face was ruddy.

"Oh, hey, got something to show ya," Gavyn said. He searched his coat pocket and pulled out his wallet. He flipped through various pictures in semi-opaque plastic covers and stopped on one of Eva. "Boy, DO I have something to show ya!" he said, grinning. She was wearing a curve-hugging black dress with short puff sleeves and a high collar tied in a bow at the neck.

"Wowza! Who's the dame?" Bennie's face lit up.

"Whoa now, this here bombshell is my wife!" Gavyn said proudly.

"Your...what?"

"Yep. Just got married."

"Golly geez, Gavyn, I leave for a small tour and look what you go and do!" Bennie's smile was beaming. "Congratulations, friend!" he said, shaking his hand huskily and slapping his back hard. "Let's go celebrate at Mac's place!" he said.

"Yeah, ok, I guess so. Gavyn hesitantly agreed.

"His is the only place always fully stocked!"

"Yeah, that's true, and fortunately, he's outta town!"

Bennie threw him a questioning look but didn't probe any further. Moments later, they were sitting side by side on the brown barstools of McNully's bar.

And sometime later, they were downing a second, third, and fourth shot of amber liquid in small crystal glasses. They talked gibberish with red-rimmed, watery eyes.

"Soooo, you mean she's rationed?" Bennie asked with both elbows on the bar, looking down at his drink. He was referring to Kate. It was no secret that Bennie had his eye on her before joining the army. Gavyn clumsily placed his arm around his friend.

"Ya. Thas wha I'm tellen you. Shess taken. So you can farget bout her. But ..." Gavyn lifted a lone forefinger; the other fingers were wrapped around the glass of booze. "Not by jus any guy," he continued and clumsily set down his drink, "Nooo, no sireebob, sheesss..." Gavyn lifted his glass with some trouble and held it in front of his face. He stared at its contents in the light. And concentrated hard on enunciating the words, but his mouth wouldn't move right, "she issss taken by no utha peson than my bahder." He laughed a little at how the word brother sounded to him.

Bennie also chuckled. Then he turned to look Gavyn in the eyes, and his head wobbled a little. His bloodshot eyes made a sudden effort to open wide, but then they quickly narrowed, and his brows dropped down heavily. "Well... thas not righ. No, iss jus not," he said, shaking his head no.

The bartender on shift that night was Freddie. He wore a white shirt with sleeves rolled up to the elbows and was leaning back on the counter, wiping dry a tray of cleaned shot glasses. He carefully watched the two of them talking, drinking, and then drinking some more.

"Bahtener!" Bennie shouted, and he held his empty glass up, but when he didn't come, he leaned over the counter and balanced his stomach over it so as not to fall face down on it, and shouted again. "Hey, Mac! Donya wanna sell somin to us?" he said, ignoring Freddie, who was a few feet away from him. Bennie looked around, but his eyes didn't focus on anything as they jutted around the bar.

"No Macs noh herr member?" said Gavyn.

"Wha?" Bennie started. "Whaddya mean, Macs not herrr? Thes is Mac's plase, you know!"

Mcnully was known around town as Mac. And outside of sneaking a few beers while underage with buddies at Mac's Pub, Gavyn didn't have any contact with him. He didn't know much about him, save what his father had told him about the fights. And what he had learned from his dad wasn't pretty. Ty and Mac had been bitter rivals in the past.

Mac had been the one who ended Ty's career in boxing with that victorious TKO, and Ty held it against him for many years. Something happened to Ty that day beyond a bruised face. He had gotten a bruised ego, too, which was much more painful to bear. His confidence was stolen unexpectedly from its safely guarded personal vault. And his self-assurance was drained from his veins. So that what lingered behind was a broken, bitter, and admittedly weak person. That day, he vowed to never let the inner wounds of defeat show, especially to McNully.

Freddie slowly walked over, polishing a shot glass, and fixed his eyes on Gavyn. "I gotta hand it to you. You've got some guts coming in here," he said, in a non-confrontational way.

Gavyn looked at him with his eyebrows pushed together and languid eyes. "Why?" he asked, genuinely clueless.

"Why?" The man snickered in surprise. "Aren't you the guy who ran off with Mac's daughter? Vegas got eyes, you know, and they snitched," he said.

Gavyn grew deep in thought and got serious. He looked down at his drink.

But Bennie, not being keen on the current situation, stood up proudly. "Yep! Thas him alrigh!" He smiled broadly. "I seen tha piturs," he said.

Gavyn lazily pulled at his sleeve, motioning him to sit down. "Yeah, we got mareed," Gavyn said, and his eyes were intent but languid when he looked at Freddy. "So? Whas it to ya?" he asked.

"Married?" Freddie snickered. "Uh, that's not how Mac sees it. He's really mad that you just up and ran off with his baby," Freddie said. "Kind of not respectable like," he added, looking at him from under his brow. "Seems that someone he knows in Vegas called him up and said I've seen your little girl in the chapel doing a quickie matrimony with some kid. Mac is on his way back here to duke it out with you!"

"I ain't fightin' wih him," said Gavyn, resolutely.

Freddie mockingly sneered, "We'll see."

Then, from behind the three men, Mac entered the bar. "Yeah, you are," he said, in a roaring voice.

Mac was a burly man with a large gut and bulging eyes. His hair was thinning in some areas, leaving mostly pink scalp to show. He would comb a few of the shiny black strands over the top. His eyes immediately fixed on Gavyn, and they shifted over to Bennie. He walked over to the men sitting at the bar and then motioned for Freddie to leave.

Freddie nodded back in acknowledgment and readily unbuttoned the collar of his white shirt and loosened his black tie. He knew what it meant to get Mac upset. He had seen it before with an acquaintance that owed him money; the man had been left face down in the red-stained sand.

Freddie swiftly moved to the opposite end of the bar and started to close down the register and mind his own business.

"I think you two have had enough for tonight," Mac said, moving the empty shot glasses away from them. Gavyn met his father-in-law's eyes with the same uncompromising look. Mac turned his attention to Bennie. "You," he said, and pointed at Bennie, "get out." His thumb pointed to the door. But Bennie didn't budge. He wasn't sure what to expect, and he could just about smell the tension in the air.

"Look, Miser MaNully," Gavyn's voice was low, and he had just started to talk when Mac grabbed him by the collar and lifted him up out of the barstool. A boxer's automatic reflex is always to swing first, ask forgiveness later, and the pardon applies only to someone you like. So, Gavyn took a wobbly swing at him over the counter. Mac grew angrier, and he responded, landing a giant fist right on the side of his face. Gavyn staggered sideways, and he fell on Bennie, who now felt the same contempt for Mac as Gavyn. He pushed his way out from under Gavyn to take his own shaky swipe at him. For several minutes, bottles, crystal glasses, and bodies flew over the tables and counter and landed crashing on the wood floor. The shattering and thumping could be heard from outside.

Mac was big, too big for Gavyn, even with his ring experience. And Mac came at him again like a tank in the middle of a war. Bennie saw the scowl in Mac's eyes, and he tried to get in between him and Gavyn.

"Hey, hey, Mac..." he stammered, "go easy now, we're leaving," he said. But Mac didn't have ears for listening right now, and he kept throwing jabs. He went in deep to Gavyn's stomach with his right, and there was the sound of air being expelled from Gavyn's lungs. Mac stepped back momentarily to view him, but Mac was a swarmer, and he continued relentlessly pummeling. After a few more punches, Gavyn's legs began to wobble, and he had trouble standing up. That was when Mac delivered the final blow, and Gavyn fell as quick and solidly as a tree when someone yells timber! Gavyn was bleeding from his mouth as he lay on the ground, and his face appeared misshapen from the trauma to the facial tissue.

Gavyn rolled into a fetal position, and his eyes closed. "You killed him!" yelled Bennie. "You, you killed him!"

Mac's face showed little emotion staring down at Gavyn, but then he turned around to look at Bennie, and his eyes were sharp and piercing. "Get outta here!" he said in a low growl that came from his gut. "You and your friend," he motioned to Gavyn's curled-up body and walked out.

Bennie kneeled down next to Gavyn to feel his pulse. It was weak, but he had one. He looked around desperately and caught the eye of Freddie, the bartender, who was sweeping and glancing. "You gotta help me. Please," he pleaded, looking down at Gavyn. "He's my buddy."

Freddie stopped and thought a moment. He could get in a lot of trouble. But when Freddie saw Gavyn up-close, he decided to help. "Alright," he said. "Come on." They carried limp Gavyn to the car and placed him gently in the back seat.

"Thanks," Bennie mumbled.

Freddie watched the truck disappear into tree-lined nebulous obscurity.

CHAPTER 17
THE MYSTERY SHIP

The golden sun had quenched its thirst. It dipped halfway into the sea and burnished the vast sky, turning it into a flaming display of fire over the blue of the ocean. It burned and smoldered until late afternoon had turned black.

Kate had returned home to find that Flynn had not called as he usually did, and she became worried. The tension between Ty and Flynn perturbed her, and she didn't trust Ty, but even more distressing to her was the widening distance between her and Flynn. Lately, he just hadn't been around as much as before, and she wondered why.

The Masons' home was masterfully built, designed by Mike himself, and it sat atop a hill that overlooked the entire bay.

Kate's room had a wrap-around bow window where she would sometimes prop a pillow on the nook bench and read with the ocean's rhythmic sound as background music. However, tonight the sea was deeply pensive and hardly moving. She looked out of her bedroom window into the blackness that fell like ink across the ocean. She could see the same large white ship that had been anchored offshore nightly for some time now.

It was no secret what went on board. There had been no efforts to conceal the boats that picked up the well-dressed strangers from the shore and transported them to the ship. For a twenty-five-cent fare, a water-taxi would transport visitors to the gambling ship, Wayan, which operated three miles offshore.

The visitors were far from regular. Women in Taffeta beaded gowns and gloves, accompanied by men in black vested tuxedos and double-breasted jackets with wide-brimmed fedoras. Kate would see them nightly from her hilltop home.

They would usually come in pairs and step out from shiny Lincoln Continental Coupes onto a small private boat that would carry six or so. She could make out the women's shadows as they lithely stepped onto the deck of the Wayan.

That night, she noticed one of them because she looked a lot like Lila. She struck her as the type that would frequent that ship. And she hadn't seen her around in a while.

Kate exhaled softly, stepped back from the window, and began to pace the floor. She glanced at her watch. A quarter to seven. Her mind jetted back to the Wayan ship, and her eyes moved about the floor. What if Flynn was keeping something from her…could he be at the Wayan? Her heart was the gun, and her mind was twitching on the trigger.

She grabbed for her coat and yelled to her mom as she hurried down the hall. "I'm going for a walk, Mom." Her voice was faint, high-pitched, and unconvincing.

Her mom took a second to respond, no doubt downing quickly the last of the shot of vodka to do so. It was a well-maintained secret that she was a functioning alcoholic, and her dad saw to it that the secret would stay that way. It both embarrassed and angered him. Kate would muddle through waves of pity and resentment, and the two would often fight over her drinking. Still, lately, Kate had come to understand a little more about what was behind the deep, dark depression that engulfed her mother.

Mike and Helena had a torrid love affair for years before getting married. She was the unattainable city girl who traveled in the circles of high society, the gorgeous brunette that everyone wanted. Not just for her status but for her looks as well.

Her father had chased her mother long enough to win the grand prize. Then, not unlike his passion for collecting model airplanes as a kid, the thrill was gone once he conquered the quest. Helena was left with only one friend to ease the loneliness, a bottle of Cognac.

"Kate!" her mom's groggy voice called to her from one of the rooms. "You can't go out tonight, hun. It's too late in the evening!"

Kate could see her mom's head pop out of one of the rooms in the hallway in her peripheral vision.

Before giving her any time to start a fresh bout of fighting and griping, Kate quickly ducked out of the house and into the brisk night air. She hurried down the concrete stairway and down the street.

Dooly's Furniture store on the corner of Crescent Street was just closing, and she could see a woman turning off the lights and pulling down the front window shades. Kate paused for a slow-moving car to go past her before crossing the street and stepping up on the pier.

The docks were quiet and dark, but the ocean was beginning to grumble. She could hear the creaking and moaning of the wooden supports under the pier. It was a long, drawn-out sound as if the pillars were in pain whenever the robust ocean waves twisted underneath and pummeled into them. It was the proverbial rhythm of the sea.

Then she heard another sound, one that made her stop to listen. Warm, honey-like musical notes from a sax broke through the chains of darkness near a corner of the pier. The sound was intoxicating, and Kate leaned back on the dock to listen, but just as quickly straightened up when the music stopped abruptly. She could hear footsteps coming out of the darkened corner, and she glanced briefly at a man walking towards her as she resumed her walk.

"Wait..." he called to her. The man was Nick Collins, a sax player who gigged on the Wayan. Nick's eyebrows came together, and he called after her. "Hold on there! Was I really that boring?"

Kate kept walking, and he smiled to himself, surprised at her resolve. Nick had been sitting in the shadows on a large crate before he stood up to follow her. He buttoned his black single-breasted dinner jacket and, still holding the sax, hurried to catch up with her.

Kate slowed her pace but didn't stop, and she snuck a peek at him asquint. She could feel the man's presence next to her as she walked.

"Know what that was?" he asked, and the voice sounded like he was smiling.

"Very nice saxophone music," said Kate, gathering her lips to the side a little.

"Thanks," the voice said. "The song is called *After All* by Johnny Hodges."

"Beautiful song," she said.

"Yeah, it is. Um… my name is Nick," he said. "Nick Collins." His hand was suddenly in front of her, and she was forced to stop walking to avoid running into it.

Kate analyzed his face. His eyes were long and the color of sage. His hair was obsidian black and neatly combed back on the sides. But the top, having more length, had a few strands that fell on his forehead whenever he made a movement. He had high cheekbones that drew attention to the mischievous gleam within his eyes.

Kate smiled and lightly shook his hand, and she had to tug a little to retrieve it. He smiled a little, amused at her wariness, and a dimple showed on the left side of his cheek.

Although she refused to admit it to herself, he somehow made her feel intimidated. That was something she had never felt before. In her unease, she started to walk down the pier again without looking back at him.

"You're not usually around here at this time of night. What brings you here now?" he asked, stepping up beside her.

Kate stayed silent, and she bit her lower lip distractedly and looked straight ahead.

Nick searched for her face. "I play nightly at the Wayan," he said, and there was a spark in his eyes. "You should come by some time." He held up the golden instrument to demonstrate, and it caught a glint from the lamp on the pier.

Kate maintained her course but moved her eyes sideways a little to glance at him again and the instrument in his hands. She was intrigued. "I usually don't have time with my studies to go to clubs much," she responded. But it was in no way a dismissal; she was curious to see what he would say.

He nodded slowly. "What are you studying?" he asked.

"I'm interested in archeology."

He raised his eyebrows, impressed, and a smile stretched across his face. "That's unusual," he said.

Kate slowed her pace. "You think so? Why?"

Nick looked down at his saxophone and idly began to wipe the glossy finish with a cloth he kept in his pocket for that purpose. He didn't want to say anything that would close the conversation, and he thought about how to answer. "I don't know. It's very adventurous," he said. "I've wondered so many things about you. I've wanted to meet you for quite a while now. I've seen you with your folks at the car races."

"Oh, you go there? My dad loves racing cars."

A light came over his face. "Yep, been racing since before I could walk!" he said, animated at having found something in common. Kate giggled, picturing a baby behind the wheel of a racecar, and he beamed at her smile.

They both stopped walking when they reached the end of the pier. There were a few scruffy men in big overalls, each with a fishing line dropped into the ocean. Nick looked down as if words could be found written on the wooden boards, then he quickly looked back at her face. The melodious sound of brass notes floated over the ocean from the Wayan. He glanced at his watch, and he gathered his mouth to the side a little.

Kate took notice of the music. "Did you say you play with the band nightly?" she asked.

"Yeah, every night." He sounded encouraged by the question. "Why don't you stop by and hear us play? I think you'd like it."

Kate smiled and looked down. "I might like it, but I don't think my boyfriend would like it," she said.

"Oh…your …boyfriend." Nick put his hands in his pockets, not resigned, but bothered.

"You're mismatched with him, you know," he said.

A small smile came to her lips. "Well, I don't happen to agree," she said.

"I've seen him before," he said.

"Oh?" she asked

"Yeah…" he said. He lowered his head, and his eyes looked like those of a fox. "At the Wayan."

Kate had been looking out at the dark ocean, but her eyes immediately darted back to his face, and they widened a little. "Onboard the ship?" she asked.

Nick nodded and looked down at the sax, inspecting the gloss on his instrument. "Yep," he said, without looking up. "He was with a redhead…" His voice trailed off a little.

Kate felt something stir inside. "I think you're lying!" she said.

His eyes widened, and he almost looked amused at her reaction, and he smiled a little.

"No, I wouldn't lie to you. Why would I start this relationship with a lie?"

"We're not in a relationship, Mister Collins!" she said sharply.

"Ah, please, call me Nick."

When she didn't respond, he added, "Okay, then how about friendship?"

"Look, I don't even know you."

"Not yet." He smiled.

"What makes you think I want to?"

"Something…I don't know…," Nick said under his breath.

Their conversation had turned cautious and cagey. Kate had become wary of him, and Nick, who had stuck his foot in his mouth, was trying not to be misread. The truth was Nick had fallen for her like he knew he would, and he was trying desperately to win her.

Now his boldness had left him, and he felt like he was at the mercy of some kind of undetermined essence that had command of the night. The moment grew tense. He touched her hand, and Kate stepped back. She scanned the pier and the darkened sand for any sign of Flynn, but there was none.

Nick persisted, "I think her name was something like Lila." He viewed her face for a moment.

He got a reaction from her. "Lila?" she asked in disbelief.

"Yeah, she's tall, redheaded…she sometimes sings on the ship. Great voice."

They were words merely spoken, but they felt like a slap to her face, sharp, stinging, and cold. Tall redheaded singer, that was her all right. Kate felt her stomach sink. "I have to be going," she said.

And Nick knew not to follow. He watched her silently as she walked hurriedly down the pier to the street. Then up the winding path that led to the house on the hill.

The music spilled out over the waves from the ship. Nick was late for the show. He readjusted his tie, walked to the crate he had been sitting on, and methodically set the sax in its case. Lost in thought, Nick snapped it closed and walked to the small boat docked nearby and got inside. He stared back at the shore. It became a misty blur in the fog as he reached the ship.

The casino onboard the ship was jumping when Nick stepped inside. Smoke rose up from each table like personal genies from a bottle, creating a canopy of fine particles suspended on the ceiling. The floor vibrated under Nick's feet to the rhythm of jungle drums. The flame was turned on high as the band played Benny Goodman's, Sing, Sing, Sing.

Nick made his way through the crowded tables and around the dance floor. Abruptly, a tall, lanky man with a thin brown mustache pulled him by his arm into a corner of the room.

"Where have you been, Nicky? We had to put Gus in for sax for one of the numbers!" he said. The veins on his neck were sticking out, and his eyes were bulging.

Nick shrugged off the grasp. "Nowhere," he said calmly. "Stay cool, Sammy...Ok?"

Sammy was making short, anxious, pacing movements, as if the world was about to end. "I can't keep cool, Nicky!" He stopped, and his eyes jetted around the room, and he breathed in to get a hold of himself, but he actually tensed up more, "You know who's in the audience tonight?" he said through tight lips. "Do you know?"

Nick coolly took out a cigarette pack, shook it upside down, and grabbed the first one that slid out and stuck it in his mouth. Sammy instinctively moved to light it, but Nick moved his hand away and did it himself.

"Yeah, I know," he finally said, in between puffs of smoke.

Sammy let out a long, frustrated breath. "If we don't play for the talent scouts from the Meikle agency, we won't get the chance we've been banking on!" He seemed to fear the anxiety he felt and tried to allay his dread by talking aloud, "Ok, ok... It's all right. We can do this tomorrow; they said they'd be here both nights...right?" His voice had calmed down, but his expression was pleading.

Nick studied his face before answering with pity-filled eyes. He grabbed his collar and readjusted it as someone would do to a kid. "Yeah, that's right, they'll be here tomorrow, Sammy." He patted his chin a little. "We can do this tomorrow. Tonight I gotta go crash," he said. He turned his back to him and walked steadily out of the door.

Sammy watched him. Something had happened. Something was different with him, but he didn't know what. He went to the bar and sat on one of the stools. In a flash, he had brandy in his hand. And he downed it all at once. Then he turned round in the seat and stared at the entrance door.

CHAPTER 18
A STRANGE FIND

The vast open sea at night is a song being written, a rhyme, a mysterious and gentle arpeggiated work of Beethoven. It is sung by the waves as they travel on the face of the ocean. And their lyrics are the rhythm of the pounding surf.

The songs of the sea were very familiar to Kate. She had grown up playing in the salty shallow waters of the inlets and swimming in the tides, usually alone, except for her nanny sitting quietly on the rocks nearby, reading a book. It was his love for the ocean and his disconnect from others that outstood most when she first met Flynn, his passion for the sea, and his preference for solitariness.

And those two things they surely had in common. As a teen, Flynn would pause his sweeping outside of The Drop-In to watch the boats docked near the pier. The smell of frying fish clung in the air as the vapors escaped the vents from a nearby diner, and the sounds of kids running on the boards of the pier were merely background noise. It had been his dream to sail out on those mesmerizing waves, to feel the freedom from the confinement of his dad, and become a captive soul of the sea.

The freedom came later in the years and culminated on a night when he experienced one of his best diving expeditions. He had been privileged to dive with the revolutionary self-contained underwater breathing apparatus, the Aqua Lung, which allowed descending to diving depths of sixty feet into the sea. This brought a heightened mystery to the silent world he had never felt before. And it gave an entirely new meaning to ocean discovery.

As Flynn became wrapped up in his nightly diving and spent more time in this newfound freedom, he inadvertently spent less time with Kate. That night, while diving with a friend, he felt something strange on his palm as he was ascending. He glanced down at it when his head bobbed out of the dark ocean and saw a black substance stuck to his hand.

"What you got, Flynn?" another head bobbed out near him, this one was bearded.

The face and beard belonged to Jack Smith, a friend who was more like a brother. Jack was six feet, two inches tall, most of it was muscle, and all of it was used for talent as a cave diver.

The two men sauntered out of the water. Jack's brown, wavy hair seemed impervious to water, and it stuck straight out when he ran his fingers through it. He swept the palms of his hands down both sides of his face, then over his short, wet, wiry beard, pulling on it as if to wring it that way. Jack's unruly hair and beard were unusual for the 1940s, but they certainly spoke to his adventurous side, and he refused to tame them with hair cream.

Jack lowered his head to look at Flynn's open palm. "What did you find?" he asked, peering down at his hand.

"I'm not sure," Flynn said. They were intently looking at a small, round, black gummy substance.

Jack poked it lightly. "Was it just floating out there?" he asked.

"No, it was deeper. It was stuck on some rocks. I felt it as I pushed off a large rock. At first, I thought nothing of it, but when I ran my hand over the other rocks, I could feel the stuff all over them." Flynn rubbed his fingers over it. "It looks like some kind of black oily substance," he said, glancing perplexed at Jack.

"It's not tar, that's for sure," Jack said, looking at it. "Tar has the consistency of fresh asphalt, and this is...slimier."

Flynn brought up a sample of the substance and rubbed it between his forefinger and thumb, then sniffed it. "It smells like something I've smelled before. Kind of like a rotten, chemical type of stench, if it could be described that way. See what you got in your car to put it in, something small like what you use for your specimens," Flynn requested, still examining the substance.

Jack hurried to where he had parked his brown 1941 Chrysler station wagon. He could barely make out the toothy grille of the car through the fog that had moved into the shoreline. Jack ducked inside and felt around with his fingers beneath the seat. A paper bag was rolled up and stuffed under it, and he peered inside for some sort of container.

He found an old Winston G.I. pack that had just one smoke left in it. How could he have overlooked that one last one? He wondered. The G.I. packs were meant to be strapped inside the bands of soldiers' helmets and carried four cigarettes. Jack had forgotten about it when he returned from service some time ago. He dumped the last cigarette, found an unused waxed paper sandwich bag he had in the glove compartment, and he lined the inside. It would have to do.

"Here," he said, reaching Flynn, who was scouring the sand for something. "It's all I got in the wagon. I lined the inside with some waxed paper I found so that it's isolated from the cigarette smell."

"Ok, good." Flynn took the pack and then looked at his face. "Old pack of cigarettes littering your precious car. Doesn't sound like you to be disorderly," he smirked.

"No, but it does sound like me to be orderly enough to find something where there was nothing to be found!" He smiled proudly.

Flynn laughed, but then grew a little pensive. He took the pack and held it in his hand a moment, his eyes shifted to Jack's face. "You know I'm glad this cigarette pack made it back, bud. Cuz, I know you carry these *everywhere* you go," he said reflectively.

Jack nodded, "Yeah, let's just say they would have been able to positively identify me, if by nothing else," he said.

Flynn scraped the gooey substance off his hand and dropped it into the pack. "I think I remember where I smelled this less-than-fragrant aroma a few years back," he said. "I think it was at a dump."

Jack nodded. "That would certainly account for the 'rotten chemical' thing. Dumps are usually like a giant bubbling cauldron of chemicals. But why is it here? This isn't the dump."

"Yeah. I'm not sure. I found another one on the sand over there. Just a very small one," Flynn said, and he gestured to the wet shore.

Jack looked to where he pointed, then back at him. "This is strange. I mean, this stuff is in the water and all over the rocks in the deeper areas for now."

Flynn nodded, running it over in his mind. Then his eyes grew concerned, and he stared out to the sea. "I think I just remembered exactly where I had smelled that before," he said and glanced at Jack with his eyes. "It was at the closed-down Huntington Way canal on the opposite side of town."

"I remember that place," said Jack, "I was just reading in the paper that Mike Mason bought the whole parcel of land there. The guy's loaded! It's a big area."

"Yep," Flynn contemplated.

The two men talked about the hows and whys. Why did it smell like something from the canal if that was on the opposite side of town? How would it have gotten here? Maybe it was some kind of covert operation of some sort. But that thought brought up more questions, like was Mike Mason involved and how, since he's the one with full access to the canal. The more they thought about it, the more it seemed too fantastical. They tried different scenarios.

"What about oil leaking from the Wayan?" Flynn threw out the idea.

"Not likely. It's too deep, and it's not exactly the consistency of oil."

"Yeah, that's true."

"All I know is that I've never seen anything like that in the water," Jack said, looking out to the pristine sea. Then he turned to Flynn. "Hey, what about your ex-girlfriend's dad? A professor of biology sounds like a good place to start."

"Not really, my ex-girlfriend, but you mean, Lila's dad?"

"Well, you two were an item for a while, weren't you?"

"No."

"Ok, ok, …touchy subject, I guess. Well, what about him? The professor. Word around is that he's a walking encyclopedia when it comes to underwater studies…always wanted to meet him." Jack's eyes lit up with admiration.

"I haven't seen him since Lila, and I broke up... I mean, stopped going out or whatever," Flynn said.

Jack laughed at his caginess on the subject. "Yeah, well, maybe we should take it to him and see what he thinks." Jack reached into his pocket for his keys to his wagon. "I'm pretty sure he still works at the Pacific Biological Laboratory, so maybe he can analyze it for us."

"Yeah, that's a great idea!" said Flynn. "Sometimes you actually get those," he added. Jack smirked.

Flynn and Jack didn't make it to the lab. The moment they were walking back to the station wagon, they heard the loud, continuous blare of a car horn from the parking lot near Jack's car.

"Who's that?" Jack asked, stopping to look.

"Looks like Gavyn's truck," Flynn said, and his voice showed unease.

"Something must be going on for him to track us down at this time," said Jack.

Bennie jumped out of the truck and peered into Jack's car. Then he looked down the stretch of sand both ways and caught sight of Flynn headed toward him.

"Bennie! When did you get back?" Flynn smiled big but froze when he saw the look on Bennie's face, a combination of alarmed, frazzled, and worried.

"Flynn! Man, I've been looking all over for you!" His voice was choked.

"Why? What's wrong?" asked Flynn. Bennie was so distraught that he couldn't answer right away.

Flynn insisted, "What is wrong, Bennie? Where's Gavyn?" he glanced at the red pickup.

"It's your brother, Flynn...it's Gavyn. He's bad."

Flynn had never seen Bennie tear up before. "Ok, hold on, Bennie, you have to try and calm down." Flynn became fearful; he knew whatever it was wasn't good. "What is it? Some kind of accident...what?" Flynn asked loudly and shook him for answers.

"No," Bennie replied dryly, and then swallowed hard. "Worse."

Flynn threw a distressed look at Jack, then back at Bennie. He tightened his grip on his shoulders and lowered his face to look Bennie in the eyes. And he spoke emphatically as if Bennie was hard of hearing. "Ok, tell me, calmly. What's happened to Gavyn?"

Bennie was nervously breathing. "It was Mac," he said, and he grimaced with his whole body. "Mac busted him up!"

Flynn's eyes grew wide. His brain ran through a gamut of emotions: shock, confusion, rage. None of it made sense. "Mac? *He did what*?" he asked, but Flynn knew what, and he didn't wait for an answer. He immediately felt the warm sensation of blood rushing to his head. Flynn moved agitatedly like a tiger being teased while in chains, devising the next thing to do. Then he stopped and grasped Bennie's shoulders hard again. "Where is he now?" Flynn asked. He skimmed past Bennie's face toward the street.

"Gavyn? He's at--" Bennie started weakly. "I—I must have passed out cuz I just remember one minute we were drinkin' – and it was night—I took Gavyn to the hospital last night." He said grimly.

Flynn swallowed hard and stared at Bennie, "—I just want to know if Mac is at the bar?" he asked, his voice was low and robotic. "I want to know where Mac is."

Bennie felt fear looking at Flynn. Maybe he shouldn't have told him, and he shook involuntarily. "Flynn, I don't know if you should go see Mac like this."

Flynn gave Bennie a push on the chest to get him to pay attention, and he spoke slowly and clearly. "Snap out of it, Bennie, I just wanna know if Mac is still at the bar," he said.

"Aaa, I don't know. We went cuz we didn't know Mac was back from Chicago, or we wouldn't have gone in the first place…but… I mean, he closes at 3:00 am, so..." he rambled nervously—he should be there opening, I guess."

Dawn had broken hours ago, but the sun was not visible through the thick fog, and the dock lights still glowed on the pier.

Flynn looked up at Jack. "Throw me your keys!" he yelled. He caught them in the air and climbed into the car. Jack hopped into the passenger seat. No words were spoken, and Jack's station wagon spun dirt as he made a U-turn and headed back toward town.

CHAPTER 19
THE RECKONING

The fog was thicker now; it was like driving through a vast cloud. The pickup was cutting through the white blocks like a knife, and Flynn was without regard for what might be directly in front. Luckily, traffic was nonexistent at that early hour, and they were in town in a matter of minutes. Flynn slowed his speed and drove into the lot.

Jack spotted Mac through the bar's window. "Mac's inside the place," Jack said. And Flynn turned the wheels, situating the car directly in front of the door. Jack had gone with Flynn, hoping to ease the tension, but he had reservations about the encounter. "You sure this is something you want to do right now, in this way?" he asked.

"Yep." Flynn's answer was short.

Flynn sat in the car, turning over in his brain methods to get at him. They could see Mac walking back and forth in the bar, closing up. Mac's mind was on what had gone on with Gavyn, and his thoughts were on his guiltlessness. He wondered if Gavyn died, would it be justifiable in court? He had taken his little girl away from him. In his head, he had basically kidnapped her, and now he had no one. Deep in thought, he hadn't noticed the car idling in the parking lot.

Jack observed Flynn, then he looked out of the window at the bar. His silence wasn't a good sign that things would go well, or at least be civilized. "Flynn… maybe you should…" Jack started to speak, but when he looked back at Flynn, he was already slamming the door of the vehicle. So instead, he just followed him.

Flynn walked steadily toward the door, glancing into the windows as he made his way to the entrance. It was dark inside, and more so with the dense fog outside. Mac had finished sweeping the main room and had turned off all the lights, save the sconces on the back wall.

The soft yellow light of the sconces highlighted artwork done by Mac's ex-wife. The fact that he held onto those pictures after the divorce was understood by most to be a soft spot for her, and he would excuse it by saying he just didn't have the time to take them down. Now, with the room in darkness, the pictures were barely visible on the wall and gave an eerie feel to the bar. Flynn caught sight of him behind the counter of the bar. Mac stood bent forward, sweeping the black & white tiles beneath the bar and around the brass foot rails.

"Hey! Mac!" Flynn's voice filled the room with its bigness.

Mac slowed down the sweeping motion but didn't stop, and he didn't look at who was at the door. He already knew who it was. And he went about his business, wiping down the wooden tables and placing crystal coasters and ashtrays on each.

Flynn walked up and brusquely knocked the neatly stacked shot glasses off the counter with a sweep of his arm and looked at Mac's face. Crystal glasses and ice cubes were swept up into the air and dropped swiftly on the parquet floor. They shattered across it and gleamed like glitter. "You looking to fight with someone?" Flynn asked. He continued with tension building in his body. "Wanna hit somebody? Why didn't you look for me?"

Mac kept sweeping quietly, but his hands gripped the push broom hard, and his jaw was rigid.

Flynn walked closer. "I know why," he said through clenched teeth, then paused as his ire was gathering momentum. "You're a washed-up mediocre fighter that wanted to feel like a big guy pummeling a, most likely drunk, young kid, right?" Flynn stood with his shoulders squared and both fists clenched. He felt the familiar surge in his blood again. The surge was always triggered by an emotional response to something. Usually, he was able to control it, but this time he did not. "You wanna stop cowering in the corner and look at me!" he called out to him.

Mac turned around like it was a huge favor to do so and faced him. He was standing a few feet away.

But when he saw the look on Flynn's face, he slowly started to move behind the bar counter.

Flynn called to him. "Want the protection of the wooden bar between us? Or maybe you got some sort of weapon behind there?" Flynn chuckled from his gut with anger. His voice deepened. "There's nothing that will protect you from me, old man! You shouldn't have touched Gavyn," he said, through clenched teeth.

Flynn charged Mac and pinned him down with his back on the bar. He pressed his arm firmly against his throat, and Mac made grunting noises as he struggled to breathe. Mac pushed back hard with both hands on Flynn's chest, and he didn't move an inch, but quickly came back at him.

"Flynn!" Jack called out to him, agitatedly. "Don't...don't kill the guy!" The momentary distraction was to Mac's advantage, and he was able to recover some from the attack.

Flynn breathed out hard, and tiny veins near his temples bulged. "Why shouldn't I kill him?" he responded with rage, and his eyes set on Mac. "Isn't that what he tried to do to my brother?"

Mac started to step toward the exit, and Flynn grabbed his sleeve and pulled it on it, tearing the shirt at the seam. Mac looked down at his shoulder, then back up with disdain. "You and your brother are just alike," he said breathlessly. "You're both dirtbags," he added with repulsion. "But especially that sissy brother of yours!"

Flynn swung him around to face him and dug both fists in the doughy part of Mac's stomach, and he bent over in pain. Then he hooked both fists to his face. Mac had no time to counter when he followed with a lunging left hook to the head, and he began to spurt blood.

"Flynn!" Jack yelled and took a few steps toward him, "You're better than this! Don't bring yourself down to the level he wants. He wants you to do something you'll regret!"

Flynn slowed his assault and momentarily lost a little intensity. Mac once again took advantage and tried to clinch Flynn. He derisively let him, but he kept his right hand free. Then, when Mac threw his first jab, Flynn brought his head close into him and ducked under his anxious left hook. Flynn threw a big counter hook to the head, and Mac felt his ears pop with an explosion of pain, and something warm gushed from them as he immediately fell back. The blood oozed from his mouth and flowed from his ears and nose. Various areas of his face were already swollen.

Out of the darkness, a voice emerged. "Hold on, hold on, a minute..." a man's dry voice broke through from a shadowy seat in the corner.

The distraction made Flynn step back and view Mac, who was on the floor, writhing in pain. Jack tapped Flynn on the arm. "Come on, let's go. It should stay here. You're wasting time on this guy."

Flynn nodded, looking down at the badly beaten Mac. "You're right," Flynn said, and a sudden vision of his sadistic dad popped into his mind, and he looked at Jack. "You're right." Flynn calmed down, and he slumped over to catch his breath. Then he looked back at Mac, who was being helped out the door by Freddie. Leaning on Freddie for support, he staggered and dragged his feet to his car.

If Mac had had any endurance left as a boxer, he had just used it up on Gavyn, and now he knew he was done as a fighter. That night, he faced his greatest fear. After he retired from the ring, Mac refused to accept that he had softened up. All he feared had come true; his legs felt shaky and numb after just a couple of swings...he was washed up.

The old man who had spoken from the dark corner stood up and approached Flynn, who hadn't noticed him sitting when he first entered the bar. The stocky man was bald apart from a little gray hair on the sides, "You're Flynn Brennan, right?" he asked, and he took a sip from the drink he was holding.

"Yeah, that's right," Flynn answered, cautiously.

"Your reputation precedes you, as they say," he said and smiled crookedly. "You're a hell of a fighter!" he stared at Flynn and narrowed his eyes as if he were dissecting a specimen he found rather interesting.

Flynn scrunched his mouth to the side and tasted some blood from the corner of it, "So I hear," he said.

"I bet! Listen..." the old man started, and he tapped Flynn on the chest lightly with his forefinger, but quickly wrapped it back around the glass when Flynn looked down at his finger and slowly back up at him.

He was stocky but solid for his age. His blue eyes were unassuming and slanted down at the corners. They stared out from a round face. He jigged a little when he walked as if he heard a jazz tune in his head, and with each step, his head, disparagingly tilted to the side, would jig too.

"My name is Harold, but you can call me Harry...if you'd like. I'm a reporter for the Woodrose Daily paper," he said.

By now, Jack had helped himself to a drink and set money on the bar. Then he sat down with it and eyed Harry, curious to know what he wanted. Flynn sat down too, and he tiredly rubbed his face with both hands, then placed one arm up on the bar and looked up at Harry. "So, what is it you want?" asked Jack impatiently.

"I'll tell you what I want, and it's from this guy here," he said and pointed at Flynn, then turned to him. "Mr. Brennan, I want to be the first to report on the upcoming matchup with you and Joey Williams...and maybe a chance at becoming the first to interview the champion?" He smiled boldly and took out a pack of cigarettes and stuck one in his mouth, but didn't light it right away; instead, he watched Flynn's eyes for a flicker of appeal.

"Not interested," Flynn said, impassively, and he stood to leave.

"What? Wait… you can't decide just like that! This is something you need to mull over...real slow...you don't seem to understand what…" said Harry.

"No, *you* don't understand!" Flynn was exasperated. "I'm not fighting Joey Williams or anyone!" He leaned his body forward toward the man and came close to his face. Let me spell it out for you, "I'm not fighting anymore. I declined it long ago," he said. "You can scratch my name off your list," he said. Flynn tapped Jack's arm and headed for the door.

Jack jumped up from his seat and slowly walked by Harry. He was struggling for something in the pocket, and when he looked up, Jack's eyes made a steady contact with his. Harry got nervous. "Here…" he said and quickly handed Jack a card. "Give this to your friend."

Jack stopped and analyzed it for a moment, then looked back at his face with an even-keeled expression. "I'd advise you to stay away from Flynn," he said in a low voice. Jack flipped the card between his two fingers. "But I'll give it to him," he added. The man leaned back on the bar with his elbows and raised his eyebrows at Jack's audacity.

"Thanks," he said, a little unnerved at the warning. "I'm confident he's gonna take me up on that interview." Jack stopped at the door and looked back at him. "Don't be," he said and walked out.

CHAPTER 20
THE WORLD OF THE WAYAN

The face of the ocean has many moods. When the wind blows fiercely, it scowls back with long tormented waves. When the sun shines hot and bright, tiny glittering lights joyfully spread out over the heavy swells. And when at times the sea acquires compassion, it flings itself up to quench the burning fire of the sun well into the night. Then all of the day's yearning is forgotten, and the silver queen makes her appearance high in the sky. A serene coolness washes over the darkened water.

Kate was not sleepy. She watched the changeable ocean from the balcony of her bedroom, and she thought of Flynn. There was a time the two of them were inseparable. A time they would tell each other of every step taken because that's what you do when you're in love and away from each other. But now it seemed to her that he had become moody, quiet, and not forthcoming. It worried more than angered her.

Those same moods of the ocean seemed replicated within her at this moment. Something was brewing inside, like when the sea slowly starts to churn. A discontentment was growing inside her. What surprised her most was that she felt it toward Flynn. Before, it might have faded as soon as she saw him again, and the stirring would subside. However, this time it bubbled steadily, not intensely, but steadily inside her.

It was 2:00 in the morning, and her eyes were heavy with unattainable sleep. She looked out of her bedroom window at the glow of the Wayan ship. The lights blinked through the fog. Colored bulbs were strung all along its bow to the mast and stern, creeping up the smokestack. The large white vessel appeared ghostly in the shrouded horizon. What a mystery that ship was to her. She had heard stories of how it looked and what took place on board, but she had never seen it for herself. The more she wondered, the stronger the pull to see it, and in a split-second decision, Kate grabbed for her coat, and she tiptoed through the hallway and out the door that night. It was a decision that would change her life.

The wet night air was fresh as it brushed her cheeks and swept back her auburn, wavy hair. Everything was still dark and quiet except three miles offshore under the moonlight. Onboard the Wayan ship, there were plenty of sounds. It ascended like smoke from a brightly burning flame of a candle into the night air.

As Kate approached the dock, she could see the water taxi pulling up to shore. She was suddenly in the company of a well-dressed crowd as she stood by the shoreline. From inside the boat, a gruffly looking, dark-haired man put one foot on the dock, maintaining the other inside the boat, and held his hand out to her. "Good evening, Miss. Twenty-five cents, please," the man said, not really looking at Kate. He was busy surveying the small waiting crowd of people.

Kate already knew the fare and was prepared to hand him the quarter, and when she dropped the coin in his palm. He smiled and looked at her, and Kate took his outstretched hand to board. The man's face was weathered- brown, wrinkled, and sullen, and it would have seemed that not many things would make those tired eyes widen, but they did when he noticed it was Kate.

"Eh, you're one of the Masons, right?" he asked, as he assisted her onto the boat.

Kate nodded her response.

"Never thought I'd see one of yous girls grace Wayan's." He waited with a toothless smile for a response, but he got none.

Kate knew what it meant for him to recognize her. She gave him a small smile and sat down with the rest of the people who were chattering among themselves. When the others noticed her sitting amongst them, the chattering abruptly stopped. The men mostly stared while the women whispered to each other.

Maybe it was the awkward circumstances, but the three-mile journey seemed to take three hours. When they arrived at the ship, everything got bolder and louder quickly. Music notes rose up as thick incense and smoldered into the night. The people were babbling again as they disembarked the water taxi. Kate was wide-eyed as she surveyed the large ship from the outside up close. The gangway to the vessel was barricaded with a steel door, and an iron mesh gate backed up by three heavy fire hoses spraying water over the side.

Onboard the Wayan was another world. It was a world Kate had never been exposed to before. Her father, who served on the Moonstone Beach City Council, would always say that he would never set foot in a gambling ship, not even breathe the same air!

He and Kate's mother seemed to have had life all figured out. It involved an endless parade of parties and cotillions, yachts, and polo matches. And Kate had developed a distaste for all that a long time ago. The problem was that no one had cared to notice.

No one but Flynn. In fact, he had introduced her to the opposite of it all. Their parties consisted of sunset bonfires at the beach. Yachts were replaced by fishing boats where they'd catch Bonita fish and mackerel, and polo matches were replaced by excavations at nearby beach caves looking for treasure. Kate took to his life right away. No more narrow people with mindless chatter. And now, as she carefully opened the door to the floating casino, she wondered just how real all the stories about the Wayan were and what she was walking into.

The sounds of trumpets, snare drums, and velvety singing voices immediately overpowered her like too much heady perfume. Tables were scattered throughout the smoky room, and they were alive with rolling dice, spinning wheels, and animated exuberant sighs, mingled with echoes of lament.

She stood near the tables and watched as cards were placed and shuffled on the glossy tabletops, and money was set down. Behind the large bar were stacks of bottled liquor. An attractive brown-haired waitress walked by with a tray of drinks, stopping briefly to wink at one of the men playing pool nearby, then disappeared through a door at the back of the room.

One of the men ordered scotch and soda, a bottle of each, and followed in a hurry.

"Don't think I've seen you here before." The voice was low and raspy and emerged from seemingly nowhere. A man with silvery, short curly hair took a few slow steps toward Kate. He was stocky with a slight beer gut that seemed to be firmly held in place under a tight-fitting tuxedo. There was a cigar jutting from the corner of his mouth. His eyes were dark and had a gleam like cut glass when he looked at you.

Kate moved aside a little in a gesture that implied there was no interest in chatting with him. He smiled a little, acknowledging her disdain, but instead of moving on, he pulled out a chair from a nearby table and gestured with a sweep of his hand for her to join him.

Kate tightened her lips at the request. She wasn't about to join him. There was something about the way he looked. He seemed to slither instead of walk, and his smile was more like a snake than a man's.

"Look, I can tell you don't like me," he started. His eyes darted about the room, then landed back on Kate's face. "But you don't know me..."

"Maybe I don't care to," Kate said, dryly.

"Well, how about if I told you something you need to know?" He tilted his head, and his eyes smiled at her.

"Like what?" Kate asked.

"I know why you're here."

Her eyes widened a little, then they relaxed when she realized there was no way he could know. "Really? Why's that?" she asked.

"Cuz you're looking for someone." He pulled the chair out a little more and pointed to it with his chin. "Take a seat."

"No. I don't think I should be here anyway."

"And why's that?" he asked, grinning. "Is the Wayan ship too sleazy for you, Kate?"

She drew in a short breath through tight lips at the sound of her name.

He smirked. "You sure of who you looking for? Cuz, I saw you walking with Nick Collins the other night on the pier." He smiled at her look of surprise and continued, "There's nothing wrong with that. Nick's a nice guy. But if it's Flynn you're looking for ...well, he's also here."

Kate's eyes opened wide. The thought of Flynn being on the Wayan could only mean one thing, and that one thing was Lila. She felt as if she had suddenly taken a blow to the stomach. "What do you mean? How do you know Flynn? Your ship has been docked here for just some months..."

He interrupted her, "Yeah, but in those few months, he's been a regular here."

In a dissenting gesture, Kate's head moved a little sideways, and her eyes fixed on his. "I don't believe you," she said.

He paused and, in a conniving maneuver, said, "Then...why are you here?"

Kate was silent again. He had her second-guessing herself.

The man stuck his hand out and said, "Oh, ah, by the way, my name is Belino Rocco, but you can call me Lino if you'd like."

Kate had first heard the name Belino Rocco when she was sixteen years old. It had become a topic of conversation or gossip for years at the dinner table. Although her father made a point of lowering his head and allowing the name to escape through a corner of his mouth whenever she was present. And her mother would turn her lips down in a scowl at the mere mention of him. It was an obvious way of protecting her from something or someone they didn't want her to know.

Kate had no interest in what to call Belino Rocco or in talking with him. When she didn't extend her hand back, he looked somewhat amused at the derision and wiped his hand on his jacket before putting it in his pocket. "I think I'd better go," she said, but what she meant was... I wish *you'd* go.

"Sure. If that's what you want to do. But you'll miss out on some eye-opening things I had to say." He smiled crookedly.

Kate's eyes lingered on him a little, and her mouth was tight as she turned back toward the entrance. Taking a few steps to leave, her legs felt strangely stiff and cold. It was a feeling she had felt before, like in nightmares when she felt as if she couldn't run while being chased. It had been diagnosed by the family doctor as anxiety. The band was loudly playing *Mack the Knife*, and the sound spilled out onto the promenade deck as she walked out of the door.

The sharp cold of night air hit Kate's cheeks as she carefully stepped down to board the small boat, and the loud music lost some intensity. She was helped by the same boat attendant who took her there. Her face felt the color; it looked…red. She welcomed the coolness of the night as they headed to shore.

Her mind was spinning as she climbed the concrete steps to the top of the hill where she lived. Thoughts incessantly tumbled. Was Flynn on the Wayan that night? If not, where was he then? But perhaps the most unsettling of them all was how Belino Rocco knew Flynn in the first place?

Shady was too mild a word to describe Belino. She remembered a time when Kate was sixteen. She was walking past her parents' bedroom one night during one of their heated discussions, and many other words were used for Belino.

"He's a drunkard and a liar!" She would hear her father's voice roar.

"Well, he's nothing like you, honey," her mother would say with an almost insulting calmness.

"Like me? No. Not like me!" he would say back with a sound of disbelief and insult in his voice.

Her mother would respond with composure. "No need to get so heated. I just meant that he's…different from us," she'd say.

"He's a murderer… dearest…," her father's speech sounded like it came from tightened lips, "maybe I can elucidate the kind of guy Lino Rocco is for you. You seem to lack--"

"--Stop it! Just stop. Before you say something that you'll regret!" her mother had said.

That's when all fell coldly silent, and Kate walked back to her room, confused, and with questions, she'd find out later, would never be answered.

CHAPTER 21
BAD NEWS AND MORE BAD NEWS

The buildings and dock of the seaside village appeared frosted under the swathe of mist that wrapped tightly around the town. And just as tightly wrapped were Kate's thoughts in her mind. Every notion reeled in her fears and worries. It left her unsettled and squirming like a fish at the end of a pole.

The lateness of the hour dropped heavily on her shoulders as her mind closed in on Flynn. And it was somewhere around 6:00 am that she finally surrendered to her heavy eyelids and slept. At noon the next day, there was a light tapping on her bedroom door.

"Yes?" she asked, with her head spinning and barely coming out of slumber.

"Kate?" her mom called from the other side of the closed door. "Kate, hun, I'm going downtown. Do you want to go along?"

"Um, no..." Kate said. She flipped her body toward the door and rested on one elbow.

"Are you feeling alright?"

"Yes. Why?" Kate asked, hoping she hadn't noticed her absence last night.

"Oh, I don't know. You just seem odd to me."

"Everything is fine, Mom. Just extra tired, I guess."

"Okay, hun. I'll see you when I get back."

"Alright."

As soon as she heard the front door close, Kate hopped out of bed and looked out of the bay window in her room. She had an expansive view of the ocean, but if she looked down and to the side of the house, the garage was visible, and she could see her mother pull out in her Mercedes.

Subconsciously, she was keeping an eye out for a straight line when she backed up. Her mother had narrowly missed one of the two stone lions that guarded the front gate on occasion. But this time, she watched her as she carefully looked behind and backed up, then drove down the winding road toward the boulevard.

Some words usually accompanied her mother's driving… tipsy, drowsy, and tired, were some she had heard. It was true that as a young girl, Kate had witnessed her mother clumsily miss her mark when throwing a wine glass at her father in the middle of one of their fights, and it had stained the wall. Her father wouldn't even duck his head anymore, knowing she would miss in her drunken state. Those nights, Kate would fall asleep to her mother's sobs in the room next to her while her father quietly tried to appease the situation.

With her mother gone shopping, the house was quiet, and Kate wandered into the bathroom and splashed her face with cool water. Taking a towel, she slowly tapped her face dry as she studied her reflection. Then she ran a warm rose-scented bath and dropped herself into the water slowly.

Her mind replayed the events of yesterday, like a movie. Something in her gut told her there was something up with Flynn. She hoped it wasn't another problem with Ty, although it wouldn't surprise her. She had never known someone as selfish and narcissistic as Ty. He was bent on living his dreams through his sons, no matter what the cost. That thought made her wonder if Flynn might be at the boxing ring, and she quickly dressed and headed there.

The Drop-In was quiet, and the windows were shut. It was odd and unsettling to see the bar, usually open for business at 7:00 am, closed down at the mid-morning hour of 10:00. She approached the door and slowed her pace when she noticed a note tacked to the front.

The heading of the note read: The Drop-In. The message read: *Due to a family emergency, the Drop-In will be closed until further notice. We are sorry for the inconvenience. Please check back here for any updates.*

Kate was stunned. All sorts of thoughts raced through her mind. Did the emergency have to do with Flynn? But why wouldn't Gavyn have contacted her? That didn't make sense. Her heart was beating fast, and she bit on her lower lip. She wondered what to do, and she decided to go back home and call the nearby hospitals to see if anyone by the last name of Brennan had been admitted.

At the hospital, Flynn was slumped sideways on a metal chair next to Gavyn's bed. He had been awake the rest of the night watching his brother. The light from the window had been shining on Flynn's closed eyes for a few minutes now. And the warmth of the sun began to penetrate into his eyes. He suddenly began to feel as if he was blind and tried to open them, but the glare was too much to bear, so he quickly shut them.

All around him, he sensed a stillness of waters dark and deep. He became aware of the blood rushing through his veins and heartbeat as it pulsed in time with the monitor next to Gavyn. All of a sudden, he was short of breath and began to gasp. He flung his eyes wide open, and his body stiffened in his chair, and it propelled forward to an upright sitting position. He was immediately disoriented, and his heart pounded wildly. Breathlessly, he looked around and realized he was in a hospital room, and then his eyes caught sight of Gavyn on the bed.

His breathing calmed, and he labored to get up, and he stood over him. He watched him as he took small, shallow breaths. Gavyn's face was puffy and alien-looking with dark purple and bluish spots around his eyes and cheeks.

Troubling thoughts snaked through his mind. Flynn slowly shook his head and cradled it in angst. It wasn't even in a ring. All this damage, and it wasn't even a fair fight. Mac had years of experience over Gavyn. Flynn felt his body tense up, and his fists tightened again. His jaw felt tight, too. He imagined Mac, overbearing, taking out his life's frustration on Gavyn that night.

The hospital room door suddenly flung open, and Eva stepped in. Her eyes were red, and they had black eyeliner smudged a little underneath.

"Hi," she said glumly.

"Hi, Eva." Her entrance made Flynn relax, and he turned back to look at Gavyn.

Eva approached the bed slowly. "Is he any better?" she questioned weakly.

Flynn scanned Gavyn's broken frame, then looked back at his face. "I don't know," he said. "The doctor hasn't been in to see him yet."

"Your dad is talking, I shouldn't really say talking… It's more like yelling at the doctors." She spoke as she gently slid Gavyn's hand in hers.

Flynn's lips formed a scowl. "Yeah, that's one thing he's really good at," he said. "I'd better go see what's up with them." Flynn walked to the door, then stopped and took one long look at Gavyn on the bed, and stepped out. He could hear two voices rising and falling from down the hall. It wasn't the doctors he was talking to anymore. One was male, the other was female, and he recognized them both. It was Kate and his dad having a not-so-unusual spat.

"The nurse at the station said that Gavyn was pretty bad. I know Flynn's here." The female voice was tense.

Ty was silent at the moment.

Kate leaned forward a little, and her eyes locked with his. "So, are you going to tell me Flynn's not here?"

"I didn't say that." He paused a moment and drew a tired breath. "He's here, but…"

"But what? What room?" asked Kate.

"Well, …it's just that you shouldn't be here," he said to her.

Kate took in a long breath of her own and let it out, then cupped her hand over her forehead. Her eyes looked weary. "Look," she said. "Whatever there is between us shouldn't get in the way of me seeing Gavyn and especially Flynn."

Neither of them had noticed Flynn walking towards them from down the hall.

Ty bobbed his head yes, slow and emphatic. "Yeah, but you see…"

"There's that word again! But what? We need to work together to bring to justice whoever did this to Gavyn."

"You really don't have anything to do here, Kate…or with my boys." Ty's lips were in a straight line, and his eyes were cold and steady.

Kate's eyebrows raised a little. "You think so, huh?"

"Yep…know so."

Kate stood stiffly and looked at Ty straight in his eyes. Her voice was low and definite. "Keeping Flynn and me apart… that's not going to happen here."

Ty's straight lips stretched a little to a smile and then gathered to the side. "We'll see," he said.

"Knock it off, dad!" Flynn said. There was suddenly another voice in the mix.

"I'm getting tired of you talking to your old man like that, Flynn!" Ty responded, and the pitch of his voice was up and tense.

"And I'm already tired of *you*…dad!" Flynn fired back.

Ty shook his head in disgust and looked down with the corner of his eye toward the floor. His eyebrows lifted. "I'm not the one hassling anyone here." He glanced at Kate. "I'm not the one sticking my head in other people's business!" he said. He walked down the hall with his lips down in repulsion toward the exit doors.

Flynn turned to Kate. His smile was shadowed with worry, and he took her by the shoulders.

"Where have you been?" Kate asked. "I've been looking high and low for you!"

Flynn didn't know how to explain what he had been up to, mainly because he wasn't sure how deep, if at all, her dad was involved in his recent underwater discovery. He became fretful at how his lack of explanation would seem. He slowly took his hands off her shoulders. His eyes jetted around the floor as if looking for an answer there.

"I...I was at the...um..." He quickly realized there was no alibi to be found, and his eyes traveled back to her face. "I was at the ring, you know, I'm usually there..." He mumbled his words and didn't look her in the eyes because he knew that if Kate looked closely enough, she would find the truth hiding for cover within his.

Kate's mouth stretched out in a tight line. "Hmm, well, that's strange," she said.

"What do you mean? Why?" asked Flynn.

"Because right before coming here, I went to the Drop-In looking for you, and it's closed until further notice."

Flynn gently kicked the baseboard that ran along the white hospital wall with his foot. He breathed out long, then lowered his head to look in her eyes. "Ok," he began quietly. "I hope you understand this. I can't tell you where I was or what I've been up to lately... I need to be sure of something...," he said. His voice trailed off, and she didn't hear any of the second part of his sentence.

"Why?" she asked accusingly. "Or maybe I know why. I was told you were on the Wayan ship the other night? Thought you didn't like that crowd?"

"The Wayan ship?" Flynn was genuinely puzzled.

"Yes, I was told you were with Lila?"

"Lila?" he asked, even more astounded. "Who told you that?"

"So, you're not denying it?"

"Denying what?"

"Nick… Nick told me," she said, and stuck out her chin a little.

"Nick?" his voice raised. Nick, who's that?"

"Nick Collins."

Flynn laughed forcefully. "Nick Collins! The sax player from the Wayan? Why would you believe anything that comes from him?"

"Shhh…this is a hospital," a nurse said as she walked by.

Flynn nodded in response and looked down.

Kate paused and then said softly, "Why not? Why shouldn't I believe him?" Flynn took a pause in a stubborn stance on the subject. But Kate wasn't just stubborn; she was questioning their very relationship and everything that had led up to it. Kate added, "You know, I find myself asking *why* a lot lately, in fact, everything that has to do with you brings up a why?"

Flynn looked down the hallway, exasperated. He was trying to think of how to ameliorate the situation. But in the middle of going over it in his head, it shocked him when Kate turned around and walked away. He threw his hands up in frustration and crossed his arms. His eyes followed her out the door, but he didn't call after her. There was a history between her and Lila. This one he'd have to wait to blow over.

Flynn felt a gentle touch on his arm, and he turned to see a nurse nudging him toward Gavyn's room. "Mr. Brennan," she started softly. "The doctor wants to see you in your brother's room," she said.

Flynn reacted immediately. He wondered if something might have gotten worse and hurried down the hall. He flung open the door to the darkened room. Someone had closed the blinds, and there was just a sliver of the sun attempting to burst indoors. The words he heard next floated into his mind like when you're in a bad dream, and your brain can't catch up with what you're hearing.

The doctor stated grimly, "Mr. Brennan, the news is not good. Unfortunately, your brother has slipped into a coma."

Flynn walked with his eyes wide past the doctor as if he was not present in the room and leaned over the bed to stare down at Gavyn. The swelling had gone down some, but the bruises were still visible and raw. Now his features had taken on a different look. It wasn't like when he was asleep… he was vacant.

The doctor noticed Flynn's look of shock and said, "Now, a lot of people wake up from comas every day…"

"What about brain damage?" Flynn interrupted him, bluntly.

The doctor paused. "We simply do not know at this time," he said in an apologetic tone. "But he's very young," he added. Flynn nodded in small, quick movements, but his eyes were not focused. He seemed to be hearing his own thoughts louder than the doctor's voice. It wasn't any consolation to Flynn. He had spent his whole life trying to protect his younger brother from situations like this one. And now, here *he* was, alive and well, and there he was shattered. Flynn couldn't find any words to say back to the doctor. They felt strangled somewhere in his throat. He simply walked to him and placed his hand on his shoulder, nodded in a small way, and walked out.

On his way out of the hospital, he saw Eva walking in. Her usually curled flaxen hair was disheveled, and her face was blank, but her eyes showed a raw pain. She undoubtedly had been told the news. Flynn called out to her, but she didn't hear him. He walked quickly to catch up and touched her arm lightly. "Eva, are you going to be alright?" he asked.

She looked through him at first, then her expression changed when she became aware of him. "Oh, Flynn!" she sobbed. "I don't know what to do!"

"We'll all get through this," he said, lowering his head to look into her eyes. "You'll be okay." He hugged her and patted her back.

Eva began to sob uncontrollably. When she tried to speak, the words would skip, and he could only make out some. Every other word was punctuated with a sharp, short inhale. "I…know…tell...him…"

"What? What do you need me to tell him?"

"I don't know…Gavyn can't hear us anyway!" Eva said, dissolving in tears. "I'm pregnant!"

Flynn stepped back a little. He was surprised at the bad timing of the news. "Gavyn doesn't know?" he asked.

"No." Her breathing was unsteady. "I never got the chance to tell him. I don't know if I even have the strength or if he'll recover enough…" Eva's body fell a little, and Flynn sustained her, gently escorting her to a seat.

"Nurse!" he called out. "Nurse!" he yelled. Two nurses came and helped Eva. Her body weakly dropped into a wheelchair, and she was wheeled into a room.

CHAPTER 22
THE SLUDGE

Flynn raced out of the hospital brusquely. His head hurt and felt as if it were on fire. Thoughts flew around like lightning strikes. "Flynn!" A man's voice trailed in softly at first, then louder. "Flynn!" He looked up to see a car idling curbside. It was a maroon-colored car with glossy ash wood-paneled sides; it was Jack's Chrysler station wagon. He waved him over from the driver's seat. Flynn approached the window in a frozen manner and lowered his head to peer inside.

"Hey, Flynn." Jack looked disconcerted at his appearance. "Hey, man, how are you holding up?" Flynn shrugged, but he said nothing. Jack looked concerned. "Hop in," he urged him.

Flynn pushed back from the car and looked over the top of it to the street. He thought a moment, then went around the passenger side and got in. Jack's eyes lingered on his friend. "You ok? How's Gavyn doing?" he asked.

Flynn shook his head, and the words spilled out slowly. "Gavyn's in a coma," he said, gravely.

Jack's face dimmed. "Oh, I'm sorry to hear that, Flynn," he said.

Flynn nodded appreciatively.

"Look, maybe it would be best if you got your mind off of this for a little while. Let's head back to my place. I've got something to discuss with you."

"Yeah, ok," said Flynn, and they sped down the road.

It was windy, and the palm trees dipped side to side, their long fronds drifting near the light post on the two-lane street. They almost blocked out the light for the station wagon as it pulled into the driveway of a beach bungalow on Sandy Drive.

Flynn dragged his feet inside and fell hard into the couch, and he rubbed his hands over his face, then swept them back over his head. He sighed long then glanced over at Jack as if he had just remembered that he was with him.

"Pour me a drink, will you?" he asked Jack, who was already behind the small bar. It fit snugly in a hollow space in the wall. "Really need one of whatever you got."

Jack glanced up, briefly taking his eyes off the liquid he was mixing into a tall glass. "Sure," he said.

"I don't know what to do," Flynn said bluntly, and he looked straight ahead at nothing. "I don't know what to do about Kate... I don't know what to do about Gavyn..." His voice tapered off dimly.

"Begin by taking a breath," Jack said, holding a glass in front of Flynn.

"Thanks," said Flynn.

Jack sat down in a chair across from him. He watched his friend as he sipped on his drink. "Flynn, this might not be the right time, or maybe it's just what you need right now… to step away from this whole thing for a while, but I was talking to Professor Redmond earlier today."

Flynn sat up a little. "What did he say?"

Jack stood and walked over to the bar. He grabbed a couple of ice cubes with small silver tongs and dropped them in his drink. "He said there's something bad going on out there." He walked back over to the chair. "He said he had to analyze it more thoroughly, but it looked to him like that sludge we found… It's toxic waste. He thinks it may be that someone is dumping waste off the Wayan ship." Jack sat back down and slouched in his seat. "And whoever it is must be getting paid handsomely for it and for his silence."

"The Wayan ship, huh?" Flynn pressed his lips together. "Yeah, doesn't surprise me."

"I'll tell you what will surprise you…there's more."

Flynn glanced up, interested. "What?" he asked.

Jack stared down at his drink. He watched the liquid and swirled it a little. Then he brought his eyes up and fixed them on Flynn. "You're not gonna like this, but..." he paused, "it's just as we thought. Michael Mason is involved in it."

Flynn stood up suddenly. He was bewildered. "It's hard to believe, and even harder to prove, from a guy honored by the local community as a model citizen and entrepreneur. Are you sure about this, Jack?" he said.

"Yeah, I took an early morning trip to the canal, got a sample of the sludge, and gave it to Redmond. So, if you're thinking of giving Mason the benefit of the doubt, just think about it…he owns that canal, so he would know what was in there."

Flynn sat back down slowly. "What about Kate? Do you think she might know about all of this?"

Jack put his drink down on the table. "Well, I don't know for sure. But if Mr. Mason is involved, I don't see how she could not have known." He paused a moment, "I mean, you don't think she was clueless to the events happening in her very own home?"

"Yeah, I think she could be unaware. You don't know their family. By what I've seen, some things are kept very hidden in that household," said Flynn.

There was a long, cold silence as the two men sat staring into space. Jack's voice broke it first. "What are we going to do with this?

"Well, first I'm going to find out if Kate knows anything about all of this, and if not, find a way to tell her," Flynn said, dryly. He gulped down the last of his drink.

CHAPTER 23
THE ONLY THING CONSTANT
IS CHANGE

A change of seasons was coming to the city of Woodrose by the Sea. The breeze stirred up the sun-dried leaves and flung them in the air, sending them scattering along the streets. Women pinned their freshly curled hair more tightly, and their hats changed from straw to wool.

After one month in a state from which many do not return, Gavyn woke up. And just as the doctor had hoped, he began to recover well, likely due to his youth. Flynn's life was slowly piecing back together again in some places, but just as quickly falling apart in others.

Flynn and Jack concluded after reviewing all they had seen that Mike Mason knew and had ordered the operation of the canal drainage. If there had been a heart-saving way to tell Kate what they suspected about her dad, Flynn would have found it. But there was none. And he approached the beach house the next day and sat alongside her on the walkway steps, searching for words in the air surrounding them.

"What's this about?" she asked, reservedly.

"Your dad," responded Flynn.

"My dad?"

"Yes."

"Well, what is it? Is something wrong with him?" Kate asked.

The moment of silence lasted a while, and Kate understood quickly that the matter was serious.

"Flynn. You want to tell me before I start guessing all kinds of bad things?" she asked, impatiently.

"Like what?" Flynn asked. He felt a brief moment of hope that she might already know about it, saving him from telling her.

"I-I don't know. You saw him with an unknown woman? I have no idea! What?" she asked, cluelessly.

Flynn's hope was deflated. That was obviously the worst she could think of right now. But it was far from that. It was something even weightier, something that could bring dire legal consequences and change all of their lives.

Kate was quickly sure that her dad's infidelity was the problem. "I already know about my dad and his flings," Kate said. "He doesn't mean to hurt my mom, it's just, well, hard to explain the whole thing."

She was sitting on the steps with her knees at the level of her chest, resting one elbow on them. The other arm fell lazily by her feet, and when her free hand found a twig, she nervously scraped the red tile on the ground. Flynn gently placed his hand over hers and stopped her hand from moving.

She felt almost afraid to look up at his face since his touch felt different. If bad news could be detected in that way, she felt it and knew it; he had something unpleasant to tell her. She slowly looked up at him.

"Kate, I don't know how to put this. I mean, maybe I should just say it," he said. He stared at her face.

"Yes," she said. "Just say it."

Flynn felt uneasy sitting, and he stood and looked out to the sea just yards away from them. The sun's brilliance was bouncing off the water, and the waves looked silver instead of blue.

"Your dad," he began, "I think he might be in some trouble."

"Trouble?" Kate grew worried. "What kind?"

"Well, Jack and I went diving a while back. The day that Gavyn went to the hospital, we ran across a substance on large rocks beneath the pier." He turned and faced her. "Kate, there's so much I have to tell you, but I don't know where to start."

"I don't follow you, Flynn. What does that have to do with my dad?"

"The substance was toxic waste being drained from the Huntington canal."

"Waste? In the ocean? I can't believe anyone in their right mind would dump something like that there. I mean, children swim there, and people fish there." Flynn nodded but stayed quiet.

Kate stood and walked a few steps. She looked down at the tile beneath her feet. "If so, then it would only be lowlife that would do that. So what would that have to do with my dad?" she asked defensively.

"Well, I think Belino Rocco is the main guy behind the whole thing..."

Flynn started to say. He stopped the next sentence abruptly when Kate began to speak.

"People like that are the most selfish scoundrels. They should be given long prison sentences ..."

Flynn bit on his lower lip. "Before we continue, I have to tell you that I don't think that Belino is acting alone."

"Oh, really?" Her eyes widened, and the naïveté made it challenging to continue, but he had to.

"Yes, I have to tell you something that will be hard for you to believe. I have reason to believe your dad is involved."

Kate stared at his face and blinked. Then she smiled as if she pitied him. "What? No. You've got it wrong. My dad? You know he wouldn't hurt a fly."

"Look, I know this is hard for you. You're close to your dad, but people make mistakes."

"No, you don't understand. In fact, you don't understand anything about my dad. He wouldn't do that." Her pained eyes searched the pavement. Instantly, she looked back at him. Her eyes were filled with ire. "You never liked my dad," she started, "I know what this is! This is your resentment speaking! It's not about my dad."

Flynn was taken aback. "My what...resentment?"

"Yes, because you must have heard the rumor about Nick and me. And you're jealous." She didn't look at him as she spoke for fear that she might lose her nerve to continue. So her eyes stayed fixed on the concrete floor, with her eyebrows slightly raised, and she tilted her head a little to the side and brought her chin out in defiance. "I bet you're also angry at my dad for buying out the land your family had years ago." Kate was rambling blindly now. Her pain and disbelief dictated her words. "It's not his fault your dad couldn't afford to stay. And you're mad at me, and you're taking it out on someone I love...to hurt me."

Flynn stood still like a stone statue staring at her. "Kate..." he said, caringly. A wash of paleness overtook his features. "You know I would never do that! I don't know what you're talking about," he said numbly. He was stunned, angry, and hurt. Kate moved away a few steps, and he grabbed her arm. "Kate, don't play with this kind of thing. This is not a game!" Kate said nothing and tried to wrestle her arm away, but he held on to it tightly. "Don't you see that you're starting something up here that's not going to end well?" he said.

"*I'm* starting up something? Is that a threat of some kind?"

Flynn's face showed confusion, "not to you!" he said.

"Oh, I see, but yes to whom? Nick?"

Flynn's face showed surprise at her display of loyalty to Nick. Then his eyes grew tense. "Ok… yeah, to Nick! Talk about a low-life!" he said, and his words were born from bitterness and bile.

"Ha! What about your girly, Lila? What kind is she?"

"Lila? There's nothing between her and me…"

Kate shook her head in disappointment and tried to pull away again from his grasp, and the struggle froze when they heard her mom yell from the top of the stairs. "Let go of her, Flynn!" she shouted in a stern voice.

Kate and Flynn looked up toward the balcony of the house. Helena was leaning over a railing with a drink in her hand. It was mid-morning, but Helena was fond of Gin Rickey and particularly fond of drinking it at all hours. Her face was pink and flushed, and her hair unkempt. Ash brown curls fell awkwardly on her face. She pushed them back with the same hand she held the drink in, and the ice clinked together as she did. Flynn relaxed his grip on Kate's arm and stood silently for a moment, awkwardly facing each other.

"Mom, it's alright." Kate glanced back at her mom. Then she turned to Flynn with a dour expression, and she looked him straight in his eyes, "Flynn's going now," she said.

Flynn's lips tightened. "We gotta talk about this, Kate," he said.

"No," she said dryly. "Not now, anyway."

"When?"

"I don't know."

"Kate! You can't ignore this…I don't understand…" he said.

Kate turned from him and started to walk to her house, and Flynn's eyes followed her in disbelief.

"Kate, talk to me!" he pleaded with her.

"I don't have anything to talk about with you." Her voice was soft and stoic.

"Yes, you do! You have to explain what's going on in your head!" he called to her.

"I don't think so…figure it out," she said.

Flynn felt confused mostly, but angry and jealous too.

"I can't believe you're going to walk away just like that," he said incredulously.

"Yeah, I am…" She didn't turn back to him but instead looked at him askew and with one eyebrow slightly lifted. "…just like that," she responded and walked up the steps.

Flynn's eyes jetted everywhere, and they landed on Helena, who was still leaning on the balcony railing. They locked eyes, and she smirked triumphantly. Flynn dropped his eyes and turned toward the ocean, and he dug his hands deep and stiffly into his pockets. A range of emotions churned inside, from fury to hurt to disbelief. He walked down the way toward the pier.

A cool mist was suspended in the air, and it caressed his face, and he could see the ocean tide rising and unleashing its wildness on the rocks of the coastline. The pounding surf seemed to echo in his chest.

With the deepening of the sun came noon, and the smell of the salty air intensified. Flynn looked out to the amber-colored horizon; its bright, crisp light twinkled like gold. But the light added no warmth to him, and he felt cold as ice inside as he walked toward the train station and waited for the next train out of the beach town of Woodrose.

After Flynn had gone, Kate spent the rest of the day in her room, quiet and alone. Sometime during the early evening hours, Helena thought she heard her daughter up and around, and she called out to her. "Kate!" her mother's voice yelled from the kitchen. "I want to talk with you, hun."

Kate didn't respond but instead showed up moments later in the kitchen, dressed in a black silk evening dress. She examined her vaguely outlined reflection in the kitchen window and adjusted her long pearls with gloved hands. Her mother's face lit up in surprise. "Oh! You look fantastic, Kate! Where are you going?" she asked.

"Out," Kate answered curtly and leaned back on the counter, her face downcast. "Just out." Her lips formed a slight scowl.

"Out? But where to? Dinner? With whom?"

"Um, yeah, dinner." She didn't want any more questions, so she gave her mom a peck on the cheek and rushed past her. "I'll be back early!" she said.

Helena stood with her mouth slightly open, watching her sprint down the walkway. She watched with despondency. The same girl who would wait for her return by the window when she was small, now wasn't interested in a mere conversation. Helena blamed herself, the nannies, the drinking…the failed marriage.

CHAPTER 24
CHARISMATIC NICK

The night sometimes wears a cape of sable, warm and comforting against the brisk cold, and the shawl that fell upon Kate's shoulders as she stepped out into the night felt just the same. She didn't know where she was going; she just wanted to get away from the prison cell that her home had become. But there was one thing she couldn't escape: her thoughts, and she found them, as always, on Flynn.

She wondered where he had gone, and she began to question herself. Had she reacted too harshly? Should she have heard him out before leaving abruptly?

But she knew there was no way she could believe what Flynn was saying to her, and it hurt her. Then she began to question Flynn. Why was he so quick to involve her dad? Why did it seem that he never accepted the differences between him and her family, especially her father?

She felt he must have held prejudices against him all this time, as Ty did. The thought of hurting Flynn back originated in a place she rarely visited, and in that dark corner of her mind, hurt him she had.

Kate looked up at the ink-blue sky of inestimable deepness. She thought of walking the strand but instead decided on climbing Lavender Hill. From there, she could see the shoreline hugging the water's edge as it curved around it, with its small twinkling lights. It looked like a glowing crescent moon in the midnight sky. The earth was still. There was only a breath of wind and the murmur of the ocean's waves below her.

"It's beautiful, isn't it?" A man's voice invaded her thoughts from nearby and startled her.

Nick Collins approached where she sat, hugging her knees on the side of the hill, but he did so cautiously. "May I?" he asked, motioning with his hand to the empty space beside her.

Kate smiled. She felt relieved that it was someone she knew. "Of course," she said quietly.

He settled in next to her. And brushed his hand along the wildflowers, barely visible in the dark, and picked one out. Then offered the pink bloom, misty with dew, to her. Kate took it and smiled at him, then looked out to the sea.

"What are you doing here? I thought you'd be at the Wayan ship?" she asked.

"Yeah, that's where I'm supposed to be right now," he smirked. "But..."

"But what?" she asked, curiously.

He leaned back on a rock with his elbows and stretched out his legs in front of him. "But, I'd rather be here with you," he said.

"Oh, I'm sure there's more to it than that," Kate said, not convinced.

"Not really." He smiled boyishly at her. "I was late for the gig, so I just decided to take a walk and clear my mind," he paused and looked at her, "I've had a lot of things, including you, lately."

Kate didn't respond, but she looked at his face. It was handsome under the moon's light. The frost of the moon highlighted his cheekbones, and his sage-colored eyes glistened.

Nick was very different from Flynn. In fact, they were like night and day. Flynn was rugged and casual and lived for adventure, no holds barred. That was both a blessing and a curse. He was always ready to jump to conclusions and quick to resolve problems with a hothead. The benefit was that although he felt the power of it and knew he was good at it, he reserved its use only for the ring or in defense of someone he loved. The curse was his dad, and his greed to exploit that gift since he was a kid.

Nick, on the other hand, was sophisticated, artistic, and very charismatic. He was known to always keep his cool under any circumstances; he, too, knew his power, and it was also a kind of gift.

Kate looked down at her shoes, and when Nick unexpectedly took her hand, she moved it away. She stood up, brushed off her shawl, and wrapped it around her shoulders again. Nick stood up too and tugged the collar of the cloak a little closer to her neck. "You always come to sit on Lavender Hill so elegantly?" he smiled.

Kate laughed, and that was good because it broke the tension. "No," she said, still giggling a little. "I was going to..." She caught herself.

"To...?" he asked, with a little more than average curiosity.

"To go to the Wayan ship for distraction," she finally admitted. "But then I thought better of it and came here instead."

Nick smiled big. "The Wayan ship? Hmm, one might think you knew I played tonight...or at least one might hope?" he said, bending at the knees a little to look in her eyes.

She pursed her lips, trying to hold back a sheepish smile, but finally gave in. "Yes, I guess I was curious to hear you play," she admitted.

Nick was more than pleasantly surprised and gently placed her hand on his bent arm. "Well, then, would you do me the honor of being in the audience tonight at the Wayan?" His eyes gleamed with excitement, and he smiled at her.

"Yes," said Kate.

The Masons were known in towns both far and near. In Europe, Mike Mason was famous for his business savvy, bringing fresh ideas to companies in need.

Around town, though, he was better known for his philandering, which he did his best to keep secret, but usually failed to do so.

Kate's mother, Helena, had more than a hunch about these affairs early on. After the initial betrayal, she learned quickly how to cope. Her therapy consisted of a shot of Gin upon awakening and another as needed throughout the day. 'Doctor's orders!' she would say. However, that did nothing other than dig a deeper trench in the marriage, and it weakened her relationship with Kate.

It was perhaps this background, with its weak and, for the most part, absent rearing, which left Kate to figure out the world and its residents all alone. Her inexperience at times made for a poor job of it, though, and tonight she found herself quickly complicating her life.

CHAPTER 25
THE STANDOFF

TWO WEEKS LATER

The streets in Los Angeles were shrouded in black with dark alleyways alternating with lighted shops. Chryslers, Lincolns, and Chevrolet coupes lined the road and were parked bumper to bumper with one or two buses by the curbside. Women with long coats and men wearing fedoras, suits, and ties congregated on the street corners waiting to cross the busy streets. The train ran through the heart of it all, and Flynn exited the train trolley on First Street in downtown.

Taking the train gave him ample time and allowed his mind to figure out the problem at hand without having to focus on driving. But the problem was, which problem first? From Gavyn's health, though improving steadily, to Mike Mason and Kate, he was overwhelmed!

The windswept streets were busy as he turned the corner on Spring and continued toward Jim's Café. The café was family-owned and run more like a twenty-four-hour diner. The lot was big, and Jim had a small victory garden out back so that all the meals were made with handpicked fresh daily produce. At this time of night, however, it would be most likely just black coffee for Flynn.

"Just coffee?" the waiter asked, as Flynn settled into a barstool.

"Yeah"

"You sure? You look like you can use something stronger," he said, smiling.

Flynn thought a moment. "It shows, huh?" he smirked back.

The man nodded, yes, and he chuckled as he poured black coffee into a cup and placed it carefully before him. "We have the best brandy in all of the state," he said.

"Alright, guess I'll have one of those too," said Flynn.

The waiter was pouring the shot when the small bells that were hanging on the front door tinkled. Flynn didn't turn back to see who entered, and he threw the brandy down his throat and then just stared into the cup of coffee.

He concentrated his thoughts on the warmth of the liquor running down his throat. Then Flynn felt a heavy-handed thud on his back, and he turned to see Bennie standing with a broad grin on his face.

"Bottoms up!" Bennie said and grinned. "Look who's here!"

Flynn's downcast expression didn't change when he glanced up at him with the corner of his eye, and he turned back around and mumbled: "How are you doing, Bennie?"

"I'm surprised to see you here at this time of night. It's past your bedtime," Bennie said, taking a seat next to him as he looked at his watch. "It's 11:00 pm. You guys train early, don't you?" he asked.

Flynn didn't seem to hear him; he just looked straight ahead at nothing. "I'll have another brandy," Flynn called out.

Flynn's sullen expression made Bennie think of Gavyn. "Hey, I haven't been to see Gavyn lately. I feel really guilty about it, you know?" Bennie looked up at the waiter. "Hey, you guys have any whiskey?" he asked all in one breath.

"Whiskey? Yeah, sure." The man poured Bennie the drink. "You guys come in here like it's some sort of bar." The server laughed a little.

"Well, it's our bar away from the bar," Bennie joked back and looked at Flynn to support the joke, but he didn't. Bennie's smile faded, and he placed his arm around Flynn's shoulders. "Hey buddy, sorry, I guess I'm looking callous about things."

Flynn shook his head no. "It's okay, Bennie. Things are better with Gavyn now. He's going to make a strong comeback, you'll see. I really believe that. He's a fighter. Been making real progress since he got out of the coma, and he's back home now," he said.

"Oh, uh… yeah… I heard that. I think so too. But I wasn't referring to Gavyn. I was talking about your ex."

Flynn turned to him and squinted; his eyes were red from the overindulgence in the fine brandy. "My what? My ex? What are you talking about?"

Bennie squirmed in his seat a little. He seemed to always find a way to open the lid on the most tightly sealed can-of-beans. "Uh, nothing, I mean, I guess I shouldn't have opened my mouth," he said.

"No, it's just that I don't know what you mean, my ex? Who do you think is my ex?"

"Kate Mason…?" Bennie said, insecurely.

"Kate?"

"Uh, yeah."

"Why do you say she's my ex?" Flynn turned his body toward Bennie and searched his face.

Bennie downed his drink in one gulp. His eyes had the expression of someone who just found an injured puppy by the side of the street. "I thought she was your ex because I saw her just now before coming here, on the Wayan ship with the sax player, uh, Rick or Nick, or whatever his name is."

Flynn's eyes were intense as he watched him speak. He was unnervingly quiet. After a minute of complete silence, he said, "At the Wayan ship, huh?" under his breath.

Bennie nodded.

"With Nick Collins?"

"Yep," Bennie said apprehensively. "Is this something you didn't know about? Did I spill the beans or..."

"No." Flynn got up from his seat suddenly. "No, it's ok." His face showed little emotion, and his eyes looked distracted. "Can I borrow your car, Bennie?"

"Uh..." Bennie reached into his pocket. "Yeah, sure." He tossed the keys over without hesitation.

Flynn caught them in the air and nodded his head slowly. "I'll be back to get you in a couple."

"Yeah, ok, take your time. I'll be right here," Bennie said, biting on his lower lip and staring down at the liquid in the glass.

Flynn's walk was fast-paced as he headed into the briskly cold, dark air of the night. The light wind felt like stinging needles on his face as he raced to the car parked a couple of doors down on the curb.

The half-hour drive on the highway felt like minutes as he pulled into the parking area near the docks. He could see the lights of the Wayan ship dancing off the dark waters. He quietly untied a stranger's small boat, taking care to not be seen by anyone, and pulled away from the shore.

The music was loud and brassy, and there was the sound of muffled singing as he approached the ship. He climbed aboard, stealthily moved along the walkway, and peered in the windows. He stopped when he saw them. Kate and Nick were sitting at a table. She had a cocktail before her, and she smiled as she sipped on it. The swirls of smoke ascending from

Nick's cigarette wrapped around them like a cozy blanket. Flynn hadn't taken notice of his tightening fists as he watched Nick.

The tension was building to a point where he might lose his sense of reason. He could see as Nick leaned over to whisper something in Kate's ear, and she threw her head back in laughter. And with that, the point was reached. Flynn burst through the entrance and knocked over anything that was in his path to get to Nick.

Kate saw him and immediately stood up. Her eyes flew open wide, and her lips parted as she drew in a breath. Nick followed her eyes and turned around to look. And that was the moment Flynn was waiting for. Flynn grabbed Nick, lifting him off his chair, and pushed his body into the tables nearby. The crowd in the room stood up and collectively drew their breath as he came crashing down, and the live music was abruptly replaced by the sound of glass flying everywhere.

Nick stood up and squared himself in front of Flynn. "Come on, fighter," he said. "I've been waiting for this, too," he smirked.

"Flynn!" Kate yelled, "What are you doing? Have you lost your mind? Stop!" She touched him on the sleeve, and he shrugged off her hand. His entire attention was on Nick. Nothing else was visible to him. Not the people, not the damage, not Kate.

Nick swung a hard one, but it was expertly blocked by a grinning Flynn. "You're nuts if you're going to take me on," Flynn said. "Tonight is your last night on earth if you do."

His fist plunged into Nick's jaw, and he flew across the gambling table. When he stood up, he was dazed and unsteady from the force of the punch, and a gash had opened over his left eye. He shook off the haziness, and there was a metallic sound of a blade flipping out of its casing. Nick crouched down a little and shifted the switchblade to his right hand, then stepped forward and swung, hoping to slice Flynn's face. But Flynn blocked the move with his arm, and it sliced the skin and began to bleed heavily.

"Nick! Stop!" Kate yelled and nudged her way between them.

"Kate!" a distressed but familiar voice rang out.

She looked to see her father as he cleared his path over to her, and he yanked her away from the precarious position between the two men fighting.

There was an immediate silence when a dozen tall men in suits descended on the area and began to clear the ship of everyone on board. Two of them struggled with Nick and Flynn as they both shook them off, and Nick left for a back room with a folded cloth over his eye. A waiter brought a heavy towel for Flynn's arm, and he held it in place as he watched Kate and her dad.

"You know what to do." Her father ordered the men with a tip of his chin, barely glancing at them.

"Dad, what's going on? What are you doing here?" She struggled to see what was happening, but her father held her firmly by the shoulders, blocking her view.

"There's nothing to see here for you, honey," he said in an unfamiliar tone.

Kate grew stiff at the strange sound of his voice. It sounded like someone other than her dad. She allowed herself to be escorted out of the Wayan by her father and staunchly dropped into the nearest boat. Why was Flynn there? Did Flynn expect to see her there? Did she still care for him or Nick? She shook off the thoughts in a hurry.

Shaking off the thought might not have been the best move for Kate. Had she reflected on it longer, she might have uncovered a hidden agenda in the seemingly harmless move by her dad to escort her out. She was unaware of the plot unfolding before her that involved Belino and her father, Mike. Kate had no idea that the scene had been a setup and that they were both in cahoots to get her away from Flynn.

Kate's mom, Helena, was stretched out on her bed, looking up at the ceiling as she puffed on her cigarette. She had shuttered the windows, turned off all the lights in the bedroom, and secured the French doors that overlooked the ocean.

The only light visible was the glow from her cigarette and the moon on the sea. It was coming on midnight, and she was alone. She no longer wondered where her husband was or when he would return. Instead, in the silence, she was lulled into a dreamlike world, making out figures on the shadowed ceiling in the dark. That was her heart's sparing way to deal with the loneliness. She did not hear when Kate came in, walking zombie-like to her room. She did not hear when her husband settled into the library for the night, falling asleep in the large recliner with an open book –the usual decoy- resting on his chest. Sometime after 3:00 am, she too dozed off in an admission of defeat to the night, and she fell asleep.

CHAPTER 26
WOODROSE NO 402 TO DOWNTOWN

The mornings in Woodrose were magical. The sun would glide in softly through the clouds as it made its way up high in the sky. Everything was gilded with a soft brush of gold, from the turquoise sea to the grassy knolls to the deepening bright blue of the sky. Everything awoke as mellifluous and luminous as honey.

However, things weren't quite as magical at the Masons' home. Helena woke up to find her husband sleeping in the library, and she didn't have a clue as to where he had been all night. Everything seemed to be crumbling around her. Michael's love interests outside of the marriage had come to a showdown. She wanted an end to all of it before it brought an end to them.

"Michael..." She shook him slightly. "Michael!" She raised her voice when there was no response.

Helena stood over and watched him. His breathing was slow, and the features on his face showed no tension. He had loosened his gold silk tie, and his white shirt was untucked. She took the decoy, closed it, and set it aside, then gave him one last push that jerked his body sideways.

That worked, and he lifted his head up from the backrest and stretched his eyes open. He looked blankly in front of him at first, then his eyes shifted, and he surveyed the body standing next to him from the waist up to her face.

"Oh, it's you," he said, lifting himself clumsily from the chair, slipping the necktie off from around his neck, and tucking in his shirt.

"Who did you expect to be standing here next to you?" Helena asked.

He ran his fingers through his messy hair that was falling every which way, and he smoothed it back. "I don't know...don't start. It's too early."
He waved her off tiredly and walked to the door.

"Michael, you're not going to brush me off like that! What time did you get home? I was up until 3:00 am!"

"Really? Waiting for me?" His tone was derisive, which compounded the insult.

"Yes, if you can believe that. I guess I'm just that stupid!"

Michael let out a breath of exhaustion. He was tired of the fighting, and he was tired of her. "Look, you know, I've said it before, maybe we should sit down and discuss our options," he said. "Tonight, I want to do that."

In his mind, the decision had been made. Helena caught herself. Options? She knew she was pushing it to the limit with him. Helena knew all he needed was an excuse to leave, and he would. What would she do alone? The war had taken its toll on everyone, even reaching the well-to-do folks like the Masons. Helena did not need to work in a factory to provide income, like some of the other women were doing. But she did feel the stress and the insecurities just as the rest.

She loved Michael, but that was only part of the picture. With him gone, so would be the safety she had enjoyed, not just personal but also monetary. He had always been her refuge.

Michael walked down the hallway and tapped on his daughter's bedroom door. "Sweetheart, I'd like to talk with you," he spoke into the door benignly.

Kate had woken up and was already dressed. She had something to do. One of them, in fact, was to talk to her father about last night.

"Be right there, Dad," she yelled back.

She peered into her dresser mirror and hurriedly smoothed rose-colored lipstick on her lips, then sat down on the side of her bed and pulled up her lace skirt to adjust her silk stockings. Her fingers fumbled with the metal clips, making sure they were attached securely to her lace garter. She stood up, took one last glance in the mirror, eyed the nightstand to make sure she had everything she needed, and she opened the door.

"Hello dad," she said, and pushed her way out, closing the door behind her as if she were hiding something in there. Kate walked toward the kitchen with a determined air. Her dad followed.

"Kate, uh…" he started, as she opened the cabinet door and peeked inside.

"Yes?" she asked, without turning around.

"I, ah, about what happened last night on the ship…"

She turned suddenly and looked him in the eyes. He dropped his and continued, "I know you must be wondering, I mean, I guess you're upset with me…"

"No," she quipped. "I'm not upset," she said,

Her father threw her a perplexed look. Kate grabbed a box of Cheerios and poured them into a bowl with milk. "I mean, you did what you thought was best…for me…for Flynn and for Nick, or at least that's what you want me to believe, right?" Kate crunched on the cereal nonchalantly as she spoke.

Her father took a few short steps and stopped. "Ok, so you are angry then."

"No, Dad. Not really, I mean, I'm more confused." She put down her spoon and gently blotted her mouth.

"Yeah, I understand that. Kate, you know you're my world. You mean everything to me!" He shook her shoulders gently, and he bent down and wrapped his arms around her as he had always done since she was a child.

But Kate didn't respond the same anymore, and she broke away and stood up to look at him. "I used to think I knew you." She said and blinked in an effort to stop her eyes from getting misty. "Well, I've since found out that you can know and trust someone all of your life and not know them at all."

"Look, I can explain this to you, pumpkin."

"Are you sure, Dad? Can you explain those thugs you were with last night? And can you explain being on the supposedly forbidden Wayan ship, Dad? Remember how terrible that place was and full of low-life people?"

"Well, it is."

"But, you were there."

He was quiet as a clam, and he felt as cold as one, too. Helena had been listening to the latter half of the conversation. She walked into the kitchen and gave Michael a look of faux surprise.

"I never would have guessed that's what the illustrious Michael Mason was up to last night!" Helena said. "What are you gambling our money or something even more sinister?" she smirked.

"Helena..." Mike started to say.

Kate's eyes jetted between the two of them, and she said, "I'm going downtown." She knew it was headed for an argument between the two, and she didn't want any part of it.

Helena snapped away from Michael for a moment. "Downtown?"

"Yes, I'll be back before night." She quickly exited the kitchen.

Into the wet morning, she flew. Past the dew glittered Morning Glory that bloomed on the white brick border by the sidewalk. They lushly draped over the edge and eagerly awaited the sun's first rays on that misty morning.

Kate found herself eagerly waiting too for the return to the normalcy that she and Flynn once knew. Being the product of a flawed marriage, Kate had always felt that she lived her life on a ship that was constantly being rocked by storms. Trust didn't come easy to her, and now it was all but gone after relinquishing that trust to two people she believed in, her father and Flynn, and being let down in the worst of ways.

So now it was all over, she thought. Now she wouldn't be able to backtrack on those feelings. Kate walked, thinking, and hurting. The sea was wild and blue, with clusters of green seaweed floating near the top. It smelled of salt and fish. The sand was warming to a golden hue as the sun broke through the fog.

It was nearing noon, and the train could be heard rumbling down the tracks, coming to a long, dragged-out screech as it stopped to pick up passengers. The sign on the front of the trolley read Woodrose no. 402. Passengers disembarked cheerfully and systematically, looking forward to a day on the beach, as others boarded.

Kate left the ticket counter with her boarding pass in hand, downtown bound. Though the pass read *Downtown,* her thoughts were somewhere else. As she settled into her seat, she looked out to the ocean yards away. The sanderlings were running back and forth, pecking at tiny prey on the wet sand. The birds' little black legs blurred from the speed at which they moved. The wind had kicked up, and the tall palms swayed as the sun caressed the green fronds' bundle at the top. They looked like tall, shapeless women with unruly long tresses.

She rested her head back and closed her eyes. She was exhausted, and the day had just begun! A longing suddenly emerged; it ran through her veins like hot liquid. Precipitately, she wanted to escape Woodrose, if only for a day.

A shadow of a memory crept into her mind. She could see the room in Paris, where she had stayed as a teen, traveling with her father on business. The Masons owned a seaside cottage in France, and when her father had business to take care of there, he would sometimes take Kate with him to Paris. In her mind's eye, she could see herself stepping into the pale blue ornate room with its high wooden ceilings and stone balcony. There was a large painting with a beautiful French woman dressed in pink in a gilded frame, and a decorative cart filled with books near the bed. She longed to be there again, quiet and secluded, away from the pain of the present time. After a few moments, the susurration of the moving train lulled her to sleep.

The sound of a man's voice woke Kate up. "Miss…" The man spoke sharply but kindly. "Miss…"

Kate could now feel his hand on her shoulder as well as hear him clearly. She blinked, her eyes startled at having fallen asleep. "Oh, I'm sorry. I fell asleep," Kate said.

"Oh, that's alright. Happens all the time on the train," replied the conductor.

"What stop is this?"

"You're at the end of the line, Miss. Twenty-third and Elm."

"Twenty-third and Elm?" she asked, peering out of the window. "How far is Oak Lane?"

"Oh, it's right down the line here. Just follow the end of the tracks and make a right."

"I hear there's a nice bookstore there?" she inquired of the conductor.

"Yep, it's called the Book Nook. Brand new. Nice place, really fancy," he replied, as he walked, surveying the seats on the empty caboose for litter.

"Think I'll have a look at the new place," she said, out loud, staring down the street.

"Fine by me!" He smiled widely.

CHAPTER 27
PREMATURE VERDICT

Kate disembarked the trolley and walked the narrow street to Oak Lane. Downtown streets, though swept, always looked dusty to her. The sun was drier and hotter downtown, and her throat felt parched. She passed a place with big glass windows and double doors with a large sign on the roof. The black letters tilted sideways a little, read The Snowbird Ice Cream shop. Kate inspected the interior of the place through the glass as she walked by. The walls were stark white, and round red seat stools and small tables dotted the floor. There were pictures of ice cream cones and malts on the wall. She decided to stop and get a cone.

Moments later, she emerged with a praline and cream ice cream scoop sitting high atop a brown sugar cone. There was an invitingly cozy bench in front of the bookstore, and she sat down to eat her treat.

Kate's people watched. Downtown was just now beginning to get busy. Kids ran in groups of two or three with reckless abandon in and out of the ice cream shop. Couples, parents, siblings, and some older folks seemed to all be out in force on a shopping spree. They darted in and out of the diverse storefronts, from deli to fine apparel; they all seemed to find what they were searching for and would leave the shops with large bags in tow.

But the harmonious quiescence of the afternoon would soon be shattered for Kate. From among those she observed, there appeared a familiar face. At first, she wasn't sure if it was actually him, but when she straightened for a better look, it was Flynn.

Her face would have taken on a different semblance other than shock bordering on horror if he had been alone. But he was walking with someone she recognized as his old girlfriend, Lila.

Yes, it was long-legged, red-lipped Lila, the same woman whose favorite pastime seemed to be flirting. Men followed her like a pack of wolves, but as soon as Flynn was mentioned, she would always drop them like a hot potato.

It was clear she had a penchant for Flynn. And it was beginning to be clear that she had been waiting in the shadows. Much like a cougar on the prowl. For that moment when either Kate or Flynn would make the first move away from the other. Kate watched them, and her heart beat fast and painfully hard. The two walked across the street to a park in the center of the city. Lila's body leaned close to Flynn when they sat down. He had his head bowed and was looking down at his shoes, and she caressed his face while he spoke with her eyebrows together, listening carefully to him.

This was surely a nightmare. Kate wanted to believe that. She ventured to think that if she walked up to Flynn right now and touched him, he would fade like a mist, and she would wake up. But deep down inside, she knew it wasn't a dream; it was all real, and Lila must have been the reason why she couldn't find Flynn on certain nights. Those nights, searching for him on the pier like the evening when she met Nick for the first time. Nick…he had warned her about Flynn's infidelity. She felt emotions churning inside her like the sea waves near her home. Grief crashed with fear, and hate tossed and stirred within her. What would she do now?

The next moment happened as if her body was disconnected from her head, and she didn't know how it happened, but she suddenly found herself standing in front of them. "Hello, Flynn," she said dryly.

"Kate!" A short breath escaped along with her name. "What are you doing here?"

"Fancy all three of us meeting here, huh?" said Kate.

Flynn's eyes moved to the side and glanced at Lila, who was smiling up at Kate.

Flynn realized how the circumstances might look. "All of *us*? Uh, yeah…I'm sure you rem--"

"--Remember your friend?" Kate interrupted. "Yes, I remember her," she said coolly.

The setting sun gave the park a deep golden luminosity. It reflected off Kate's face. Her eyes glowed like burning topaz, but especially so when she looked at Lila.

Lila thought of Kate as a spoiled brat and a boyfriend snatcher who would do it for the ego boost and just because she could. She knew her kind, she thought. Kate ran on a different track; in fact, the two ran on opposite sides of the tracks. Lila thought that Kate had a code of morals that took the thrill out of nearly everything pleasant.

Kate, on the other hand, knew the likes of Lila. She thought of her whenever she would hear the term *cheaper by the dozen*. To Kate, Lila was one of the dozen.

Lila brought her chin down and smiled with her eyes fixed on Kate. "Nice to see you," she said, in a phony-sounding voice.

Kate ignored her. She stared at Flynn, who stood up and reached out for her hand. "Kate..." he started to say, but she stepped back firmly, avoiding his touch. "How could you do this…to me…to us?" Her words were ragged with emotion. A tear betrayed her and ran down her cheek; she wiped it off quickly and angrily.

She gave him no chance to speak, and her voice tightened. "I'm leaving, Flynn."

"What do you mean, Kate? Where?"

"I told you before…if this would ever happen…"

"Kate, you've got this wrong."

"Isn't that what they always say?"

"No, I mean it, though."

"It doesn't matter anymore. I won't be my mom. I won't endure that kind of relationship, and I told you so."

"I don't believe you would leave me." In his eyes surfaced angst. "This is not what you think!"

Kate looked at the quietly snickering Lila, then back to Flynn, and her eyes grew cold. "I don't care what you believe, Flynn, I'm leaving. May you find comfort in her garishly tacky red lips!"

Flynn moved as if he were in a haze. He reached out to her, but Kate turned and quickly moved toward the street. She flagged down a nearby taxi, and it sped away. There was no amount of nice words, kind thoughts, or encouraging ways to comfort Flynn after that. He knew Kate would never allow him to explain the situation now. Not after seeing him with Lila.

What Kate didn't understand was that Lila was an old flame, but not the kind of flame Kate perceived her to be. In Kate's mind, she was a never-waning, hot, burning fire. Which Lila would allow to smolder but never burn out entirely, so it could easily be rekindled. But the rekindling never could happen because, try as she would, Flynn never saw her as anything but a friend.

Kate had an inherent weakness, a fear, and it was of ending up in a loveless, hostile relationship like her parents. It was a fear that grew out of childhood trauma of seeing the constant fighting without really understanding the dynamics of the situation. And this fear was genuine to her and clouded her judgment entirely. Flynn did not understand this about Kate. He was sure of his feelings for her and lack of them for Lila, and he tried telling her so. However, with her past condemnatory beliefs and the current situation, he was sure it was the death of them.

The truth of the situation was far from conflictive. Flynn had gone downtown to meet with Robert Redmond, the biology professor, and Lila's father, to talk more about the substance he and Jack had found under the sea. He hadn't planned on meeting up with Lila and, in fact, had no idea she would be there, but when she was, they discussed his concern about the findings under the ocean.

The distress over the crisis that Flynn felt and Lila's support, genuine or not, was mistaken by Kate for a rekindling of affection between the two of them. She thought Flynn might have been acting out of spite for her friendship with Nick. In her hurry to judgment, she had ruled on a premature guilty verdict.

After Kate left, Flynn boarded the train back to Woodrose, not really knowing what he would do or say to Kate, but just wanting to see her. However, while on board the train, he quickly lost his nerve, not knowing the best way to approach the situation. He didn't disembark in Woodrose but stayed aboard until the last stop on the ocean route to the town of

Serpentine, where he walked and thought among strangers strolling on the shoreline.

CHAPTER 28
AN UNDERWATER LODE

The sun looked large and dark gold in the sky as it took a last bow of obeisance into the mighty sea. And when its glow faded, a parting gift appeared, as the darkened sky scattered tiny diamonds in a grand display of light.

It was evening when Flynn stepped off the train back at Woodrose and looked up at the innumerable stars. The night was clear and crisp. A hand patted him on the shoulder. "You know what it's a good night for?" Jack's voice came out of nowhere.

Flynn didn't startle easily, and he looked down at the ground and shook his head no. Jack took in a breath. "I heard what happened downtown," he said.

"Wow, news travels faster than light around here," Flynn replied glumly.

"Lila called me. She's concerned..."

Flynn waved him off. "I don't want to talk about it."

Jack nodded. "Ok," he said. He watched the sky along with Flynn for a moment. "You know what I think you should do?"

"No...can't imagine, but I feel some good, time-honored words of wisdom coming on," he said.

Jack laughed. "Well, yeah, sort of. I think we should go diving again. I'd like to bring up more of that stuff as evidence," he suggested.

Flynn looked at him with his interest piqued. He nodded, yes. "I think that's a good idea. Finally, a good one!" he joked. Jack shook his head, smiling.

They started to walk to Jack's car, and Flynn paused a moment, placed his hands over his head, and interlaced his fingers. He looked out to the ocean, and his eyes grew serious. "I can't believe these guys are doing this," he said. "Everybody in this town will be affected if they haven't already been. You know, I was worried about bringing Kate's dad into this because of her. But now, after hearing the professor's dire warnings, I feel it's the only thing I can do to help her and everyone else!"

Jack looked at Flynn. "Yeah, I agree. We have to do this," he said.

The two went down to Jack's place and geared up. Then drove back to the pier and stepped lightly around the boats to avoid being spotted. Jack started up his small boat, and Flynn placed the diving gear, Jack's homemade rebreather, and two frogman rubber diving suits inside.

They plunged into the watery deep, disturbing the ocean's calm. The Wayan ship was quiet tonight. Belino Rocco had a system going; every Monday night, they would go dark. It was becoming clear that it probably had something to do with the illegal dumping around his ship.

Jack's cave diving expertise had come in handy, if not crucial, in the discovery of the dumping. Diving for him was not a sport but a way of life. He forayed into underwater caves with snorkels fashioned from garden hoses and handcrafted spears, and squeezing into small spaces to bring up some of the gunk came easily to him.

At the time, the only commercially available equipment was crude goggles and Corlieu fins, and even these were hard to come by. So Jack made do with homemade goggles and arm power for swimming. This was the degree of his love for underwater hunting. And Jack was shrewd and alert when it came to the darkness and water. He'd always find his way as if he had built-in radar attached somewhere on his body.

Submerged in the waters of the ocean, visibility was low and became lower as sediment clouded the water. Jack knew they would have to go very much by feel. The two men floated in the watery darkness and probed the rocks along the sides with a long pole to avoid raising clouds of unsettled muck around them. Jack quickly located something, and in the bubbly silence, he tapped Flynn on the sleeve and signaled him to follow. Flynn swam over instantly to look at what it was. There was a big, round metal object wedged between some rocks.

Jack ran his hand along its side. It was a white metal drum, and there were many beneath it. The cylinders had words and numbers running up the side of them, and on the lid, two letters, FM.

Flynn looked up toward the surface of the water. He could vaguely see the shadow of the pillars from the pier. They must be right underneath the area where the Wayan ship is anchored, he thought. Jack motioned for Flynn to look at something else he had found on the side of one of the drums. They could make out the numbers 504 and Huntington Way written in small black letters. They looked at each other, and Flynn motioned to go up.

The sound of air burst forth from both of their mouths, disturbing the quiet of the night as they clamored on the boat and took off the diving gear. "504 Huntington Way, that's the canal," said Jack, catching his breath and rubbing his head with a towel.

"Yep." Flynn's mouth became a tight line. "The very same." Flynn smoothed back his wet hair, and the water drops fell on his shoulders and ran down his back. "You know, I remember it as a kid," he said. It was unspoiled then. "It was a neat place where Gavyn and I would go swimming. We'd go looking for garter snakes and hunt out bullfrogs to bring back home. Then they unexpectedly closed it off and set up an illegal trespassing sign that was there for years."

"Well, now we know why it was being transformed into a waste dump by FM, whoever that is." He thought for a moment, and then Jack said, "It actually sounds like it could be the initials for Frontier Manufacturing, that big building over on Olive Street."

"You're right. Wonder what the manufacturing hours are? If that would add up with the Wayan shutting down on Monday?" said Flynn.

"That would be interesting," Jack said.

"If that's what Belino's been up to, he must be getting a lot of cash from that little venture," said Flynn.

Both men looked at each other, and Flynn was first to drop his eyes; he stared down at the floor. The moment of silence fostered thoughts, uneasy ones. "And just who would have that amount of cash handy?" he spoke gently into the night. "Paying for an operation as big as that?"

Jack leaned back on the boat and rested his elbows on the teal cushioned seat. "There's just one person I can think of. Mike Mason. I think he is expanding his interests, and he won't stop until he owns this town down to the sand crabs, though they do try to hide under the sand from him."

Flynn chuckled. "In vain...he's going to buy that sand right from under them!"

Jack nodded, laughing, "Yep. He's the one guy who would have that cash around here. You know how much he'd be able to develop on that land? He would rake in the bucks!"

Flynn bobbed his head slowly. "Yeah, I agree. But that kind of waste would need to be safely contained, removed, and buried."

"Yep. And removing it in that way would be very costly. So, I think Mason thought, why go the costly route - meaning the legal way. When he could just approach Belino, who is already getting paid by the Frontier Manufacturing people to dump the waste. And offer him additional money to get the sludge out and find another place? That way, he would be able to clean it up a bit and develop it for less from his pocket. Then I figured Belino needed a cheap place to dump all that waste, and lo and behold, he found a free one! A place where no one would ask any uncomfortable questions, what better place than Davey Jones locker?"

Jack looked up at the giant moon over the water and examined it as if the answers were written on it. "Mr. Mason surely is involved, and he, Belino, and Frontier Manufacturing will surely do time for it in the big house. Another thing I've seen is him talking and taking long rides with Belino in shiny black limousines on many occasions…very secretive type of meetings. What could those two characters have in common to go on lunch dates? And they almost always headed down the way of the canal."

There was a long, quiet moment while they both let that sink in. Flynn unexpectedly started up the boat. It was now nearing midnight. "Where are we going?" asked Jack.

"Let's go check out the canal."

Jack straightened up in the seat. "Oh," he said, "You wanna go right now or in the morning?"

Flynn smiled and shook his head at his friend's idleness. "Now, Jack, right now," he said, as he looked out at the approaching shoreline.

On land, Flynn and Jack followed a truck that was headed toward the canal. At a little past midnight, it was an odd road to take. There were no rest areas, no population nearby to catch a snooze or a meal, and this made them suspicious.

Their suspicions proved to be right on when they saw the trucker turn into the Huntington Way canal. They drove behind him with their headlights off so they wouldn't be spotted, and when the truck stopped at the channel, they maneuvered underneath the cloak of a tall, shadowy tree.

The vantage point was excellent, and they could see the truck's red lights come on; they glared brightly as a dire warning when he put on the brakes. The trucker flung the driver's door open and hopped out. He adjusted his heavy gloves and surveyed his surroundings as he walked to the back of the vehicle.

A long hose-like apparatus connected to the back of the truck was released into the canal. There was a gurgling noise that went on for a while. The man was busy doing something inside the cargo area of the truck, after which he disconnected the hose and quickly got back inside. He started up the engine and took off back down the same road he had come. They followed again closely but undetected back to the town of Woodrose.

Flynn parked nearby, and they could see the man, who was then joined by two other heavily muscled men, unload the drums onto a boat. Jack looked at Flynn. "Do you recognize any of these guys?"

"Nope. They're definitely not from these parts."

"Yeah, that's what I thought. Wow, looks like we caught them red-handed doing the dirty deed."

"Yeah, and I bet those deeds don't come cheap," said Flynn, and they both smirked at the quip.

"Wonder specifically what kind of substances are leaking from those drums?" Jack asked.

"That's exactly what I was in downtown talking to Lila's dad about."

"What did he say?"

"I'll tell you verbatim because, after the first word, I was lost! He was able to isolate halogenated solvents, chlorinated compounds, volatile organics, and heavy metals," said Flynn.

"Are you kidding? I can't believe they're putting that stuff in the ocean and so close to shore!"

"They probably didn't expect the leak," said Flynn, "And they were sloppy about dumping it. Bypassing the legal areas used to dump toxins was way cheaper. And Belino preferred to do the dumping at low or no cost to him, in the deep, dark sea, without anyone's permission or knowledge." Flynn brought his lower lip and bit on it. He squinted his eyes, and they shifted to his friend's face. "I wanna go back to

Huntington Way in the morning and see what it looks like." He said.

Jack stared at him, looked away, then back again at his face. "What for? We have all the evidence we need. We know how they do it, when they do it, and where," he reasoned.

"I noticed one other thing going on. There was some sort of liquid burning on the east side of the canal. Didn't you see it? The guy opened the spigot and let some sort of liquid run out into the canal."

"Well, Professor Redmond said they sometimes burn off some of the waste in the canal. I don't know, maybe what's left behind?"

"I think we've stumbled upon a massive operation," Flynn said.

Jack's brow got tiny lines, and his eyes tightened. "That might be true, and if we have done so, we have to be careful. I think we're dealing with something here that's bigger than all of Woodrose," Jack said.

Flynn nodded slowly, "Are we talking Mafia?" he asked. His expression showed the pieces were falling into place for him.

"Yeah, that's what I think. And those guys don't mess around."

"I understand," Flynn said. "I'll be careful. Just want to check things out in the morning light."

CHAPTER 29
THE CANAL AND THE DREAM

Daybreak came, and the wind whistled over the empty field of the Huntington Way canal. Still, the watercourse remained motionless, murky, and dark.

Flynn walked alongside the bank with the neckline of his t-shirt pulled up over his nose to escape the noxious fumes. He stooped down where the truck had been the night before, and he could see evidence of the sludge's displacement. The barrels were fifty-five gallons each, and there must have been hundreds in the back of the truck that night.

He put on a glove he had taken with him and scooped up the black sludge with his forefinger. Flynn rubbed it between his fingers and thumb while he thought. It felt gummy and viscous even with the gloves on, and it was stygian black. Flynn thought of something, and he stood up and got back in his truck. He drove across town to the nearest public phone booth in a Shell gas station to call Jack.

The glass door on the wooden booth was stuck, and he had to nudge it open with his hands. When inside, he reached into his pocket, pulled out some coins, and dropped in thirty-two cents for the call. A clang sounded when he dropped each dime in one of the three slots at the top of the metal payphone.

The town where Flynn was calling from was mostly undeveloped and desolate. But for some reason, someone saw it fit to put a gas station right in the middle of it at the crossroads of two dusty roads. Across from the station stood another building, which was a dairy farm. From the phone booth, Flynn could see a man loading crates of glass bottles filled with milk into the back of a delivery truck. Flynn watched him absentmindedly as he listened to the phone ringing at Jack's. After a couple of rings, he picked up.

"Hello?" Jack sounded busy.

"Hey, Jack…" he spoke into the phone loudly.

"Yeah, what's up?" Jack could hear a loud rushing noise from the cars as they drove by. "Where are you? At a highway?"

"Yeah, I'm off Long Street. The canal's almost drained completely now, but it still has sediment of some kind along the bottom and sides. I think I'm going to have to take it to the authorities. They won't stop otherwise," said Flynn.

"Seems to all be going according to plan. Next, they fill it with dirt, and no one will know it was ever there," Jack responded.

"They must be busting their chops trying to get that done since he won't be able to build there until it's all completed. Hey, are you going to be there?" asked Flynn

"Yeah, for about another hour," said Jack.

"Alright, then I'm stopping by to…" Flynn was suddenly distracted when a swirl of dust caught his eye up the way on the long, straight road. It was a roadster, and it was speeding toward the station. The stylish car was out of place there, to say the least, and as it approached, Flynn recognized it as Michael Mason's car.

"Are you still there? Flynn?" The voice sounded small and distant through the receiver.

Flynn stood shocked to see Mr. Mason pull up to the gas station. Not only was a sports car out of place in the barren town, but he was too; it was nowhere near his home. What could he be doing traveling through here?

"Wait…hold on a minute," Flynn spoke low and with his mouth close to the mouthpiece of the phone.

"What? What did you say? Hey, I think the reception's going…"

"I'll…a…I'll talk to you later," Flynn said. He was distracted, and his eyes were glued to the car. "I'll call you!" He hung up quickly to the sound of Jack's voice fading into the receiver as he hooked the phone back. Then he opened the door of the booth and stepped out.

Mike Mason's car did not pull into one of the pumps, but instead, it rolled around to the back of the gas station. Flynn followed the vehicle with his back pressed against the wall so as not to be noticed. Mr. Mason pulled up next to a large rig like the one he had seen at the canal. Flynn's head dropped back a little against the wall.

"Mr. Mason!" The big guy he had seen that night stepped out of the truck and animatedly shook his hand.

Michael Mason was a soft-spoken person, and he rarely raised his voice unless he was in an argument with his wife. When it had nothing to do with emotion, he was calm and always collected, and in control. Mike shook the man's hand and smiled. His body leaned forward toward the man's face, and Flynn had to get closer to hear what he was saying.

"When do you think it will all be clear?" Mike asked the man.

"Well." The man straightened up and looked around with an air of importance. He was getting a lot of attention for his work. It wasn't just anyone who could handle a job as large and corrupt as he had. "I'm thinking maybe two days more," he said.

"Two days?" Mike Mason's mouth grimaced, and he looked stern. "Your men said it would be done today."

"Today? Nah, no way. Look, you want me to be cooking with gas? I gotta do it right."

"We're paying you over the top. Believe me, you wouldn't want Mr. Rocco to get upset."

The man squirmed a little at the mention of Belino's name. "Yeah, I know, but I can only go so fast."

"Find a way to go faster." Mike Mason nodded slowly as he spoke for emphasis. "Ok, you get me?" he asked.

"Yeah, yeah, I get you. I know the likes of the guy you're in cahoots with, you don't gotta tell me twice."

Mike Mason relaxed his posture, and his chin stuck out a little; his eyes were set on the man's face. He didn't say anything again, turned around, and got back into his car, then drove off. The burly guy watched him leave, then pursed his lips and shook his head. He got back into his truck and clattered past Flynn toward the canal.

It was noon, and the sun was at its highest point when he returned to Woodrose. Flynn stood overlooking the bright blue of the ocean from a window in Jack's house. He sipped on the water as he spoke about what he had seen and heard.

"So that's it," he said, staring out to sea.

"Well, I can't say I'm surprised." Answered Jack.

"You know… there's something else that bothers me," said Flynn

"Mike Mason's involvement?"

"Yes, he's rich."

"Yeah, very, and?"

"And why would he get involved with someone like Rocco and his crooked dealings when he's already set for life?"

"Where's there's that much money, there's bound to be a tangle."

Flynn looked bewildered at him. "What do you mean, a tangle?"

"Well, I'm not so sure he's a bad guy, per se. Possessing the essence of greed is not an unlawful act in itself."

"Maybe not, but that doesn't change what he's done to his family. Mainly Kate because of that greed."

"I understand your point, Flynn. Maybe you're right. We're going to have to alert the authorities on that dumping either way."

Flynn grappled with how and when to do it. He wasn't sure if he should talk to Kate first about what to expect. She probably wouldn't listen to him at this point anyway, maybe it would be better to just get it taken care of. He and Jack decided to dive again and check what, if anything, was new with barrels.

The water was clear and blue at the top, but as they dived further down, it took on a cloudy appearance. It looked like an undersea swamp with the overgrowth of algae everywhere. Flynn and Jack spoke in their underwater sign language about the cloudiness and the increase of dead fish floating belly up. Not all of them would ascend to the top of the waters and float; some would sink to the sand, and they could see their mouths open, upside down. Flynn signaled to go up, and Jack followed. They rushed out of the water and swam to the boat.

"There's an increase of dead fish," he said to Jack. "And did you notice the newly sunken barrels half-buried under that boulder?"

"Yeah, I saw it. It's just as Professor Redmond said, the fish are dying from what seems to be a lack of oxygen, anaerobic decomposition that leads to eutrophication, he told me."

"Eutro—what?" Flynn asked.

"Eutrophication is the term for suffocation. The fish died from lack of oxygen."

Flynn shook his head, and he felt pity and anger.

Night arrived, and the moon showed a crescent and was glowing. A veil of glittery mist made its presence known at the docks, snaking its way around boats that bobbed in the dark waters, and encircling the hills and train station. Flynn was poring over a map, marking, and calculating reference points to show the exact areas affected and where the barrels could be found. And when he was done, he called out to Jack.

"Jack! Hey!" he yelled toward the rooms of the house. When there was no answer, he searched the areas of the big, elongated home. Jack lay outstretched and snoring on a big chair in the library. A rolled-up magazine was halfway out of his hand. Flynn slipped it out of his relaxed grip and glanced at the cover. It was a journal on cave diving. The man on the front actually resembled Jack. He glanced back at his snoring friend. He chuckled, rolled the magazine back up, and tapped his head lightly with it.

Jack weakly flailed his hand, thinking maybe it was a fly overhead. Flynn laughed again quietly and left the room. He wondered if he should stay the night or go home. But he

decided staying at Jack's would allow an early start to the
Bureau of Investigation, and he got comfortable on the couch.

OLD PHOTOGRAPHS SPEAK without words to the heart
and to the mind, and Flynn wanted to hear what they had to
say about him and Kate, and where things might have gone
wrong. He dug in his pocket and pulled out his wallet. He
carried two pictures of Kate. In one, the two of them were
standing in front of the train depot when they were very
young. She had snuck out of her house to meet up with him
when he returned from overseas. Flynn was in uniform, and
Kate was wearing a butter-yellow colored dress with white
trim on the collar, short white gloves, and a wide-brimmed
straw hat. Flynn smiled to himself, remembering that day.

The memory came back as swiftly as the wind. That day,
the wind was breezy and blew about them mischievously.
Every so often, Kate would impulsively throw up her gloved
hand to catch her woven hat just before it flew off into the
depot's parking lot. He had never seen eyes so expansive,
vibrant, and gold. He remembered when she whispered, "I'm
crazy about you," as they watched the waves glimmer in the
sun.

"No, not that much." He remembered saying to her, trying
to coax her into admitting more.

"Yes, I am!" she had insisted. Her insistence appealed to Flynn's immaturity, and he continued the game.

"Oh...I don't know..." He rested his elbow on his knee. And placed his chin in his hand to cover the smile on his face.

"Flynn!" she finally fired back, exasperated, crossed her arms in front of her, and turned from him.

"See?" he said. "I frustrate you!"

And when Kate turned back to look at him, he was suddenly in front of her face, and he kissed her deeply.

He stayed close to her face. "I love you, Kate, though that's not really what I feel... I mean, I can't put into words the depth of it. The word love is too flat, hazy, and overused. What I feel is the most sincere thing I've ever known. To tell you the truth, it's so strong I'm even afraid of it."

Kate looked into his eyes and examined the blue and beauty within them. She wished she could reach into his mind and read the inside of it. At times, it was as if she actually had. Kate sometimes wondered if she knew more about Flynn than Flynn himself. And maybe that was true. Flynn would never have admitted fear to anyone. That was not the way his father brought him and Gavyn up, but with Kate, everything was different.

"I want to marry you, Kate. There is nothing else in the world that can compare with this love we have."

Kate's eyes glowed and were shiny with tears. "I accept!" she shouted, forgetting the people around her who all looked over to see what the excitement was, and she flung her arms around his neck.

Flynn was so involved in the reverie that he hadn't noticed, while lying on the darkened couch, he had been smiling broadly, as he remembered all of these things. Flynn could hear the waves of the ocean wildly pounding against the darkened shore; they, too, seemed lost in their search for equanimity. *What's happening to us, Kate?* He whispered to himself, but the dark offered no response. *Whatever it is, I will fix it, and things will be the same as before.* He spoke out to nothing, but in his heavy-eyed state, he could see her standing before him as he fell to sleep.

CHAPTER 30
BELINO'S MOVE

While Flynn was fast asleep, Kate was wide-awake. It was 1:00 am, and the night had just come alive on the Wayan. She was sitting at a table at Nick's request. He had something to show her. The waiter brought Kate a French 75 and set it in front of her carefully. She smiled up at the waiter, and he bowed down slightly and moved away to the next table.

She sat alone and looked down at her drink. She had never been much of a drinker; living at home with her mother had made her shy away from it, but tonight she was going to celebrate. She was tired of the worries, heartbreaks, and lies. It was time to start something new. But these words were born only in her head, not her heart, and she didn't feel them very deeply.

What she did feel was loneliness, ostracized by those she loved in one way or another. Flynn, her dad, and her mother all seemed to have their own agenda, and none of it seemed to have included her. Kate took a sip of the cocktail: champagne, gin, and a twist of lemon.

She stared into her glass, and suddenly she noticed the music had changed tempo. The beat was now on simmer, the lights were dimmed, and on stage, a female singer with a passionate voice began to play the piano. Her voice was sultry but sad as she sang *One For My Baby* by Frank Sinatra.

Kate fought the despondent feeling building up as those words struck her deep inside. She stared down at her glass.

"Must be lousy…" The voice of Belino Rocco broke through the music. Suddenly, his face was close to hers.

"Pardon me?" Kate asked. She moved to the side a little uncomfortably.

"Oh, I said, it must be lousy being lonely on a night like this," he said, extending his hands up to the ceiling and smiling that crooked smile of his.

"No, I don't know what you're talking about, really. You seem to always come out of nowhere, don't you?" asked Kate.

Belino laughed softly. "Yes, I can see how it might look like that. But you see..." he paused and outstretched his hands, "I own the place."

"So you like to slither around in it, huh? You don't fool me with your nice guy approach. I know your kind."

"Really?" He was genuinely surprised. "How's that?"

She smiled a little but stayed quiet, looking at her drink.

He stayed quiet too, but he was no longer smiling as he stood next to her and observed her for a moment. "You're nothing like your dad." He threw out the words and watched to see what reaction he would get. But Kate didn't give one, and she avoided looking up at his face and stared straight ahead.

"I don't like you very much, Mr. Rocco, but my guess is a lot of people don't," she said.

"Oh…" he started, and he breathed out with exaggerated indifference. "Some do, some don't…" he paused and looked for Kate's face. "But your dad does."

Kate stood up abruptly, and Nick appeared, seemingly out of nowhere, and took her hand. He glanced at Belino, then back at her. "You're not leaving, are you? Is this guy giving you trouble?" he asked lightly.

"I'm feeling tired," she responded.

Nick waved off Belino, who sauntered away with a small smile. "Look, I know he can be a pain, but let's ignore him and not let him ruin our night." Nick lowered his chin and looked at her; his eyes danced as they always did with excitement, light, and spontaneity. "Tell you what, let's just get out of here," he said and took her hand, leading her through the maze of well-dressed guests, booze carts, and gambling tables.

They took the short trek to shore on one of Belino's boats and docked it nearby. The long strip of dark sand looked mysterious and lonely. In its perpetual motion, a sweeping wave from the sea would periodically lap up to their feet and slip back in. It looked like a sheer gossamer scarf gliding over the surface of the firm, wet sand.

Nick and Kate talked about their differences and similarities. They both understood the power of money, and they both knew the allure of comfort, but he could not discern the mechanics behind the needs of the poor. The everyday townspeople like Flynn. Nick was quick to point out. "I have to admit, I still don't understand how you and Flynn ever became an item," he stated quietly.

"Why?" she asked, already knowing the answer.

"I guess because of the differences between the two of you." His eyes moved sideways to peek at her face. "You know, it's the age-old, beautiful girl too good for the guy from the wrong side of the tracks thing."

Kate's mouth tensed up, and she looked uncomfortable with the subject. "Let's not talk about that. I find myself having to explain my situation with Flynn to everyone, and I wouldn't want to start having to do so with you, too," she said.

"Ok, but let me just say this, if you find yourself having to *explain a situation*, as far as I'm concerned, that seems like the situation might not be right."

Kate looked straight ahead at a small hill at the end of the sandbar. It was shadowy and dark, but she could see the outline of the sagebrush, and it was frosted by moonlight with a mysterious white glow.

"But who should decide that but Flynn and me?"

"Fair enough," he conceded. Nick stopped walking and turned to her. He placed his hands on her slender shoulders. "I'm interested in you, Kate. I think you probably know that. I believe the two of us should be together instead of your frequently disappearing boyfriend."

"I kind of figured you thought that," she said, smiling. "But what makes you say that?"

"What? That your boyfriend is the disappearing kind?"

"Yes."

"I've observed you on several occasions looking, no more like searching, high and low for him…at the docks, by the train…"

"Well, you don't know the reasons why or the situation…"

"There's that word again," he interrupted and smiled, looking down at the sand.

Kate wanted to be mad at his somewhat cavalier attitude, but couldn't when she looked at his boyish expression. He was a multi-dimensional character, a sharp-dressed, sophisticated sax player. Still, somewhere deep inside, she could see the outline of a mischievous boy. "You know, sometimes you act just like a kid that loves to play pranks...clever as a pirate!"

Nick was very pleased with her assessment of him. "And you are a real live mermaid."

He turned to her and put his arms around her. Under the glaring eyes of the moon, Kate somehow felt a pinch of betrayal of Flynn, for she was warmed by his embrace. The ocean had once again calmed its agitation. It seemed to be a conspirator to the serenity of the moment. Kate became uneasy at their closeness, and she pulled away.

"I have to go," she said

"Why? Because of him?" He stepped back and examined her eyes.

"Yes and no."

"Kate, the guy is not one of us. He's...he's rough, and not just around the edges. I mean, the guy wouldn't know the first thing about being with a girl like you."

"But you do?"

"Yes." He took her by the shoulders again. "I can give you anything you want."

"I already have that."

"I can give you loyalty." His voice went down to a whisper. "I would always be there for you..." His lips touched the top of her head, and he kissed her forehead.

Unexpectantly, a light beamed into Nick's eyes from the parking structure up the way. He winced, and Kate noticed.

"What is it?" she asked, turning back and following his eyes to the lot.

"Just someone's headlights, I guess, they were just so bright."

Kate looked down, then back up at him. He gazed at her and smiled.

"I really do have to go. My mom must be worried and…I don't know, I just should check in on her," she said.

Nick nodded, slowly agreeing. He was happy that they had this time together, and he saw it as the beginning of the two of them. They walked to the parking lot, and Nick opened the door to his pearl-colored Cadillac. While closing the door, his eyes scanned the empty lot for signs of the car or whatever it was that had shone that light, but there was nothing, so he got in and drove Kate home.

The Cadillac purred like a cat as it idled in front of Kate's home. She bade him goodbye with a peck on the cheek before exiting the car and entering her home.

"Mom," she called into the dark, quiet house. "Mom? I'm home." She spoke softly as she searched first the living room, then her mother's bedroom. Kate found her sprawled on her bed, still in her street clothes. "Mom…" she said softly and shook her head when she noticed the open sleeping pills by her bed. She nervously counted the pills left, but there was just one missing. Kate was relieved and twisted the cap back on.

"Kate? Is that you?" her mother mumbled thickly in the dark. She held up her head weakly and squinted at her.

"Yes, it's me," Kate said. "Go back to sleep." Her mother relaxed back into the bed and slept.

Kate went to her bedroom and undressed in the dark. Her mind was on a million things at once. She was too tired to take apart the situation with Nick right now. The word, *situation* made her smile. He had used it so often that night that it felt like a word they had christened, and that somehow made her nervous. The fact that she found herself giggling at the overuse of it was confusing to her. Although it amused her to think back on him. It was, after all, Nick who had used it to describe her circumstances with Flynn and in an unfavorable light.

Kate didn't want to think about it anymore; she was exhausted, and she crawled into bed. It was around 4:00a.m. when a noise made her glance at the clock on her nightstand. She recognized the footsteps as her father's, and she heard him slowly close the door to his bedroom. Kate closed her eyes again and drifted to sleep.

CHAPTER 31
THE TRIP

The seagulls swooped low and noisily flapped their broad white, black-tipped wings as they landed on the wooden railing of the wrap-around deck at Kate's house. The cream-colored sundeck faced the ocean, and Helena would often have her morning coffee alongside her husband before he headed to work. This Monday was no different from the rest, and Kate could see them through the open French doors discussing something. Stella was busy in the kitchen, setting down a carafe of coffee and two shiny plates brimming with a breakfast feast on a tray.

"Hello, Kate, my dear, would you like something this morning?" asked Stella.

"No, thanks," Kate called back as she whisked by her toward her parents.

"Not even coffee…?" Stella called after her, then shook her head and smiled.

She knew Kate was always on the run, but she wished she would sometimes stay around longer to chat; sometimes it looked to Stella like she could use the company.

"Mom…dad…" Kate broke through the existing conversation.

"Kate, honey," her dad began, "why don't you sit down with us for a moment?"

Her mother looked her over quickly. "Where are you going?" she asked, noticing her classy ensemble.

She was wearing a navy blue suit with a white lace blouse underneath the jacket. Helena smoothed the ribbon-hugging waistline of the coat and tugged at it a little as she spoke. "You look like you're going somewhere special," she said and smiled brightly.

"Yes." Kate adjusted her doe-skinned short gloves and checked her veiled hat in a small mirror for straightness. "I'm leaving for the airport," she said matter-of-factly.

Stella had stealthily arrived with the tray, and she was setting down the plates. She handed the newspaper to Mike Mason as was her usual custom, and he took it and placed it down in front of him without unfolding it.

"Where? The airport? Why didn't you tell us about this?" he asked accusingly. "Kate, I don't like it when you make plans like this without consulting us first."

Kate placed her hand on her hip as if getting comfortable for the discussion. "Well, I guess I thought it best not to wake you last night."

Her father threw back his head slightly. "Oh! I see. So you went ahead and made plans on your own, hoping to sneak it by us?" His eyes landed on hers like lead.

"Dad, I think I'm old enough to do that kind of thing without asking first..."

"Old enough? What does age have to do with it?" His cheeks suddenly looked sunburned.

"Mike..." Helena reached out and touched his arm.

Her father ignored the touch. "What if I told you that you don't have permission to go to France?"

Kate smiled and lowered her face but said nothing.

"You're not going!" he said. "End of conversation!"

"Well, it's not much of a conversation when all you say is no, Dad!"

"That's because that's what I mean...no!"

"Mike..." Helena's voice rose in an attempt to salvage the conversation.

"I've got enough to worry about without you out and about in Europe, alone!"

"Mike..." Helena insisted.

"What!?" he lashed out in frustration.

Helena pursed her lips and dropped back into her seat. "Fine, you handle it! You're good at it... I forgot," she said, biting back with sarcasm. He threw her a look, then turned his attention back to Kate, and there was the sound of a car horn.

"Oh!" Kate said, relieved to be rescued. "That's my taxi!" She hugged her mother and kissed her cheek, then turned to her dad. "You're too handsome a guy to have this furrowed brow," she said, smiling and leaning down to kiss his forehead. Kate peered into her father's worried brown eyes. "Don't worry, papa," she said. "I'll be right back." She sprinted down the hallway. "I'll be staying at Liliane's, so you don't have to be concerned," she called back as she exited the door.

Helena turned to her husband and placed her hand over his on the table. "Don't worry, she'll be alright," she said softly, patting it. "You worry too much."

Mike dropped his chin and stared at the table. "Yeah, I do. But with reason," he said. "Why do you suppose she took off like that?"

"I have a name that goes with that question...Flynn Brennan," her mother replied. "Call it mother's intuition, but I have a feeling she's trying to sort things out with him, and this is her way." She poured herself coffee and inundated the black with cream. "Maybe spending time with Liliane will help," she said.

Liliane Lauberge was a French girl whom Kate had befriended on an extended stay in France when she was nine years old. The family lived near her parents' summer cottage, and when Kate noticed the new clan, she quickly snuck out to inspect the kinfolk.

Sneaking out was something Kate had become accustomed to since her mother and father strictly forbade any communication with children from lesser wealth. But to Kate, most of the time, those were the kids who didn't mind getting muddy while in search of sunken treasure in a nearby riverbed, or climbing trees without worrying about their expensive clothes. And adventure was very much a part of Kate's childhood fantasies. The two became close friends and regularly exchanged correspondence during summer visits to the Masons' Cottage in France.

The Lauberge home was a ten-minute walk from the Masons'. Both were close to a bustling, artistic, and picturesque village where the two young women, upon reaching their teens, would spend time eating in outdoor cafes. And unbeknownst to their parents, capriciously sampled some liquor in the local bars and bistros. Those were summers of enchantment, which Kate would never forget.

Liliane had naturally bronzed skin that always appeared suntanned, even in the winter, and full waist-length wavy brown hair. She had plump lips that pushed slightly forward from the rest of her face, and her eyes were the color of Manzanilla olives.

CHAPTER 32
LILIANE IN FRANCE

Kate had rested on the plane. When Liliane picked her up from the airport, it was 7:00 in the evening. They greeted each other with an exchange of kisses on the cheeks and went straight to their favorite sidewalk bistro. They sipped on a glass of wine and caught up on the news from the last twelve months. Of course, the main subject was Flynn and newcomer Nick, whom Liliane had become acquainted with through the letters sent from Kate. Liliane always seemed to be on double speed, and she did everything quick, including talking. Her lips puckered when she would speak. "I don't know… as soon as I got your phone call, I knew something was not right! Is it Flynn?" she asked, taking a sip of the wine. Her speech was always quick and confident, but her words, especially in English, were sometimes roughly put together.

"Yes…" There was a long, suspenseful pause. "I'm not sure where to start." Kate looked down at her glass and then sampled the wine. "Oh, this is good!"

"Yes, it's Châteauneuf-du-Pape!" said Liliane.

"I like it! This calls for seafood, yes?"

"Yes! I agree!"

Liliane struck a match to light her cigarette; it was a nasty habit she had picked up in the years of her rebellious youth. She drew on it long and stared at Kate with intrigue. The rising smoke made her eyes water, and Liliane spoke through a squint. "You don't look like before," she said.

"What do you mean?" asked Kate.

"Lost in love and the fantasy of it. That's how you were, remember?"

"Lost, I am. In love, I am also, but the fantasy part, well, I guess that might not be as strong as before," Kate replied.

Liliane leaned forward in a quick motion and locked into Kate's eyes as she snuffed out the remaining part of her cigarette. "Why?" she asked bluntly. "What has happened? I don't think I could live without that part of love!" she said, and casually dropped back in her seat and glanced at the passersby. The street was vibrant, and women with jaunty, angled hats and cinched-waisted dresses strolled by, accompanied by men in dark suits and Fedora hats.

Kate smiled, and her eyes twinkled at Liliane's candor. She had always admired her friend for her self-determination and frankness. Those two things would often escape Kate's grasp in her small, contained, affluent world. There were rules to follow, and if one dared to stray from the regulations that governed the well-to-do in her circle, there would be quite a reckoning.

But what kept her the most in line was not the barring from the country clubs and being blacklisted from social functions, not even the blackest dread of being wiped from the family's will! No, not one of those things meant much to Kate. Especially when compared to the look of disappointment in the eyes of those she cared about. But Liliane was free to do as she pleased, freedom that came from knowing that you can't lose what you don't have.

The waiter approached their table and set before them two Cognac Shrimp with Beurre Blanc. Kate smothered the shrimp in the sauce with her fork. "This smells so good!" she said. Either Kate was hungrier than she had anticipated. Or maybe it was the intoxicating aroma, Kate found it difficult not to put the entire jumbo shrimp in her mouth. She instead resorted to a nibble so as not to burn her lips.

Liliane giggled at her self-control. "Now see, I could not do that! I simply eat the whole big shrimp and deal with the burn later!"

Kate laughed, and it felt good to her. It released the bottled-up tension with her parents and Flynn. That night was a pleasant time, and the wine and the food warmed them. After the meal, they had dessert and espresso and lingered at the Bistro until closing. Then they walked down the cobblestone street that led to Liliane's house. The road was empty, for it was now past midnight.

"How are your parents?" Liliane asked.

"Ah, my parents…the same, I suppose. A little fighting here and disagreement there, but they somehow stick it out."

"Hmm…"

"Hmm, what?" Kate smiled at her friend.

"Maybe that's a lesson for you to learn. Right in front of your face, no?"

"I don't know what you mean?"

"Well, it's like this. This is how I see it. Your parents fight, but make it work, right?"

Kate nodded, "Yes…and?"

"Why do you suppose it still works?"

Kate thought a moment. She looked down at the darkened roadway, beautiful in the shadows of the trees with multi-colored stones lining the path. "It works because they want it to. Because after all is said and done, they love each other too much to let it go," she said. As she spoke and thought, she tilted her head to the side, and her eyes fixed forward but on nothing in particular in the dark, as she reflected. A contemplative quiet fell between the two, and the only sound was of the tall trees as they soughed overhead in the varying Parisian winds.

"So you think I'm being hasty when I get mad at Flynn for being absent with no explanation whatsoever? Or because he chats with a girl even if she is a past interest, such as Lila?" she asked.

"If that's as bad as it gets, yes!" Liliane smiled upbeat.

"How much worse *can* it get? Maybe I'm missing something here, but someone who loves you should want to be around, right?" asked Kate.

"Yes, but do you know all of the reasons why he is not? You said in a letter that it was a mystery and that he didn't want to talk about it right now…well, why not give him some space and see before you make a decision on your future?"

"Well, I know it has something to do with my dad. He wanted to tell me about something he says is crooked."

"With your dad?" asked Liliane.

"Yes."

"I do think you're missing something here, as you say, but I think it's a nice long conversation with Flynn! Find out what he is trying to tell you!"

"And now about the other one, Nick…"

"What about Nick?" asked Kate.

"Do you love him?"

Kate paused. "I'm not sure what I feel…But I do feel something."

"More than what you feel for Flynn?"

She paused again. "No."

They reached the house, and Liliane opened the door and turned on the light near the entrance. The wood floors shone golden, underneath rose-colored throw area carpets. The kitchen was white with a small chandelier hanging over the polished wood table and chairs.

Liliane walked with Kate to the guest room. "Get some rest, dear friend. In the morning, we can talk some more and figure this all out. I promise. You won't leave here until it's settled in your mind and heart! Bonne nuit amour!"

Kate smiled and gave Liliane a warm embrace. "Bonne nuit, Lily!
What would I do without you?"

"Not have any fun?" she asked, and her eyebrows arched mischievously.

Kate giggled at her irrepressible impishness.

THE NEXT MORNING, she tidied her bed, showered, and joined Liliane at the kitchen table for breakfast.

"Bonjour mon amour! How did you sleep?" Liliane asked as she poured coffee and arranged croissants on a plate.

"Very well, thanks! I always sleep well here."

Kate brought the coffee cup up to her nose, took in the rich aroma, and smiled a deeply satisfying smile. She had missed France for many reasons, and one of them was the coffee. She began to sip it slowly and broke open a croissant.

"I was turning everything over in my mind last night," Kate said.

"Everything about Flynn or your parents?"

"Both, I suppose."

"Kate, you say to me Flynn is never around anymore, but what if it's your parents' fault about that?"

"What do you mean? Because they might purposely keep him away?

"Maybe that's the crooked thing he was talking about? Who knows?"

Liliane scrunched her lips in the middle and tilted her head from side to side like a palm tree swaying in the wind as she spread jam on her pastry. Then she took a bite and fixed her eyes on Kate's face. "Purposely or not, if I were him, I might be put off by the whole …he's not good enough for you thing…that you say, your parents do, no?"

"Well, yes, my mom has never made him feel welcome. She wants me to marry someone who will keep me comfortable. You know, Flynn is a dreamer. He was forced into boxing by his dad, but his real dream is ocean biology."

"And did he not pursue this?" asked Liliane.

Kate pressed her back against the chair. "He wanted to get the money needed for his studies by boxing, but I'm afraid I got in the way." Kate's lips gathered to the side. "I talked him out of the important money-making fights, you know, the big ones that carry a lot of risk of injury or worse," she said, and her eyes showed defeat. "I don't know if I did the right thing, but I couldn't stand by and see him destroy himself to feed his father's self-centeredness."

Liliane watched the small bubbles that lined the rim of her coffee cup burst in the hot liquid. "Yes, I understand, I cannot blame you for that," she said softly.

Kate's eyes watered, and her throat felt tight. "What if he's gone for good? What if there's no returning to what we had?"

Liliane patted her hand lightly. "Well, now let's keep things together, you know, in perspective."

"You think I'm overreacting, don't you?" Kate asked, and her lips turned downward.

Liliane smiled. "Somewhat," she said. "I mean, if you look at it from my eyes, you see a woman terrified of something that might not be the way she thinks."

Kate nodded. "What should I do?" She pressed her friend to come up with a solution, but deep inside, she knew the decision was ultimately up to her alone.

Liliane placed her elbow on the table and rested her chin on the palm of her hand. "Well, I think you know what I am going to say."

"I have to decide for myself." Kate scrunched her mouth sideways.

"Yes...and?"

Kate thought a moment. "Things could be worse than this...?"

"Yes! And something else…give him time, mon ami!" she said, with a quick wink of her eye.

Kate felt a sudden rush of embarrassment. "Guess I am overstretching a bit and panicking," she said.

"Oui…" Liliane started to say, and she brought a match up to light a cigarette. "Let me tell you a little story," she said, and she breathed out smoke and shook the match until the fire was out. "It's a true one, and there is something to take away from it. A few months ago, I got a letter from Monique Lesaire. You don't know her, but she is a friend I met through my cousin. I hadn't heard from her in a long time.

Anyway, she wrote in an attempt just to catch up, but ended up telling me about how her life had gone over the past several years, the good and the bad. And she said to me that she had met this man, Luc, a journalist, and they fell in love. It was the first time she had been in love, so you can imagine the depth of the feeling. But then the war broke out, and he told her he would have to leave to join.

She told me then, 'When he left, it felt as if the whole world had lost all color, and I saw everything in gray.' She heard very little about him beyond the fact that he had sailed for Malaya in 1941 with his regiment.

During the war, she had a string of boyfriends, including one older man…an officer who wanted very much to marry her. But then, he too was posted abroad. Nevertheless, she confessed to me later that not one made her feel the same as Luc had.

Then out -of -the- blue …as you like to say… one night, in 1945, she got a telephone call from Luc. She was in disbelief, and she agreed to meet with him right away. He arrived at her door with his kitbag, straight from the troopship that had brought him home from four years in a Japanese prisoner-of-war camp!

Monique was shocked. 'C'est impossible!' she said to me. 'I couldn't believe my eyes.' Liliane paused a moment, and her voice grew somber, and she shook her head and looked down at the table. "This was not the young man she had known. Misshapen, pitted, scarred. Only the eyes were the same, she told me."

Kate listened attentively. "What did she do?" she asked.

"She accepted his marriage proposal!"

"What?" Kate's eyes widened.

"Oui, she did!" Liliane threw her arms up. "Yes. This is why. She said that when she looked at him in this way, her heart bled. That night, Luc took a train to Marseille to visit his parents. Her heart did not go with him, she told me, but her pity did."

It was silent in the kitchen for a few moments. Liliane looked down at her hands and twisted a ring she was wearing reflectively and continued. "Over the next few weeks, she could not get the image of Luc out of her mind. She would come to visit me and say, 'I cannot stop thinking about the ghastly humiliations he must have suffered!'

Not long afterward, they met in London, where Luc had suddenly lapsed into a coma for two days with malaria, and Monique came to a fateful decision. Here was the challenge given to her for peacetime: Could she help keep this man alive and help him to get back into life again? Monique loved the spirit of the man, but that was all that was left of him."

Kate sat half in horror, half in sorrow. "How sad…for both of them," said Kate.

Liliane shook her head slowly, no. "She decided to marry him in that state."

Kate's eyes screamed, *what*? But she said nothing.

"It was not to be a storybook romance. And Monique told me later, 'I shall never forget our honeymoon. My husband was mentally sick, as well as physically. He could not eat what he wanted after being starved for so long. He could not play card games without getting dizzy, nor drive a car. He wept when he went to the cinema. All his mental scars would come out all the time. I was horrified, shocked at what I had done.' She confessed this in tears to me," Liliane said.

Then she paused and glanced at Kate's face, perhaps wondering if she should continue or if this was too much for her right now. Kate's eyes were misty and red-rimmed, and her eyebrows were raised in the middle as if in physical pain.

"Should I continue?" Liliane asked.

Kate nodded emphatically. "Yes! Please just go on…," she said.

Liliane nodded back. "Alright. Well, over the next few years, Monique lavished gentleness and sympathy on her new husband, who had managed to get a job with an oil company. On one of her visits, I asked how things were going, and she said, 'Not so well. The more I give him, the more I am rejected,' she told me. The truth was that Luc was no companion and was challenging to handle.

He was quiet, morose, and joyless. His work drained him and left nothing for anyone or anything else. However, Monique did not give up. They stayed together, and they did a little traveling. But ultimately, Luc relapsed into the introverted, difficult, and silent man he had been when he got back from service, and he grew ill again. For the last year of his life, he was looked after by caretakers. They told Monique that her husband was 'dead inside.'

"That must have been so difficult to hear. I just can't imagine that," said Kate.

"I agree entirely," said Liliane. "After his death, Monique moved away to England. I will never forget the words she wrote about that time: 'The eyes that so haunted me when Luc asked me to marry him were still there when he died. I have to live with the thought that I don't know whether I ever really did anything for him.' I suppose…" Liliane glanced at Kate and noticed her eyes were teary. She paused and warmly patted her hand. "This is not you and Flynn, Kate. I brought this up because I think it might be good for you to examine your feelings. What do you imagine you would have done if you were Monique?"

"Flynn is an extension of me," Kate said, as she gathered herself and blotted her tears. "It would feel like suicide to leave him under those circumstances… I would have stayed." She patted her nose with a tissue from her purse.

"And what if he never returned as the Flynn you know now, such as Luc, who did not?" asked Liliane.

Kate took a breath to clear and calm her mind. Her eyes fell on Liliane's face with a weighty look in them. Then she looked down at the table. "When I'm with Flynn…" Kate stopped and stared at the glossy wood top, gathering her thoughts. "My heart doesn't beat, it trembles," she said and glanced up at Liliane briefly. "Being near him, it brings light to my soul. It's the same light that I see in his eyes, and it transcends his being into my being. It's like a crystalline light that is the essence of him, and it reflects in his eyes and his smile…" Kate's voice trailed off, and she gazed into space as if she was seeing him in front of her.

"That's an absolutely beautiful feeling, Kate! Liliane's smile quivered. And it's a very unique one."

Kate's smile was short, and her eyes had a pensive look. "Yes, I know it's different and rare," she said quietly.

"I would help you if I could in any way, but you know love, this is *your* heart, and only you know what is right for it."

"I know, Liliane," Kate said. "You've helped me so much. I'm so glad I came to see you. Everything is getting clearer in my head and heart now."

CHAPTER 33
WHISTLEBLOWER

Just before dawn, a silver line appears on the horizon, and it glitters on the sleepy ocean and spreads its platinum light to wake up the hills. That hour of the day was enchanting in the town of Woodrose.

In the soft lilac sky was the sound of whirring as hundreds of starling birds took to flight in a twirling, ever-changing pattern. The indigo-colored, metallic sheen of their wings would catch the light of the rising sun, unfurling an iridescence in the sky, and all was quietly waking.

Flynn awoke around 7:00 in the morning, and after a fitful sleep on the couch, he didn't rouse Jack. He took his documents and grabbed the keys to his Jeep that had been parked outside for two days, and drove off, headed toward downtown.

He drove fast, but no matter how fast, he couldn't escape that dream last night with Kate. It was a good dream. He remembered so many details that life had a way of burying away in one's mind.

Reliving those days had brought a realness that renewed him and an urgency that made him double his efforts to remedy things with Kate. Whatever it would take, he was willing to do. There was just one big obstacle: her dad. And as soon as he showed this evidence to the FBI, he would surely be subpoenaed, and that would make things complicated with Kate.

But Flynn believed in the two of them and the strength of their love. Nothing would get between them unless they allowed it, he thought. He was hoping that he could work things out with Kate despite whatever mess her dad had gotten into, even if he was the whistle-blower.

Flynn parked in a concrete structure downtown and walked sturdily down the street toward City Hall. The building was the tallest in the city with thirty-two floors. When he arrived at the door, a gold plaque read: Timothy Jones, Detective.

Flynn was early for the appointment, but Mr. Jones was already there, and he escorted him into his office. Mr. Jones sat down across from him. His desk was neat and shiny, with no papers or books, just a picture of a woman in a fur coat smiling, which Flynn assumed was his wife. After reviewing the documents, Mr. Jones turned to him and lowered his head, peering over his glasses at him. His mouth was in the shape of an o. "Mr. Brennan," he said, blinking slowly. "You have got quite a case here."

Flynn breathed in and exhaled slowly. "Yeah, that's what I thought too."

"You, uh, you have uncovered…" He set his glasses back on his face correctly and examined the papers again. "Young man, you may have made a huge, albeit corrupt, discovery!" His face tilted to the side a little, and his small, clear blue eyes were stern and set on Flynn's face. Flynn sat motionlessly, then rubbed his palms on his pants nervously and nodded in agreement.

"I'll have to contact my colleagues, and I will be in touch with you. Now, you know we will probably need you to recount what you have seen and heard as a witness in a court of law." He held the papers up to his face as he spoke, then lowered them and looked him in the eyes.

"You willing to do that?"

"Yes, of course," Flynn answered. "I am as concerned as anyone would be about what they are doing."

"Yes, but…" Mr. Jones voice sounded like he was talking with his mouth full. "You are aware that you're dealing with the bad guys, right?"

Flynn nodded but said nothing.

"And by bad guys, I mean the Mafia."

Flynn nodded again, and millions of thoughts raced through his brain at that moment; Kate, Gavyn, Jack.

"Alright then, Mr. Brennan." Jones stood up; his stocky build meant his belly touched the desk in front of him when he stooped over to shake his hand.

The two men shook hands, and Flynn, with his mind still reeling, walked back to the entrance. He took a moment to stop and look back at Mr. Jones. He had sat back down at his desk and was dialing numbers on the black telephone. Flynn turned back around and walked out.

Outside, the sun was warm, and the city bustle was slower than usual, being a Saturday. Flynn felt relieved that it was out of his hands and in someone else's who could do something about the problem. He decided to walk the downtown streets and clear his mind a little, and he ended up doing so until late, stopping by a stand to get a hot dog and a newsstand to get the paper. Flynn arrived back at Woodrose and checked in on the night shift workers at the Pyrotechnics plant, as he was accustomed to doing. His job as an overseer meant he worked odd hours with several inspections throughout the day, with his last check-in being at around 1:00 am. After this, he would usually do paperwork in his office until 2:00 am every night. The plant job had been a temporary situation to fill his pockets, but now that he had declined the fights his dad had offered.

The warehouse was always empty at that time of night, with just a few overly eager workers. They needed the extra money badly or had nothing better to do with their nights.

Hyder Sykes was one of the latter mentioned. He was much shorter, fatter, and older than Flynn was, by a good twenty years. Still, he excelled at swimming and diving and was nicknamed "T-Bone Sykes" because of his diving expertise. His talent had been well celebrated in the town after several people had witnessed him skillfully diving off the pier on his time off from work.

Hyder was at his workstation handcrafting fireworks. He had become a Louisiana transplant when he, upon visiting the coastal area of California one day, decided to set up roots near the Pacific waters.

"Flynn!" he called to him as soon as he saw him step inside the warehouse. Hyder's voice was reedy, and his demeanor could, at times, appear menacing. But deep inside, he was just another kind-hearted soul.

"Yeah?" Flynn responded tiredly, on his way to the office in the back.

"I've been here since eight this morning, and I'm fixin to stay here until this here rocket is complete!" he said, and looked down at his hands and nodded as if reassuring himself.

Flynn walked over to Hyder's station, and he spread his arms and set both palms down in front of him on the desk and leaned forward. He looked him in the eyes with that steel-like security that Flynn had an overabundance of. But then he smiled and spoke softly to him as if he were a small child. "Don't go expecting any help from me, Hyder Sykes. I just got here, and you took this on all by yourself." He smiled, and his eyes glinted lightheartedly. "Plus," he said, "I'm about to head home...to sleep!"

Hyder smiled and shook his head. "You're no help! Looks like I'm a going to be celebratin' all by myself when I let this baby go!" he said.

Flynn chuckled. "You'd better not let that baby go!" he warned him. "Do you know what happens when you stay too long here, working like that?" he asked Hyder. Hyder shook his head no, smiled big, waiting for the punchline, and went back to looking at the rocket component in his hands.

"Well, when you get home...and you're about to drop dead from no sleep, you close your eyes – and... I think about my girlfriend, Kate - but maybe you can think about your pet alligator or something since you're single and all. Anyway, you close your eyes, and there go the colors," he said, with his face up towards the ceiling.

Hyder followed his eyes up to the ceiling, but there was nothing to see, only wood beams. "Where? What colors?" he asked, searching the roof.

"The rockets...there go the rockets, over and over again shining in your brain." Flynn gathered his lips to the side, and his eyes smiled. "Know what I mean? The colors your heart makes," he said.

Hyder's eyes were wide, and he nodded slowly and emphatically. "Uh, yeah, guess so," he said. He set down the piece he was working on and looked at Flynn's face.

"Listen, first of all, I ain't got a pet alligator...!" he said.

Flynn chuckled.

"And further, I ain't single!!"

Flynn's eyes widened in surprise. "What? You didn't tell me you were married!"

Hyder made a small kick with one leg as if there was a rock in his way, and he turned his head to the side a little, and his face flushed. "Well... she ain't much to look at, but she sure can cook!" he said, and laughed big. "But I have just one complaint I'd like to file with ya."

"Cooking's important," Flynn replied, and he straightened up to leave. "Have you seen what they serve over at Annie's place? He asked Hyder.

"Never been there. It takes a certain amount of smarts to be a cook, you know! And far as I can deduct Annie's solid concrete from the eyebrows backwards," said Hyder

Flynn laughed. "Yeah, and her food tastes like that, too! Well, old man…" Flynn glanced at his watch; it was 2:00 am. "What was the complaint about? I'll take care of it for you…"

Hyder's face lifted from his work, and his eyes shone happily for the moment. Only seconds later, his entire expression would drop. Flynn was standing by Hyder's work desk, about to leave, when there was a deafening sound. Everything moved in slow motion – even the boom was delayed at first, with a thunderous sound that followed. It was like an immense pressure bubble that built around them, then exploded.

CHAPTER 34
THE SCARS BENEATH THE SKIN

The last thing Flynn saw was an expanding ball of white fire, followed instantly by a short, flat sound; the sound was hollow, loud, and definite. His body was thrown back against the wall by a thick, invisible force. The world seemed to have been sucked into a wormhole, and everything fell deafly silent and black. He was engulfed by a hot, searing pain.

Flynn never knew what happened immediately after the explosion. People in the town rushed out of their homes, shaken awake by the blast. Some thought it was thunder from an impending storm that was rolling in. Still, most thought it was yet another California earthquake that had hit.

Maximo, the supervisor of the factory, was asleep in one of the offices in the plant when the blast hit, and it knocked him out of bed. He would later describe it to the news reporters. "The next thing I knew, the office building was ablaze! I wrapped a blanket around me and ran out and over the fence to safety," he said.

A series of smaller blasts followed the initial one, and they caused a colorful fire when the occasional skyrocket launched itself out of the blaze. Firefighters were the first on the scene, and residents watched from across the street as they carried out the wounded amid the long flames, with the fire licking at their arms.

Sadly, not everyone got out, and Hyder Sykes died that night.

On the other side of the street, a homeless man stood in shock as they pulled out Flynn and laid him on a gurney. "He's dead!" said the man, and he shook his head sorrowfully. "Step back, everyone. I think the man is dead!" When the ambulance arrived, they placed Flynn carefully onto the stretcher and rolled his pale, ragged body into the back.

One of the first at the scene was also the owner of the warehouse. Nobody knew if he was there to look after Flynn or his own interests, but he did offer help. He got the best of care for Flynn and had him flown all the way to New York, where they had the best trauma care center immediately that night.

It required weeks of intense treatment before Flynn was lucid enough to understand what had happened. It had been an explosion. Perhaps a firework that accidentally went off, triggering the blast…or a bomb. The incident was under investigation.

The blast had damaged Flynn's legs, and shrapnel had struck his face. While it left some superficial scarring, it was the shockwave of the blast that left him with significantly impaired sight. However, he was lucky to be alive, the doctors had said. Had the explosion occurred when he was in his office, it would have killed him.

Gavyn was the first to visit him, and eventually, when given the all-clear, he took him home. "How are you doing, buddy?" he asked quietly.

Flynn shrugged a little. "Not sure. Better, I guess."

"What does the doc say? They called for me to pick you up, so here I am!" Gavyn smiled big and leaned over him.

"The blast injured my leg pretty bad…and…" Flynn was having trouble talking, and he seemed to swallow a lot, perhaps to ease a residual dryness that comes from heat exposure.

"Maybe you shouldn't talk right now," said Gavyn.

Flynn moved uneasily but stiffly beneath the sheet as if every bone in his body was in searing pain. "No, it's ok. I had better talk now…"

Those words confused Gavyn somewhat. "Yeah, ok. But let's wait to get you home and get you comfortable…ok? Got a real nice apartment for you here. You know, New York ain't so bad. I kind of like it here!" Gavyn said in an attempt to enliven Flynn's somber state.

Flynn nodded and swallowed again.

Eva stepped closer to Flynn and patted his hand gently. "I'm glad you get to go home," she said.

Flynn was unfocused. He hadn't even heard Eva speak, and he suddenly noticed that she was holding a small bundle wrapped in a soft cloth, and he stared at it as if he had never seen a bundle before.

"What's that?" he asked, at the same time as Gavyn chimed in. "You'll be up and running in no time, champ!"

Flynn smiled weakly and nodded, but kept looking at the bundle. "What do you have there, Eva?" he asked. He squinted to make it out and hoisted himself up slowly, clumsily like a walrus coming out of water. His body felt like dead weight and useless, and his thoughts seemed to be disconnected.

Eva glanced quickly to the side at Gavyn's face. She was shocked to realize that Flynn didn't seem to remember that she and Gavyn had a baby. Gavyn shared her concern but didn't show it. Instead, he nodded reassuringly at her, and she cleared her throat.

"It's a...it's our baby girl. Remember, we had a baby?" she said, and her voice picked up some excitement with the mention of her daughter. Then she eagerly unfurled the cloth and held the baby up for Flynn to see.

Flynn waved his hand weakly as if he were fanning himself. "Bring her closer. I can't see very well from here," he said. He was breathless and making what seemed a tremendous effort to look.

Eva glanced once again at Gavyn, unsure of the best way to deal with this situation, and then inched a little closer to Flynn. Both Gavyn and Eva knew Flynn had been left with some vision problems after the accident, but they had not known the full extent of it, and they were now wondering if it was worse than they thought.

Flynn strained his neck forward to see the baby. It wasn't until he was just three or four inches from her face that he softly smiled and said, "She looks like you, Eva," And dropped back into the bed.

Eva smiled, with relief and delight, and her arms relaxed as she held the baby in front of him. He appeared to be the same old Flynn, she thought. But was he? "Thanks, Flynn," she said. "But, you know, I think she looks a lot like Gavyn, too."

"No…no… thankfully no!" responded Flynn with some distress. Eva couldn't tell if he had grinned or grimaced as he fell back on the bed.

"Well, I guess I'll bring you your new wheels…" Gavyn said nervously. It felt like Flynn was on every word he and Eva would say, looking and watching them to see if he caused them perturbation over his condition. He rolled in the wheelchair and set it up for himself. "Well, here you are. It's not the latest Cadillac, but it will have to do for now," he said, but his cheeriness sounded thin.

Flynn grunted and groaned as he lifted his body from the bed. He used up almost all of his energy just getting to a sitting position, then used up the rest to swing his legs over the side. Flynn sat still for a moment with his feet dangling over the edge of the bed, waiting to regain more strength. Then he slowly set his feet on the floor.

One of his legs was badly damaged and heavily wrapped. He had no sensation in that one. However, the other leg was still usable. He leaned on that one and placed his arm around his brother's shoulder. Then, he dropped heavily into the wheelchair and made a loud noise that came from his lungs. It sounded like a balloon losing air abruptly, an indication of how weak he was.

Flynn's mouth turned down as if he just bitten into a tart lemon and said, "Take me home, I guess." And he didn't lift his head back up again the whole way home.

Gavyn tried his best to keep things light. It had been a very trying experience to deal with and to get Flynn in the car. "You can consider yourself *lucky*," Gavyn started to say, with an emphasis on the last word.

"Really?" Flynn responded, not at all in the mood to hear why.

"Yeah, dear old dad came by to see you when you were knocked out the other day."

"Pfff!" Flynn's chin moved upwards slightly. "Who cares?" he said.

"Oh, I know. I know you don't care." Gavyn's eyes shifted back to him, then at the road. "Me neither. I just thought you'd want to know, that's all," he said, examining the traffic ahead.

There was little noise in the car, save the cooing of the baby every so often. The sound made Flynn smile a little. "You didn't tell me what you named her?" he asked.

"Oh, Flynn! I can't believe we forgot to tell you!" Eva said, smiling broadly. "Her name is Helen Rose, after my mom," she said, smiling down at the baby in her arms.

"Helen?" Flynn asked, and then clamped up and didn't say anything else for a while.

The name Helen reminded him of Helena, and he wondered about Kate. Gavyn talked and talked throughout the long way home; it would be more of a discussion with his wife about marital things. One of the subjects was the proper way to bring up a child.

"We have to set rules, Eva, rules!" Gavyn argued.

"She's a girl, so it's different," Eva responded.

"Ha! A girl! Those are the hardest to bring up!"

"How would you know, hun? Anyway, I don't think so."

"Well, you don't have sisters, so you wouldn't know either!" Gavyn stated, and his head bobbed with a self-confident air.

"You don't either, Gavyn. What do you want to bring her up like a boxer?"

"Haha! Yeah, maybe…if she wants." His eyes danced around the street, unflappably.

Eva shook her head, and a small smile betrayed her frustrated expression.

He continued, "Besides, I'll tell you why it's harder. They follow their heart first, then their mind."

"Oh, I see, so if I had followed my mind with you instead of my heart, that would have been better?" She smirked.

"Well, that's different…," he said, and quickly closed the topic.

FLYNN SHUT IT ALL OUT. His distressing thoughts were enough to keep his mind occupied for the moment. He had a lot of questions that needed answering, but he didn't know where to start. He started with Kate.

"Who else came by to see me?" Flynn broke through the petty argument between Gavyn and Eva as though they had been quiet all that time.

They stopped abruptly and looked at each other, deciding quickly who was going to tell him about Kate. Gavyn took the role on the fly, and he glanced in the rearview mirror at him. "Ah, Flynn, I think you should rest first before we start chatting."

Flynn stared out of the window. "I'm not really that tired," he said glumly.

Gavyn's mouth tightened a little. "Well, let's see, uh, Jack…Jack came by," he propelled his voice to the back.

Flynn was still and quiet. His lips were in a line, and his eyes downcast. "Are the trees moving in the wind?" he asked.

Gavyn's eyebrows collected in the middle, and he glanced at Eva, who looked back at Flynn. "What? What did you ask?" he asked, worried.

Flynn cranked the window of the car wide open and stuck out his hand, "Well, I can feel the wind…" he responded. "And I can see a blur of long brown poles with green on top, but I can't tell if they're moving," he said.

Gavyn grasped the wheel and looked straight. Eva could see a small muscle bulge on the sides of his jawbone, and she knew he was feeling stressed.

"Flynn," his voice was uncharacteristically low-keyed. "I think you should rest for a while." He glanced back at his somber face. "We're here anyway," he added and pulled the car into the driveway of Flynn's apartment.

Flynn's place was on the second level. Gavyn had wanted it specifically so he could see the ocean every day when he woke up and before going to bed. However, things were different from what he had expected, and he hadn't taken into account the wheelchair. Something he would never have thought he'd see his big brother in.

Climbing the stairs was just another hurdle he'd have to deal with now. They took a while figuring out the best strategy for climbing with his injured leg. And trying to do so without the wheelchair, and another while carrying out the plan. Flynn did what Gavyn would have expected, and somehow he climbed them, and they folded up the chair. The curtains were pulled closed, but Flynn didn't notice the darkness. With help from his brother, he got into bed, and he fell asleep in a matter of minutes.

Gavyn closed the bedroom door behind him, gave out a long breath, and touched his forehead with his arm, like when you check for a fever, then looked at Eva. "I don't know what to do with him," he said solemnly. "I can't believe this happened. Guess I was hoping he'd be better by now. I hate seeing Flynn like this."

"We have to give him time," said Eva. "A lot of what you see is medication; he's still heavily medicated."

"Yeah, but what about his sight?" They looked at each other and sat down in silence in the living room, and Eva rocked the baby to sleep.

CHAPTER 35
REGENERATION OF A STARFISH

E vening came, and with it a feeling of suffocation for Flynn. The air was black, and it felt black with heaviness. He awoke and could hear voices in the living room, and he recognized Gavyn as one of them, but he couldn't make out the other male voice. He was not able to move, and that, combined with the fuzzy sight, made it all the worse.

The blurry eyesight he was hopeful would clear with some time. However, his leg was severely mangled, and the doctors still held the position that they might have to amputate it. He wished he could hear what they were saying. He was sure it was about the accident. When he thought back on how it happened, the timing of it all, and the fact that Maximo had all the safety precautions in place, he knew it couldn't have been an accident.

Outside in the living room, the muffled voices were speaking in a low-tone for Flynn's sake. Gavyn didn't want to bring up with Flynn anything that had occurred, not yet. But he wanted answers for himself.

"What did you say it was? Did you say a hit? On my brother?" he asked the man sitting opposite him, in a hushed voice. The man was dressed in a gray suit and black tie, and his shoes were shiny and black. His fingers were wrapped around a tall glass of iced tea that Eva had given him, and he picked the lemon wedge off the side of the glass and dunked it in the liquid.

"Thank you," he said dryly, as she handed it to him. He sipped from it a little and set it down to answer Gavyn's question. "Yes," he said. "It was a hit. The explosion was a bomb placed in the vicinity of your brother's office; it was meant to kill him. We figure whoever did this knew your brother's work hours, and they picked two in the morning to make sure he was there."

Gavyn felt fear creep in. "But why? Who are they?"

"Well…" he took another sip of the drink and set it down on the coaster again. "We are sure of two things…one, your brother is familiar with whoever it is that did this. And two, it was meant to shut him up or stop him from doing something."

"I don't get it. I would know if Flynn was involved with something. I know everyone that he knows."

"Everyone? You can't always know the other third-party connections that might arise. Look, I'm not at liberty to talk any more about this case. Your brother upset some powerful criminals. That's all I can say. Maybe you can ask him the details when he wakes up."

Gavyn paused a moment and looked down at his shoes. Eva went near her husband and sat on his lap. She wrapped her arms around him, and she kissed his cheek.

The man stood up and handed Gavyn a card. "This is my number at the bureau. It's my direct line. If you see, hear, or find out anything more from your brother, anything at all, please call me right away," he said. "Oh," he turned around at the door, "and thank you again for the drink. Great lemonade!" he said to Eva.

The man smoothed his hat with his fingers and placed it on his head, and turned to Gavyn. "Hopefully, your brother will be up to speaking with me soon." He tipped his gray fedora and walked out the door.

"What was Flynn doing downtown that day?" Eva asked, picking up the half-empty lemonade glasses that were left on the table.

"He was going to see somebody at the Federal building or something like that. That's what Jack said anyway."

Eva brought her eyebrows together. "I wonder if Jack knows more about this than either one of us?"

Gavyn nodded slowly. "Yeah, I was wondering that myself. He's been really quiet about the whole thing. Honey, why don't you stay here with Flynn? I'm taking a flight out to Woodrose to visit Jack."

AFTER LANDING IN Los Angeles, Gavyn took a taxi to Woodrose, where he was dropped off in front of Jack's place. His house sat on a hill overlooking the ocean with a wrap-around deck. It was where Jack kept much of his collection of rare and exotic seashells. And some of the living stars that dwell under the sea. He collected them for himself but also sold some to museums or private buyers.

And it was on the large wooden deck where Gavyn found him. The yellow glow of a small overhead light that was strung on the roof washed over Jack's face as he sat buried to his eyeballs in his masterpieces. He was carefully placing the precious, fragile shells in a box and checking on the blue starfish he had discovered that morning. He didn't notice Gavyn standing there at first.

"Jack!" Gavyn called out as he stepped onto the deck. "I hope it's alright, I dropped by... need to talk to you about Flynn."

Jack looked up and let the instruments he was holding in his hands drop, and straightened his back. His brown hair appeared to be wet, and its waves were unruly, but his eyes were bright as lemon quartz, and at times, they seemed to penetrate your mind with a look.

"Yeah, sure." His voice was deep from the gut. He seemed bewildered and worried to see Gavyn at his place. "Is Flynn doing worse?" he asked.

"No. No, nothing like that. I mean, I guess he's doing as well as can be expected for now."

Jack nodded, relieved, and he swept his arm in front of him, inviting Gavyn indoors, and the two men stepped inside.

"Have a seat," Jack said and walked to the kitchen. "Wanna beer?" He called back to him with his head buried in the refrigerator.

"No, thanks," Gavyn responded. "Some water, I guess, would be good."

Jack sauntered back in with his usual casual gait. He placed a glass of water in front of Gavyn, and he sat down. He took his wide hands and pressed his thick hair back.

"What can I do for you, Gavyn?" he asked. Jack was known for his altruistic disposition and kindness among his friends. He was the guy to go to when in trouble or distress, the always-supportive friend.

"I'll be straightforward with you, Jack. My brother thinks the world of you, you know that, right?" he started to say.

Jack smiled, and his eyes crinkled at the sides. "It's mutual. I highly respect Flynn. I see a younger me in him."

Gavyn gave an understanding nod. "Well, I thought I'd talk to you about what happened…the so-called accident."

Jack hung his head and looked at the floor, then quickly looked back up as if he had found something there. "I do know what happened to Flynn," he said dismally. He leaned back on the sofa. "You know your brother. I told him he shouldn't go alone to see the FBI. He didn't listen."

"That's what I'm here about. Who was Flynn dealing with? Why did they try to kill him?" asked Gavyn.

"Oh… you know less than I thought!" Jack said, but now the cat was out of the bag, so he continued. "Flynn and I discovered something when we were diving a while back. It's a long, convoluted story, but I can tell you that what we found was illegal. What they were doing was harmful. Mike Mason, as well as the guy who owns the Wayan, are both involved."

Gavyn was trying to keep up with the information being fed to him. The Masons are involved, and it was illegal stuff? Those two things did not go together in his mind. "Ah yeah, I know the guy you mean," he responded, trying to wrap his head around it all. "You talking about Belino Rocco?"

"Yeah, Belino. He has been running an operation dumping hazardous waste in the ocean. They're paying him to do it." He shook his head, sorrowfully. "I can't begin to tell you what that will do to sea life and people swimming there."

"Dumping waste? How?"

"Well, there was toxic waste in the Huntington Way canal dumped by Frontier Manufacturing. Mike Mason bought the land, and he hired Belino to siphon it out cheaply and put it somewhere else. Belino decided to use the ocean. They have,
who knows how many thousands, I suppose, of leaky drums that are discharging millions of gallons of wastewater daily there."

"Wow, I never would have thought Mike Mason would be involved in something like that," said Gavyn

"He has the money and motive to clear out that canal," said Jack.

"It was Dr. Redmond..." Jack started.

"Lila's dad?" asked Gavyn.

"Yeah, Lila's dad. He examined what we found and isolated the chemicals. He said there would be grave consequences if they weren't stopped. So, your brother went downtown to talk to the people he thought could take action. I personally believe it was Belino's henchmen who tried to stop Flynn before he was able to talk to the Feds. I've been thinking of going to talk to the detectives about it so they would know there's something behind all of this, and it wasn't an accident."

Gavyn sat quietly, thinking. "They know."

"The FBI knows?"

"Yep. They're investigating it as a hit."

Jack looked down and nodded. "I'm glad. But all I really want is for Flynn to recover," he said.

"Yeah, me too. I'll tell the bureau what you said, or better yet, maybe you should contact them downtown," said Gavyn, and he dug in his pocket and handed him the detective's business card.

"I'd be happy to," Jack said, taking the card.

Gavyn stood up and walked to the French doors. He stared out at the quiet white glow of the moon over the serene ocean. A fresh evening breeze with its salty tones swept in through the open double doors of the deck, and a strong smell of parching starfish and brine filled the room. It was a damp scent but not like the humid, clammy smell of drying kelp when the tide came in, and it washed up on the shore.

"You know, I don't know if I should feel mad at Flynn or bad for him," Gavyn mumbled, staring out. "I mean, I'm kinda mad because he should have thought about his family and what consequences his actions could bring. I mean, that was a big thing to take on."

"Well, in his defense, I believe that was exactly what he was thinking about…his family—you and Kate. He talked about the effects the pollution would have on not only us today but also your kids later on. He didn't want that kind of world…you know how he is."

Jack leaned over to the side table by the couch, where there was a box with one of his specimens placed on top, and he picked it up. "Flynn is like this starfish," he said, holding up a bright purple organism. He half-smiled down at it. "Complicated but interesting."

Gavyn turned back around and walked over to Jack. He looked at the purple and orange starfish in his hand. "That's a really unique one," he said. For the moment, the starfish held his attention, and his weighed-down mind felt a transitory relief.

Jack pursued his interest. "Did you know that one of these can weigh up to eleven pounds?" he asked, sharing his enthusiasm with him.

"Wow, no, I never would have imagined that."

"They're not a fish, and there are around 2,000 species of starfish." He paused a minute, staring down at the sea creature, then continued. "You know what I think Flynn has in common with these? It is the most amazing thing of all… they can regenerate. Sometimes it can take a while –even up to a year- but given their unique ability to renew, they can regrow a lost limb."

"Wow! But I don't think Flynn has any limbs missing, though," said Gavyn. "So that won't do him much good."

Jack nodded with a smile. "No, but in Flynn's case, maybe he can regrow what might seem to him as a lost life."

A high-pitched trilling sound came from the table next to Gavyn; the phone wanted attention. "Wonder who that is?" Jack said and grabbed the receiver. "Hello?" he talked into the quiet of the room. "Yes."

His eyes shifted to Gavyn. "He's here…yes, of course, I'll put him on. You're welcome, miss."

Gavyn walked over to him. Jack cupped his hand over the mouthpiece. "I think it's your wife," he said, handing him the phone.

"Oh, I hope it's ok, I gave her this number in case of anything. Since she's looking after Flynn."

"Yeah, of course, it's ok!"

Gavyn's smile was halfhearted. "Thanks…" he said and took the phone. "Hello? Hi honey, is everything alright?" His voice dropped a little. "Oh really…ok, well, I'm on my way. I'm taking the first flight back today."

"Everything ok?" Jack asked

"Not sure. Eva said that Flynn is insisting on talking with me immediately. Listen, thanks for the water, the talk, the friendship." Gavyn shook Jack's hand, and they both smiled.

"Keep me posted on Flynn, will you? I'd really appreciate it," Jack said, walking him to the entrance.

"Of course. I'll be in touch," Gavyn replied, and the door closed behind him.

Gavin could hear Flynn's voice in the background when he was on the phone with Eva. "Tell him to come right away!" he heard Flynn say in a raised and raspy voice. His mind was racing through scenarios. They flashed before him like scenes from a flick at the theatre, and none of them were good.

CHAPTER 36
A REQUEST

Some hours later, he arrived to find the apartment dark, with only the light from Flynn's room and one down the hall where he and Eva were staying, glowing yellow. He walked to Flynn's room quietly and peered inside.

"I'm awake," Flynn said in a strange-sounding whisper as if his vocal cords were frozen. "Come in, Gavyn." The dense voice broke through the dark.

"I'm here," Gavyn responded and drew near to the bedside.

"Listen, I've got something vital for you to do for me," he said.

"Ok. I'm listening…"

"I need you to promise me…listen, are you listening?"

"Yes. I told you I was."

Flynn swallowed painfully and slowly. "I want you to do something for me."

"Ok…what is it?" Gavyn whispered in the dark.

Gavyn stood like a statue by his bed. Only his eyes moved about, searching for the meaning behind

Flynn's request. "Flynn?" he asked again in the silence, and his voice floated in the dark.

Flynn's voice sounded fainter now. "You don't have to..." There was silence again.

Gavyn felt uneasiness in the room, and he started to move about, distressed.

Flynn followed his shadow with his eyes. "Ok, look..." His voice was much softer now. "I have a lot of things wrong with me now. I have no use of my one leg...probably gonna have it off in a few weeks...my eyesight is bad, I can't even see the scars on my face...they must be bad too." He fell silent.

Gavyn went near to his bed again and looked down at his brother. "Flynn, you were there for me when everyone thought I wasn't going to make it through, you were there...helping me every step." He spoke quietly to him. "Whatever you want, I'll do."

"Then tell Kate..." He weakly moved his lips.

"Tell Kate... what?"

There was a pause as Flynn coughed a deep, growling cough. "You know," he whispered.

"No, I don't, Flynn. What do you want me to tell her?"

Flynn made an enormous effort to speak. "The obvious, tell her the obvious..." He stopped for a moment while he coughed a low, cavernous cough. Then he continued, "that I'm dead."

"Don't say that, Flynn!" Gavyn protested, with anguish.

"I don't want her to see me like this. She needs to move on. It's ok…" There was a heavy silence in the room for a moment. "Promise me you'll do this right away, ok, Gav?"

Gavyn's throat was tight, and all he could do was nod a yes. Then he watched Flynn's expression slowly fade from a slight grateful smile to a grimace. Then it eased into alleviation, and he closed his eyes, and his lips parted slightly.

Gavyn stared at his brother for a few moments. Was he still breathing? He seemed so still. Gavyn placed the back of his hand near Flynn's mouth and felt his weak breath, and he was relieved to know he had fallen asleep. He heard someone shift near the doorway. Eva had been standing there.

"How long have you been there, hun?" Gavyn asked.

Eva was silent and signaled with her hand for him to follow, and they went into the living room. "Flynn sounds so weak," she said.

Gavyn sat down next to her. He folded his hands in front of him and nodded.

"Gavyn," Eva started, cautiously. "Is Flynn going to be alright?"

"I don't know, Eva." Gavyn's voice sounded weary and distraught.

"He needs to stay positive," said Eva.

Gavyn nodded. "It's just like Jack said. Flynn is a complicated but resilient person. He has always healed…you know, growing up, my dad used to hit us with anything handy, bats, bottles, coat rack, anything. When he was drunk, nothing was spared. Many a swollen and bruised eye Flynn got, mostly protecting me from him. But he always took it in stride. I never knew how he was able to, but he always seemed to heal like it never happened."

Eva's face was downcast, and her eyes were misty. "I hate your dad for what he put you guys through!" she said.

"He's not worth even that, Eva," Gavyn said, and he stood up. "Now it's my turn to support Flynn.

Eva looked guardedly at him. "What if he doesn't heal this time?"

Gavyn's throat sounded pinched. "Flynn wants me to tell Kate that he's gone."

"What? You mean dead? Why does he want that?"

"Yeah. Because Flynn says he wants her to move on."

"But that's unfair, she should know the truth!"

"Yeah, maybe, but I promised him, and I have to do it now."

Eva hugged him. 'When and how?"

"He wants me to do it right away, so I'm booking a flight back to Woodrose tomorrow." He kissed Eva and gave the baby a small, delicate kiss. "You take care of this little one till I get back? Ok?"

Eva smiled as she looked at the baby, then up at him. "Don't be long," she said.

CHAPTER 37
FR1-5295 AND THE NOTE

When the plane landed the next day, the sun was draped in mourning. The clouds were heavy, low, and black, and the air was thick with droplets of rain. Gavyn took a taxi to the docks at 11:00 in the morning. Large round drops of water fell on his windshield, and the wind knocked about the long palms that lined the road.

When he arrived, the boardwalk was deserted. He walked past the train trolley. Flynn would have liked seeing the tracks today, he thought. They were being torn up to make way for more modern forms of transportation. Although at the present time, the train work had been abandoned over concern of the coming rains.

Gavyn stood in front of his old man's place, The Drop-In. He wasn't so sure he wanted to drop in, but Gavyn thought he could call Kate from there and set up a meeting place.

He walked inside to find the place uncharacteristically quiet. The ring was deserted and, for the first time, tidy. A small television set sat on a wooden table in a corner, and it was televising a fight. Gavyn paused to see it. The black and white picture showed two men as they pummeled each other mercilessly.

"You know what that is?" His old man's voice came out of nowhere and seemed to echo in the vacant room. Gavyn turned to glance at him and then back at the television. He didn't answer him, but that didn't matter to his father, who just continued. "It's a special fight. Today is a special day," he said, with a twinkle in his eyes, and he too drew closer to the television to watch. "It's Joey Wallace!" he said, and his eyes brightened. "Joey's fightin Rex Hombard. You remember Joe, right?" He turned his face and leaned close to Gavyn. "You met him here once."

Gavyn broke away from watching the blows to confront his dad. His dad had a striped towel around his shoulders like the one they put around a patron at the barbershop. He looked as carefree and as gluttonous as ever. It didn't matter much to Gavyn, not anymore. He had lost that gleam in his eye and the heat in his blood for boxing. "Yeah, I remember him," he said.

The fight ended, and the crowd cheered with the same intensity with which his father threw down the towel he had on him. "Damn! He's better than that!" he said, and his face flushed red. "That no-good Hombard thinks he can bring down anyone! Ha! Just wait till I set up that matchup." He rubbed his palms together, smiling, and turned suddenly to Gavyn. "Oh, by the way, did I tell you about the new thing I'm working on?"

Gavyn's whole body recoiled instinctively. Whenever his dad was working on a new thing, it was trouble waiting to happen. "No," he answered. "Dad…" he said, facing him directly. "Aren't you wondering about Flynn?"

His dad frowned stiffly. "Flynn… Flynn, so he got in over his head…so he got what he deserved. You don't mess around with guys like that!"

Gavyn felt heat rise to his head and a pull in the muscles of his right arm. He swung and planted his fist on Ty's jaw, sending him crashing back on the tables. "I kinda figured you'd say something like that, Dad. It doesn't matter anyway."

Ty's eyes were bugged out, and tiny spider veins protruded from within them. He stood up. "You got guts doing that to your old man, he said, pointing his finger in Gavyn's face. "You know it's that kind of attitude that made you a loser as a fighter."

Gavyn drilled into his brain with his eyes. If he could, he'd take that very small organ apart, piece by piece. Ty stepped back, a little uncomfortable. He could never say he truly knew his sons. He wasn't sure of what they might be capable of because he never took the time to know them as men.

Gavyn turned and stormed over to the bar area, looking for the phone. The bar top was glossy and without a speck of dust. Reaching over the top and directly under where the lemons and ice were kept, he grabbed a black phone that was at the very corner and pulled it out. He took out a piece of wrinkled paper from his back pocket with Kate's phone number, FR1-5295, and began dialing it. His hands quivered a little as he waited for her to pick up the line.

He could feel his dad's presence like one would feel a shark circling while swimming in deep waters. Gavyn was hoping she'd pick up soon, and she did after the third ring.

"Hello?" Her voice sounded small and distant, though she was only 10 minutes away. She had slept in that morning, having arrived late the night before, after spending time with Liliane in Paris.

Gavyn slouched over the phone and turned his body away from wandering Ty. "Uh, Kate? This is Gavyn. I only have a minute to talk, so please just listen…"

"Ok," she spoke slowly and hesitantly. "Where's Flynn?"

"That's what I want to talk to you about." His voice was dry and mechanical. Ty sauntered to the back of the bar and was pretending to wash, holding up to view the already clean glasses with perked up ears. Gavyn's eyes flitted sideways, then he pressed his lips on the mouthpiece of the phone. "Meet me at Lupe's Café. Can you?" he asked.

"Yes, of course. When?"

"Right now, if you can."

"Ok, I'm on my way." She hung up immediately, and the dial tone could be heard as Gavyn placed the phone back on the cradle.

His eyes moved slowly to where his father stood with both hands planted on the bar. "Some kind of trouble?" he asked, and although the caring was fake, the interest wasn't.

Gavyn set the phone back under the bar, and his eyes fell on his father's face. Ty was bleary-eyed, unshaven, and chewing an old, unlit cigar. His manner was as gruff and mean as ever, and it was evident he had been drinking. Gavyn looked him over, stocky and with a fat belly and high blood pressure, that was a bad combination for a bad guy. He didn't say anything to him, and he hurried out the door.

OUTSIDE, THE DARK clouds warned of impending doom. The surf was the highest he had ever seen, and the rain had begun to drill down upon it. Gavyn treaded against the blowing wind to Lupe's Café. When he stepped inside, the winds and surf were immediately silenced.

"Where's everybody?" he asked the waitress who was setting bills and paper in their respective slots in the cash register.

"We usually have a good crowd, but today…" She shook her head, no.

"Maybe the rain kept them home," he mumbled, distractedly.

She looked up briefly from counting, then back down and finished, and placed the green bills face down systematically in the register. "Those little ole raindrops?" she asked, playfully. "I wouldn't blame them if they stayed home, though. Try the cyclone of the century! They expect winds to reach 75 miles per hour! Can you imagine that?" She paused and looked outside. "Makes me nervous," she said. Gavyn looked out with his eyes wide and could see the trees thrashing about in the steady rain. Nothing even close to a cyclone had ever happened in Woodrose.

The storm had also reached Kate's house, but it wasn't in the form of rain. Her mom was in the kitchen, pouring coffee, bickering with her husband while her dad read the newspaper calmly. He spoke into the paper without looking up at her. "It's morning, the sun's barely up, Helena, give it a rest, will ya?" he said, drained from the constant squabble.

"Speaking of time, it was around 2:00 in the morning, Mike, not 11:00 pm as you claim."

Kate could hear her voice raised and tense. She peeked in carefully to not be discovered and could see her dad sitting at the table with a cup in hand and eyes glued to the paper. He was, as usual, taking more interest in the news than whatever Helena had to say.

Her mom walked over to him and yanked the paper down with her hand. "Did you hear anything I said, Mike?"

Mike put the cup down, neatly folded the paper, and placed it on the table in front of him, then he kicked back on the chair and crossed his arms. "Ok, Helena, is this what you want? My full attention? Well, you got it now," he said.

"Yes!" she continued, and now that she did have it, she said, "that, and a little decency too!" She paced in front of him, jittery as if her emotions were about to explode like a rocket. "Maybe staying at home with your wife every once in a while instead of gambling or gallivanting around town as everyone knows you do!" she said.

Mike followed her pacing with his eyes. "You know you look beautiful when you get angry like that?" he said.

"Stop patronizing me, Mike!" she yelled back.

"How do you know that's what I'm doing?" he asked slyly.

His notice of her did help a little. She had come to the point in their marriage where any attention was, well, at least, attention from him. However, it didn't resolve anything, and she still felt frustrated.

Helena turned away from him in a dramatized loathing. And looked out of the window that faced the garden in front, out towards the ocean. Her eyes traveled to the horizon and fell on the sea. It looked troubled, as if something was causing it distress and making it turn on itself. As she stared at it, her mood instantly changed, and she dropped the tension, swapping for worry and alarm.

"Mike?" she said softly, watching the ocean's wildness. "Mike? Have you seen the conditions out there?" Her voice rose a degree.

He dropped the paper when he heard her concern. And moved next to her to look out of the window. What he saw stunned him. "I've never seen the ocean as angry as that!" he said, in a hushed tone and moving his lips slowly.

"It's so dark," said Helena.

"Where's Kate?" They said simultaneously and looked at each other.

"She told me she was going out this morning." Her mother's voice sounded uneasy, with a little guilt woven in between.

"How could you let Kate go with how it is out there?" Mike demanded to know.

"Mike, I thought the sun would be up and shining, as usual. I thought it was going to be as hot as it has been this past week. I had no idea it would turn this way." Her eyes filled. "Go find her, please!"

But by then, Kate was well on her way, and neither one of them knew where to look.

CHAPTER 38
THE DAY THE SEA TURNED ON ITSELF

Winding down the steep road from her home to the pier proved to be difficult. The sky was throwing buckets of water on the windshield of Kate's car, and the Plymouth's wipers had a hard time keeping her vision clear ahead of her.

The slick road reflected a golden shimmer where the headlights shone as she turned into the café. Not a soul was in the parking lot, and for a moment she panicked, wondering if she had heard Gavyn right. She glanced up at the flickering neon light flashing, Lupe's Café. That was the name she remembered him saying. It was a struggle against the noisy wind just to open the car door. Her hat flew off. And her hair, which had been pinned up, came undone in seconds as she ran inside. The waitress looked up at her, standing in the doorway, a soggy jumble. "You look like a mess!" she said.

"Yeah, and I feel like one too." Kate smoothed back the locks of wet hair and tried to pin them up again. "It's quite the rain event out there," she said. When she looked around, the place was empty.

"Uh-huh, I know. Like I was telling the fellow here before you, it's more like a cyclone! I know because I'm originally from Florida –I just got hired here- and we get a lot of those…"

Kate searched the empty seats with fretful eyes. "Fellow before me?" she asked, "Do you know his name? What did he look like? When did he leave?"

"Whoa, whoa, one question at a time, please." She smiled and lazily held her hand in front of her with her fingers spread. "Let's see answer number one… I don't know his name, but he comes in here once in a while." She perked up suddenly. "Oh! He's cute too!" But then her body slumped back down. "But he has a wedding ring," she frowned.

Kate hurried her along, nodding. "Go on," she said.

"Ok, sooo, where was I? Oh, yeah! Number two… what's he look like? Well, like I said, he's really cute…tall with sandy blonde hair and hazel or brown eyes, I think..."

"Yeah, that's got to be him!" Kate broke into her sentence. "Where did he go?"

"Oh, well, hmm…let's see, I think he said he had to go make sure a boat was tied down or something like that. He sounded really upset about something. But he said he'd be right back." The woman looked out toward the boats with concern. "He's still not back, though…geeee, it's terrible out there!"

She seemed to suddenly remember something that might be important. "Oh, you know what? He left something here, maybe it's for you." The waitress searched beneath the cash register and retrieved an envelope that she had tucked there. "Yeah, he left this." She examined the envelope. "It's addressed to a …Kate. Is your name…"

Kate snatched the letter from her hands and examined it. "Yeah, it's me," she said under her breath and opened it in wonder.

"Dear Kate," it began, "I don't know how to start this letter. I'll begin by telling you that I was set on meeting you here today, but something came up, and I had to resort to leaving you this letter...." Kate walked to one of the booths, read it, and slowly sat down and continued reading. "You're probably going to hate me once you read this because you won't understand why I had to tell you this way. The reason you can't find Flynn anywhere is that...I'm sorry...I don't know how to tell you this, but Flynn is dead. He died in a..."

Kate froze, and she stopped reading. Her eyes widened, and she looked straight ahead.

The waitress had been watching Kate out of curiosity when she noticed her blank stare. "Miss, are you alright?" she asked. Kate was in a daze, and the waitress was in a panic as she watched her paleness grow and extend to her lips. "I'm going to call someone. I hope there's someone by the docks still!" she said.

The woman helped Kate recline in the booth and ran outside, hoping to get someone to help her. The first person she saw was an old man fighting the wind with a tackle box and a fishing rod, but he looked like he couldn't even hold up the pole, so she looked past him and saw a young man getting out of a shiny black car. She could hear a few words over the raging winds.

"Look, I told you, I'll be a minute. Just wait here," the man said and leaned in the driver's side window.

"Excuse me! Excuse me, sir?" The waitress's voice boomed over the churning ocean.

The man happened to be Nick Collins, who was there to board the Wayan ship and retrieve belongings before the storm hit. "Yes?" he asked the woman who was flailing her arms. He smiled, a little puzzled as to why she'd be out, soaking wet with frazzled hair, yelling at him.

The waitress waved him over. "Look, I have an emergency! I don't want to slip and fall. Can you come in here, please?" she yelled.

"Ah, yeah, sure!" Nick responded quickly when he realized it was an emergency and not that the woman was going through some strange, psychotic state. When he walked in, he was shocked to see that the emergency involved Kate!

"She's in some sort of distress," the server said, while she dried herself off with a white towel from the cafe.

"She doesn't look good. I've got a car outside, and I know her. I'll take her to the hospital right away," he said. He gently picked up Kate, who fell limp in his arms.

"I hope she'll be okay," the waitress said. She wrung her hands as he placed her in the vehicle. "She got some sort of bad news…"

Nick nodded and smiled, not really listening to her. "Thank you!" he yelled back to the woman as they sped off.

The storm had been sudden and ruthless, and by noon, Woodrose was experiencing the full brunt of it. Tourists were caught unprepared by the sudden cyclone. A few had even been setting up for a day at the beach when it hit. They ran for shelter, trying to dodge the sharp needles of rain falling from the black clouds overhead.

When the winds hit fifty-five miles per hour, lifeguards closed the beach, and schools were closed for the day. Dozens of unsuspecting people were out on boats or swimming, prompting the Coast Guard and Navy to conduct rescue operations, saving many beachgoers. However, the train was not so lucky; the rains washed away a 150-foot section of the remaining tracks.

There were some 5000 people who were left without electricity, and 2000 telephones lost service. Communications throughout the affected area were disrupted or rendered impossible. Windows were smashed by the force of the wind, and it took out several at The Drop-In.

Day turned into night in over a matter of minutes when the sun was blotted out by the dark clouds. The Wayan ship's anchor chain snapped in the gale-force winds, and it drifted helplessly toward shore. By evening, the vessel had grounded on the muddy coast.

As soon as word had gotten out about the impending cyclone, Belino and the rest of the crew all took boats to shore, abandoning the Wayan. Belino watched from the boardwalk as the ship swayed and bounced high up and then crashed back down with each massive wave. Ocean breakers pounded away at the wooden superstructure. He immediately knew what he had to do, and he called for his limo…and passport.

There was more to be seen as soon as daylight hit the region, but eventually, the rain settled down to a steady fall. The elegantly dressed people who would frequent the luxurious Wayan now braved the rain, wet mud, and sand to watch and lament the ship's breakup in the surf. Gambling tables and roulette wheels were among the equipment littering the shore for hundreds of yards.

IN THE MORNING, the shoreline was unrecognizable when the sun broke through the clouds. The ocean lapped up gently on the sand as if apologizing for the last night's destruction, and the sun's rays warmly embraced the hills.

After the storm hit the town that day, many of the residents were forced out of the area. The poor could not afford to reconstruct their residences, and the rich vowed never to undergo something like that again and chose to leave for the brighter city lights.

CHAPTER 39
SOMETHING FOREVER GONE

At the hospital where Nick had taken Kate, the corridors, though shiny and bare, somehow offered warmth to the contrast of the dark storm that day. Nick paced up and down the hallway, waiting to hear how Kate was doing. Finally, after what seemed like hours, the doctor appeared from her room, and he stepped out in his white coat with his slick gray hair brushed back and wire-rimmed glasses. He looked up and around the hallway, then caught sight of Nick.

"Are you Mr. Mason?" he asked dryly.

"No, I'm Nick Collins, a close friend of Kate's. Is she alright?"

"Yes, I believe so. She needs to rest. These sorts of things can happen when folks get bad or shocking news."

"What happens now?"

"Well, the good news is that once the reaction to the news has passed the initial shock stage and the symptoms, such as the paling of the skin, physical freezing, and the like, the person gets better on their own. You just have to be supportive and let the news, whatever it may be, sink in." He looked at Nick's worried face. "She'll be alright, son. You can take her home."

"Thank you," Nick replied. He walked past him into the room where Kate was resting. She looked pale but alert.

"Hello, Kate," he started. "Are you feeling better?"

Kate was surprised to see him at first, and her eyes widened in expression. Then she smiled gratefully when she realized why he was there. "Was it you who brought me here?"

"Yep." He smiled amiably and kissed her hand; it still felt cold and looked colorless. "And I'm taking you home as well," he added.

"How long have I been here?" she asked.

"About twelve hours," he replied. "You actually missed the whole drama."

"What drama?"

"It's all over the news," he said and walked over to a radio next to the bed. He turned the dial and tuned into the 24-hour news channel.

The news reporter's voice blared. "We just experienced a tropical cyclone that started yesterday morning. There was a lot of damage, very extensive, in fact, the train, the dock, the pier…all were impacted! The homes that were lined up neatly by the shoreline…they're gone too, and as I hear it, some people went with them." The reporter's voice grew somber. "This is a somber day, perhaps the saddest day that Woodrose has ever experienced." With those words, he ended the broadcast.

The drive home was quiet, and Kate didn't want to talk about what had gotten her in that state. She thanked Nick for his help but insisted on going straight home, and she did.

NIGHT HAD JUST fallen on the town of Woodrose. The beach was silent again, resting from the day's agitation, its waves were shrouded in black, and it too was in mourning.

In a darkened room, a female voice spoke gently into the blackness. "I read somewhere that all rivers lead to the sea," she paused a moment, then continued, "but it never fills up. No matter what, no matter how hard you try, things can only go the way they were meant to go...it's an endless cycle." Kate spoke out to no one as she lay on her bed, looking up at the ceiling. She rolled onto her stomach as if guarding her pain.

Flynn was gone, and so was the burning light inside her soul. Something had changed in her, something was forever gone. Flynn had taken it with him, but that was all right because that's where it belonged. And she would always live waiting...waiting...

Kate didn't know if she had cried out all of her feelings or if she had finally surrendered to her worst fears, but somehow she felt a strange peace overcome her.

She felt the night wrap its sable shroud around her like a blanket, and a sound as smooth as honey flowed in. "Kate..." Her mother's voice broke mildly through the darkness. "Kate, dear, don't cry anymore," she whispered. "Tomorrow, things will look better." Helena knew she wasn't listening, but she wanted to comfort her in whatever way she could.

And it was true that she didn't hear her. At the moment, Kate was deaf to everything around her but her own inner voice. She leaned over and took a book from the very back of the drawer in her nightstand. The book was a gift from a close friend, and Kate had barely read it, but tonight she felt an impulse to. In the cloak of night shadows and quietude, she lit a candle. Its glow, though small, illuminated a marked page of the book she was holding.

She rolled limply on her back on the bed and read softly from it. "Ecclesiastics," she said, forming the words under her breath. *"What does a person gain from all his hard work At which he toils under the sun? A generation is going, and a generation is coming, but the earth remains forever. The sun rises, and the sun sets; Then it hurries back to the place where it rises again. The wind goes south and circles around to the north; Round and round it continuously circles; the wind keeps making its rounds. All the streams flow into the sea, yet the sea is not full. To the place from which the streams flow, there they return so as to flow again."*

Kate thought a while on those words until her eyelids became burdensome, and her hands weakened their grip, finally surrendering to sleep. The open book dropped on her chest, and she slept.

CHAPTER 40
REBUILDING A LIFE

The healing light of autumn had come to the seaside town of Woodrose, and with it came a veil of mist that rose up from the sea. Now, a few years on, Kate watched it climb up to the sky, high to the clouds, like a floating kiss. In her beloved hills of lavender, Kate would sullenly retreat to watch the late afternoon and its brilliant display of light.

The clouds would be filled with golden shimmer as they prepared for the night. Her thoughts were never very far away from Flynn. She thought of him in silence, in quiet places, and in the stillness of night. These memories were kept locked in a treasure chest in a corner of her mind.

Night fell around her, and the stars glittered so close that it seemed she could touch them. The time had gone by quickly, and now she was ready to head for home. She stood and paused a moment to gaze out at the dark ocean. The midnight blue sky deepened and celebrated the brilliance of the living sparks of light and their glory.

Kate felt compelled to turn back to the sea, and she made a wish, a profoundly deep request, one she knew would never be granted, but she blew it out to the waiting waves.

The next morning, she walked the streets of her seaside town. Kate had a decision to make, and it would not be an easy one. How things had changed! It had been three years since the storm, and it had redesigned the area.

The pier had been rebuilt, and it was now stronger than before. Every dawn brought a dreamlike fog to the hills and ocean, and at noon, they were bathed in brilliant sunshine. The docks were different, too; there were new art galleries, boutiques, and a new coffee shop to replace those that had been battered or washed away by the storm.

The Wayan ship had been demolished by the monster waves that day, and three people died on board. Among the dead was Lila.
After that, her father, Dr. Redmond, moved his lab to another state, taking Jack with him.

The worst thing of all to her was the destruction of her family. Much like the Wayan ship, it was imploded, and the remains were scattered about. Her mother filed for divorce immediately after learning about her father's involvement with Belino Rocco. Belino was not among the dead on the boat and couldn't be found after the storm.

Mike Mason took the brunt of the law with no one else around to share the blame, and he got prison time. It broke Kate's heart to see such an ambitious, intelligent man broken down to that point.

Kate remembered the Woodrose of old as she stepped up onto the pier and walked the length of it. She sorely missed it and those times, but time kept moving, and she had to, too.

She was waiting for someone, and that someone came up behind her and wrapped his arms around her waist. "Have you been here long?" Nick asked, with a twinkle in his eye.

"No, I just got here," said Kate.

A bearded man walked by, noticed the two of them, and stopped to hold up a rope with five fish attached to it for them to see. "Catches beginning to slowly come up in the winter months," he said.

Nick put his hands in his pockets and examined the catch. "Doesn't look too bad to me," he said, smiling. He was in a great mood.

"Ha!" the old man grunted, "there's usually twenty on here, boy!"

Nick nodded, and the dimple on his left cheek showed. "Well, you know what they say, a bad day of fishing beats a good day at work!"

The old man threw back his head with laughter. "You got me there, that's true, that's true," he said, and kept walking.

When the old man had passed, and they were alone on the boardwalk, Nick turned to Kate. "Kate...you know I'm not one to beat around the bush with things, so I'll come out and ask." He dug in his pocket and produced a ring box. "Would you do me the honor of marrying me?"

Kate did not look surprised; she was expecting it through the natural course of life and events after that day. She took the ring box and opened it slowly. The diamond was large and glistening. As she put the ring on her finger, one of the facets caught the sunlight and glistened a brilliant blue, and it shone just the same as Flynn's eyes used to in the sun. And Kate felt a sharp pain traverse her heart.

Kate's face became set in sadness, and she was silent. Her immediate response was to give back the ring, but when she looked at Nick and scanned his warm, handsome face full of hope and aspirations, the two things she thought died that storm-ravaged day, she knew she had to move forward.

And so she did, along with the people who remained in Woodrose. They all picked up their personal broken pieces, emotionally, financially, and physically.

Nick and Kate bought a house in the valley part of the state. Nick had surprised her right after the wedding by pulling up into the driveway of a Queen Anne-style home in the town of Blackwater Canyon. "A home fit for a queen," he had told her.

CHAPTER 41
THE CASTLE OF BLACKWATER

Kate was in love with her new Victorian home. It sat on farmland with bushes of blueberries and strawberry vines growing lavishly. The outside of the house was red brick with a steeply pointed gabled roof and a wrap-around porch, the same bisque color as the large bay window's trim. The roof had ornate shingles that resembled fish scales, and they finished the look of the house as icing does on top of a cake.

It was a beautiful, stately home with all the charm of a lady-in-waiting. The inside of their home had the same intricate detailing as the outside, and Nick had spared no expense in imparting the house with decorative woods. Exotic eastern oak and Bird's Eye maple were used for doors, mantles, and window casings.

The Collinses lived some years there, and for the most part, everyone was happy, but to different extents, for there was nothing that could ever fill that void inside of Kate. This isn't to say that she didn't try. There was a side of her that felt compassion and love for Nick, but it was not the same as what she had felt for Flynn. There was no dreaming together, no breathtaking moments to cherish.

At times, Kate would confide these things to her mother. But unfortunately, her mother never had much to say about anything, and ultimately she was left alone to deal with it all.

The heart is complex and can be stubborn. It took some time before Kate's heart found a way to adapt to its new home, and it formed new arteries around the old ones that were no longer usable, and it beat a new life outside of Flynn.

After a year, Mike Mason was released from prison, and much to everyone's surprise, he and Kate's mother gave it a go once again. They stayed the long, golden summers with Kate and Nick and sipped on cocktails by the pool and tunes like *Until* by *Tommy Dorsey*, escaped the RCA record player, and floated over the setting sun.

Autumn came in stronger in Blackwater Canyon than in Woodrose, and the fall season blushed with leaves of bright crimson and burnished gold. Soon after, its march toward winter brought a dark brown hue to the leaves. Neighbors bundled up in soft, lightweight scarves because, though it was winter, it was a California version of one. And the weather would never nip at your nose or sting your cheeks.

A walk by the nearby lake situated on the grounds of the Collins home offered a spectacular sight as the grip on the drying leaves weakened, and they detached from the branches. A rain of muted colors floated and swirled down, caught on a wind, onto the shadowy waters. Whenever Kate stayed long enough into the evening, she would catch a view of the evening stardust cascading its brilliance on the face of the glassy blue lake.

One day, Kate awoke reeling from a nightmare, her heart beat was heavy and fast. It was dawning, and Nick was fast asleep. She got up, moving gently as a cat, and made her way to the kitchen. It was a feeling she hadn't felt before. Ninety percent of her felt fine, but there was that ten percent of ill-feeling. She drank water, and as she did, she heard Nick's footsteps upstairs. He would soon leave for work.

Work for Nick was different now, and he held an underwhelming type of office job. He no longer played the sax. It was put away in its red velvet-lined case, and only occasionally, when Nick would get a craving to play, would the Selmer have a chance to sing its honey-dipped tones. On those days, his shadow could be seen under the porchlight serenading the stars. But he'd had no qualms about trading in the nightclub life when he married Kate for a job as an accountant in a nearby town. And three years into the marriage, he was happy that way.

"Nick?" He heard his wife's voice from the kitchen call to him. It sounded strange to him, and he didn't finish tying the knot on his tie and went downstairs.

"Yeah? I'm over here. Where are you?" he asked and searched the first room downstairs.

"I'm in the kitchen," she replied, and her breathing sounded labored.

Nick moved quickly to the room. "What's the matter? Are you sick?" he asked.

"Yeah, I feel dizzy."

"I'll call the doctor," he said and left quickly to call the family physician.

He stayed with her, helping her to lie down on the couch until he arrived.

The doctor asked about her symptoms when they had begun, and precisely what she felt, then he turned to Nick. "I'm going to have to run some tests to be sure that it's what I think it is. I'm taking her with me back to the clinic," he said. His voice was low and kind.

Nick stood motionless, his eyebrows tensed over his eyes. "Ok. Should I follow you?"

The doctor was unexcitedly moving things around in his black bag, and he stopped, dry, straightened his back, and lowered his glasses on his nose. His dark eyes peered over the metal frame like he was about to say something significant, but instead, he said, "If you wish," and smiled a little. Then he bent down again and clasped the bag closed. "But you don't have to. It's nothing to worry about, really." He came close to Nick and patted his shoulder. "You'll see," he said.

"Nick…" Kate started to speak; she made an effort to sit up.

"You shouldn't do that, Kate," Nick said, helping her to sit, then he swooped her up in his arms as you would a small child who has hurt their knee, and carried her to the doctor's car.

"Should I go with you?" he asked.

"No, you heard the doctor. He's just going to check me out and see what's the matter. Something like this happened to my cousin Peggy a while back," she smiled, reassuring Nick.

"What did she have?" he asked, gently lowering her on the seat.

"Anemia...and she's fine now, so don't worry." She smiled weakly at him, and Nick nodded a couple of times and stepped back from the side of the car. He watched it disappear down the road, then got in his car and drove to work.

CHAPTER 42
THE FROG TEST

Kate returned home feeling better but with no answers. The examination went well, and the doctor took a urine sample to send to a lab. She would hear back from him in a couple of days. Of course, in the interim, she called Liliane just to chat, but mostly to confirm what the doctor didn't want to until the tests were back.

"Liliane! It's me, Kate! How have you been?" She spoke into the phone as she pictured her pausing the sculpting she did in her room to reply.

"Kate! So great to hear from you! All is fine here, mon ami!. What's new?" She was, in fact, sculpting, and she wiped the clay from her hands as she spoke.

"Oh, not too much," Kate began, but Liliane could detect something in her voice.

"Hmm…not much, eh?" asked Liliane.

"I got the frog test done today."

"You mean the Hogben test?!! Katie, I cannot believe this!" Liliane called excitedly into the phone.

"Yeah, the doctor didn't want to tell me that's what he was doing, but I saw the test name on the vial."

"Have you told your mother?"

"No, not yet. I want to be sure, and I didn't tell Nick anything either, you know, he's a worrywart."

"Worrywart! Haha!" Liliane laughed and said, "Great phrase to go with the frog test!"

The frog test, or Hogben test, was a test done on the African Clawed frog to confirm pregnancy. Doctors would ship urine samples to frog labs, where technicians would then inject female frogs in their hind legs with a bit of the urine. Making them extremely angry, but also something else. The animals were then placed back into their tanks, and in the morning, the techs would check for telltale signs, which were frog eggs dotting the water. If the female frog had ovulated, that meant the woman who provided the urine was pregnant. The human hormone chorionic gonadotropin had kicked off ovulation in the frog.

It was the second day of September, Nick had left for work, and Kate was busy when she got the official notice from her doctor. He called to congratulate her and Nick and wish them well. Nick was ecstatic, and Kate was excited, too.

"One day," Nick told her, "not too long from now, we'll see the baby running through that garden of yours." He smiled and looked out of the window as the movie played in his mind. "I can see you now, trying to keep up with him…"

"Him?" she asked.

Nick twisted his body halfway back to look at her. "Ahh, yes, that's true. It could be a little Kate," he said and smiled at the thought. Then he turned to face her. "We haven't thought of a name!" he said eagerly.

Kate smiled. "Yeah, I had been thinking of bringing that up with you," she said.

"Hmm…" He rubbed his chin while thinking. "I'm sorry, Kate, but I imagine it's a boy!" He grinned at her.

Kate shook her head, smiling at him. "Well, alright, but it's on your head if, when *SHE* is born, we only have the name Fred to use."

"Frederika!" he said, poking fun.

"No!" Kate chuckled.

They were up half the night coming up with names. They would laugh but scratch the name off the list instantly if they remembered some odd-looking or peculiar-acting relative that already had it. The next morning, Nick had just left for work when a red Hudson pickup slowly came up her street and rolled to a stop by the curb in front of her house. The man inside the car did not get out. Kate was outdoors in her front yard, trimming the last of the roses and gathering them in a bouquet to bring inside, when she noticed him.

She straightened her back and sheltered her eyes with her hand. Curious to see who was parked in front of her home. At that moment, her mother's car pulled into the driveway, and Helena got out, making a big fuss about something. "Kate! Come see what I found!" she yelled gleefully.

Kate turned her attention to what she had brought. It was a large box, and something was moving inside it. Kate smiled widely. "What is it, mother? What do you have in there?" she sounded excited.

"Oh, Kate!" she called to her as she walked back to her car to retrieve something, and she ducked inside and pulled out a soft yellow blanket with tiny ducks decorating the fabric. "I had this specially made for the baby!" she yelled, holding it up. "And I'm hoping the little one will really love the new puppy!"

At that moment, the engine of the truck abruptly started, and the red pickup hastily pulled away from the curb. Kate's head turned quickly to the side to see if she could catch who was in it, but it was too dark inside to see. She slowly crossed her arms in front of her like she felt a chill, but it was more to appease her angst because there was a feeling attached to the pickup. She thought she had seen it before...she remembered Gavyn had one just like it.

"...You know?" Kate's mother's voice trailed in. "Katie hun, did you hear me at all? What are you looking at, dear?" she asked. She followed her eyes to the street.

Kate's lips were slightly parted, and her eyes were distant. "Nothing," she said under her breath and then turned to her mother.

Helena's face brought Kate back to the present place and time, and she repeated softly, "nothing..." She smiled, but there was a trace of sadness in it. "I was just admiring the tree in the front..."

Her mother analyzed her for a moment with concern, but then dismissed it and said, "Oh, Kate! You and your trees…!" And she picked up the box and carried it inside. "Come on, let's get this little guy out of here before he suffocates!" she said.

Kate opened the large box and looked inside. It was a puppy disguised as a bear cub, for this was the furriest black Newfoundland puppy she had ever seen! Kate gently lifted him from the crate, and the puppy's legs hung limply; his soft-brown eyes were round, big, and helpless. She cradled him, smiling down at his puppy face, then back up at her mom.

"Mom, he's absolutely wonderful! I think I'll call him Bear! Nick's going to love him! Thank you," she said and kissed her on the cheek.

Kate tugged playfully at the dog's ears. "Did you hear that?" she said tenderly to him. "I'm going to call you Bear because that's what you look like…so you better fatten up and live up to it!" The puppy's eyes were alert and showed little white, and he wagged his furry tail.

Her mother sat down on the couch, exhausted from a morning of shopping, and whipped out a cigarette. She fumbled in her brown leather envelope purse for a lighter and lifted out her white embroidered handkerchief and tan gloves and set them on the coffee table in front of her, then rummaged again. "Where is that dang thing?" she mumbled under her breath.

She dug up a small vial of perfume, a coin purse, face powder, and a mirror; her hand fanned the lining until she felt the silver lighter. "Ah!" she said, blissfully happy to have found it. She looked admiringly at Kate and the puppy. The cigarette end glowed red as she stuck it between her red lips, and the stick jigged in her mouth as she spoke. "You're welcome, darling," she said and took a puff.

"Kate, dear, how have you been feeling?" She watched Kate as she brought a small saucer of water for the puppy and set it down.

"I'm okay," she said, concentrated on the puppy. "We'll have to get him some food today," she thought out loud.

"Well, I'm glad!" her mom continued. "Because when I was pregnant with you, I felt miserable the whole time."

Kate looked around for something soft and found a throw on the couch. She brought it for the puppy and made a bed for him, setting him on it carefully. Her feet moved back a few steps to watch his reaction. The puppy took small steps toward the blanket, sniffed around it cautiously, tucked his tiny snout under a corner, and lifted it a little. Once it was puppy-approved, he marched onto it, scratched a couple of times at it, and settled in.

"I think he's going to be happy here," Kate said, smiling at him.

"Oh yeah, I'm sure he will be," said her mom.

The days went by fast, and when Kate looked back on them, it seemed like someone drilled holes in the hourglass, and all the sand spilled out because before she knew it, she was already three months into her pregnancy.

At about six in the morning, Nick kissed her cheek and whispered, "I've got to be at work early this morning."

Kate rolled on her back and softly moaned. "Oh, no…why? I was hoping we could work on the baby's room today!"

Nick's face stayed close to Kate's. "No, baby, not today. But I absolutely promise tomorrow we will have the entire day for it." He kissed her on the lips and smiled. "I'll be back soon," he said, grabbed his car keys, and left.

Kate got up and fed the puppy. He jumped on her lap after eating and snuggled while she drank her coffee. She thought of last night's conversation with Nick, and she spoke quietly to the pup. "No way is my baby going to be called Eunice even if it is after Nick's grandmother!" She smiled and stroked the puppy under his chin.

Then she took out the paper where they had written baby names, and she went through them all once more. Kate rubbed her belly and looked into space. Her mind came to rest on Flynn, and she quickly felt guilty for thinking of how their baby might have looked. She bit her lower lip as she thought of the red pickup. Kate glanced out of the window. Winter had sent its forewarning with heavy rain that morning.

CHAPTER 43
FOUR STORIES UP

December rain had come in from the west, and it was beginning to bear down on the town of Woodrose. So far, they had accumulated two inches along the coast in the morning hours, and more was expected.

Gavyn peered out of the window at the rain; it felt good to be back in Woodrose, he thought, although it would probably slow him down a little on the commute to his job downtown. After the move to New York hadn't panned out as they thought or wanted, he and Eva had decided to buy a small house in their hometown and set up roots there, a place to raise their girl, Helen Rose.

Now with the trolley gone, he drove his red pickup every day to downtown to the Benson Construction site, where he worked as a bricklayer.

By the time he got to work, the rain had become an annoying drizzle. It was the usual party atmosphere when he arrived that morning. Co-workers, Frank and Russ, were on the fourth floor mixing cement to be used in the four-story apartment building in the Coyote Mint district of town. It only took Gavyn stepping off the long wooden ladder and onto the scaffolding for the jokes to start to fly.

"Heya, Gavyn!" Russ greeted him with a grin.

"Hi, Russ…" Gavyn responded and tipped his cap to Frank, who saluted back. Frank continued his conversation, "So Russ, the guy walks into a museum and says… *And this, I suppose, is one of those hideous caricatures you call modern art?*" Frank giggled to himself as he was telling the joke.

"Yeah, and…?" asked Russ

Frank continued, "So he says …*nope, that's just a mirror!*"

Russ and Frank belted out a laugh and looked at Gavyn to join in.

"Ah, you guys gonna go down that road again? It's too early in the morning, and I got a headache," Gavyn complained.

"What road? The joke road? I don't know the way there." Frank laughed and looked at Russ. "Do you know the way, Russ?" he asked, fidgeting with some wood pieces.

Russ glanced at Gavyn, then back at him with nervous eyes as he tried to hold back a laugh. "No…," he said quietly. Russ was soft-spoken and rarely got angry or confrontational with anyone. But he did love being a sidekick to Frank!

"Why don't you tell another one quietly?" he said and glanced again at Gavyn. "You don't mind if he tells the gag quietly, do you?" asked Russ.

Gavyn was unloading the large bag he carried with tools for his job and carefully placing each one in front of him on the floor. He checked and counted each device to make sure he hadn't forgotten any.

He didn't look up but mumbled back to them, "No, I don't care."

Frank had the green light, and so he began, "Ok! Well, here goes. The teacher was describing the dolphin and its habits, so she said..." He put on a high-pitched voice, "...and children... impressively, a single dolphin will have two thousand offspring..." he paused a second for effect, then continued, 'Goodness! Gasped a little girl in the back row. And how about married ones?'

The two men burst out laughing and convulsively chuckled at the joke, and Frank's ears turned red, and his eyes watered from the exhaustion of it. When he caught his breath, he looked at Gavyn. "Did you hear that one, Gavyn? What did you think of that joke, funny, huh?" he asked, grinning.

Gavyn glanced at them over his shoulder, "Wanna know what I think? I think you're both fatheads. That's what I think," Gavyn replied, bothered.

Frank waved his hand sideways at him. "You're an old fuddy-duddy, you know that?"

"Ah, don't snap your cap, Gavyn..." Russ said quietly. "We're just having a little fun, that's all."

"Well, I'm not here to have fun. I'm here to work! And you two would be better off if you took to being more like me than Laurel and Hardy," said Gavyn.

The two chuckled and eventually got quiet and returned to working on the cement. A couple of men in gray suits showed up. They walked along the scaffolding surrounding the perimeter of the building, analyzing something.

Frank noticed them and yelled, "Hey, boys, I hope you got your capes with you cuz we're four stories up!"

A couple of the men looked over. "What was that?" one of the men asked. He had a head of shiny and neatly combed hair. It wasn't that he was hard of hearing, but he didn't understand what Frank meant.

Frank chuckled. "Aaah, someone give this guy a dime, so he can buy a clue!" He turned and grinned at Gavyn, who was manually mixing the thick gray cement. Gavyn didn't look at him, and Frank continued talking to the men. "It's a long ways down, is what I mean. So unless you're Superman, it won't be pretty."

The man looked at Frank as you would a dead bug and then turned back to the others. Frank shook his head at him. "Ya, see? No sense of humor whatsoever," he said. He glanced back up at the man who had his back to Frank. There was just something about his nicely starched white shirt and black pants that bothered Frank. So he called out again. "You boys here to work or just admire the view?" he yelled to them as he placed one brick on top of the other.

The men all turned around again; this time, they focused on him. "What business is it of yours what we're doing here?" One of them, a burly, dark-haired, bushy-browed man, walked over to Frank, and the others followed. Gavyn was still working on the cement, and he glanced up at them with his eyes, then at Frank.

"Hey…" Gavyn said, unobtrusively. "Maybe you should give it a rest, Frank. Who knows who these guys are?"

But Frank was indignant at their body language, the way they walked up to him and challenged him like that, and he stood up and pushed his chest out. "I'll ask whatever I wanna ask," he said. Russ noticed the commotion and quietly stepped over to watch.

"I think you should go back to your lowly job and mind your own business," the glossy-haired man said.

Frank stood up straighter, pushed his chest out a little more, and looked around in disbelief. "You hearing this? This guy's got the guts to challenge me like that and call me a lowlife!" he said, and looked at Gavyn and Russ.

Gavyn stood up, slapped the cement off his hands on his pants, and slowly walked over to Frank. "Look, this isn't worth it," he said. "You get caught fighting up here, and you can forget about that pay raise you wanted. Foreman Hank won't have it, you know that."

Frank listened. His eyes set next to him on the floor, and he nodded. "Ok, you're right." He stuck his chin out towards the man. "It ain't worth it!" he said disgustedly.

The man stood staring at him and waited for his next move, but when there was none, he shook his head and shrugged. The other men had walked back to the other side of the building, and the glossy-haired man joined them.

Frank twisted his mouth toward the man. "Idiot!" he said, a little under his breath. "The guy thinks he's a regular Cary Grant. Oh, and thanks, Gavyn, didn't stop to think bout the raise."

Gavyn nodded and wiped the sweat from his temples and forehead with a bundled cloth he carried in his back pocket, especially for that.

Frank turned to Russ. "I wonder how much they're paying those guys nowadays?" he asked.

Russ shrugged and mumbled, "That's above my pay grade. If you wanna know, ask Hank in the construction office," he replied.

Frank paused a moment. "Nah, I was just wonderin."

They worked on in silence for a while. The sound of scraping metal and hammering was the only thing to be heard, but not for long. Frank thought of something new to share. "Hey Gavyn, know what I'm gonna do in a couple of weeks?" A brightness came over his tanned, leathery face.

"No, what?" Gavyn asked, stringing a line that would act as a level for the bricks.

"I'm headed to Wrigley Field!" he said, amplifying his chest and smiling. "You been there?" he asked.

"To which Chicago or Wrigley Field?" asked Gavyn.

"Either one."

"Yeah, I've been to Chicago, went to a fighting match there." For the first time, Gavyn stopped what he was working on and looked out over the buildings. The city was all washed in gray, and billows of smoke could be seen from factories in the distance. Frank examined Gavyn's face. It was unusual to see him have any type of expression and much less one of sentiment, but he could swear he saw his eyes get misty.

Gavyn didn't look back at Frank but continued to talk and looked out into the distance. "My brother Flynn won that fight," he mumbled. For the moment, on the roof of the building, his memory was engulfed by the sounds and sights of that prize-winning boxing match. And he stood with his body rigid and his thoughts remote.

"Hey!" Frank hit his sleeve with his hand. "Hey, Gavyn!" He made his voice sound mystical. "Come back, come back!" He chuckled, looking at his faraway face. Gavyn became aware of him and ducked back down to work.

Frank began to lay out the bricks according to Gavyn's line. "It's like I was telling you," he said. "I'll be going to the World Series in Chicago!"

Russ came from around the corner of the building with a sack of cement thrown over his shoulder. He stepped carefully around the tools and bricks. "What did you say, Frank?' he asked and gleefully chucked the bag down.

"I'm going to Chicago for the World Series!" Frank yelled.

"Beat me, daddy eight to the bar!! How come you get to go? Any spare tickets?" Russ was hopeful and beamed with excitement.

"I might...I might..." Frank strung him along for a bit. He loved to tease his friends that way, but by now, most who knew him knew better.

"Aw, come on, Frank. You got any or not?" Russ asked.

"Yeah, you know, come to think of it, I think I can get one for you!" Frank replied. He was even more excited to be going with a buddy.

"I'll blow all my lettuce on it, so I don't care how much. Just let me know," replied Russ.

Gavyn shook his head from side to side disapprovingly. "That's going to be what, seven dollars from your paycheck for the entrance, plus taxi, plus plane ticket!" he said.

"Well, don't forget, you're the only one here that can't afford it on account of your wife and kid," Frank boasted. "We were smarter. No wife, no kids, means more money for ourselves!" He smiled broadly.

"Golly, I've never been on a plane before," Russ said apprehensively.

Frank looked at the younger Russ. He would forget that he was only eighteen years old. "Ah, it's nothing!" He tried to reassure him. "Right, Gavyn?" he asked.

Gavyn was laying brick over brick carefully, wiping the excess gray mortar that would squish out in between the layers with his trovel. He stopped and looked over at the two of them. "Yeah, that's right," he said, nodding slowly.

"Gavyn, you've been on one of those big birds, right?" Russ asked nervously. "What's it like?"

Gavyn stopped and turned to him, and he placed his cement-covered hand on his hip. "When I flew, it was so smooth…" his hand mimicked the plane flying, "that when the plane was halfway down the runway and started to climb up, none of us even realized what had happened. Until we saw the orange fields rushing away behind us and the factory lights of the oil derricks winking through the murk of Signal Hill ahead."

Russ stood with his mouth open, looking at him. "Gee, that sounds okay, I guess." His eyes looked out into nothing, and he tried to imagine it.

Frank laughed and patted his back. "You'll be okay, kid! We'll be there before you know it."

Russ smiled and nodded.

Gavyn grew quiet again and went back to work. His mind was heavy with thought. Something was eating at him, something he needed to do, but he just couldn't seem to get himself to do it. He hammered loudly as he thought. The sound was more of a dull thud than the metallic sound of nails. He liked hammering; it felt like it helped to release his tension and somehow made him think better.

Some hours after lunch, the foreman bricklayer dropped by to view the work being done that afternoon, and it all looked good, he said. That was good news for Gavyn, who wanted to get a raise. Things were already good for him and Eva, but with the baby, he tried to make things more comfortable.

The rain had let up around 7:00 in the evening, and Gavyn packed up his bag to leave for the day. He stashed away his tools and took a moment to wipe his face down with a dry towel. The sweat would have to work as the cleaning agent until he got home to shower. Gavyn waved to Frank and Russ. "I'm gonna skedaddle," he said.

"Oh yeah, me too…see ya tomorrow!" Russ said.

"See ya later," Frank joined in.

THE RED PICKUP had a little trouble starting up, and he waited for a minute to try the engine again, so he wouldn't flood it, then cranked it again. That time, it fired up as if it had fallen asleep and suddenly awoken, and Gavyn began the long drive home.

It was 7:30 at night, and the fog was creeping in. He drove past the newly built May Co building. It had a huge gold-tiled cylinder with *May Company* written on its façade that hugged the corner of where the cross streets met. It looked modern and sleek to Gavyn. Downtown was looking like the city of tomorrow, and it had changed quite a bit. He was probably the only one in the world who didn't like the change, he thought to himself. A big smile grew across his face when he heard a song stream in over the car radio. Maybe Bing Crosby was trying to tell him something with his song called *The San Fernando Valley*.

"Sing it, Bing!" Gavyn said under his breath, smiling. That's what he liked too. No changes, just easy breezy living. By the time the Philco Radio Hour had finished, he had reached Marine Street.

He detoured from his usual way to go down a road he hadn't driven since Flynn's calamity. The factory was up a small hill, and you made a left at the light to reach it. Gavyn climbed the hill slowly; it was hard to make out the traffic light with the fog now heavier, but as he got closer, he saw the green shine, and he made a left.

Although it was dark and cloudy, he could see the skeleton of the once two-story factory. It had been left in place to rot, with the owner inexplicably leaving it in disrepair. Pieces of gray concrete had fallen away, exposing the dark, burnt interior, and the windows were all blown out. He drove by slowly, eyeing it as if he would find some sort of incriminating evidence of something that had happened years ago. But there was nothing, only a man in a suit walking his dog. The man observed Gavyn suspiciously, and Gavyn picked up his speed and drove on.

CHAPTER 44
DAYS GONE BY

The next morning, a gold light permeated the thin clouds leftover from yesterday's rain in Blackwater Canyon. It created long, shimmering rays that fanned out from each cloud and extended to the ground. Kate awoke from sleep disoriented. She had fallen asleep on the couch. Her brain felt sluggish, and she couldn't process the fact that Nick had not returned home last night. She had fallen asleep, waiting for him to arrive.

Her heartbeat felt feeble, and she felt a weakness in her bones that made her body tremble a little when she picked up the phone to call her mother. The phone rang a couple of times.

It was 7:00 am, and her mother was up having coffee. She sauntered over to the phone, yawning. "Hello?" she said groggily.

"Mom?" she spoke, but Kate didn't recognize her own voice. "Mom, something's happened," she said

"What is it, Kate?" Her daughter's voice woke her up. "You sound alarmed."

"I am. It's Nick. He didn't come home last night."

"What? How can that be? Did you two fight yesterday?"

"No! No, mom...everything was fine when he left," her voice cracked.

There was a firm knock on her door at that moment. "Oh, hold on, mom," Kate let out a long breath of relief. "I think he's here. He probably forgot his key!" she said breathlessly into the phone receiver. "I'll be right back, I'm going to let him in," she said, placing the receiver on the table.

"Ok, hun, I'll hang on. Bop him over the head for me, will ya?" her mom yelled into the phone. She, too, was relieved, and she smiled and shook her head as she waited.

The muffled voices were hard to hear over the phone, but it was more than one male voice, and Kate's mother became worried and called out to her husband with the phone still up to her ear. "Mike!" she yelled, cupping her hand over the receiver. "Mike, come here quick!"

Mike Mason rushed over to her with a towel still draped around his shoulders from shaving. "What is it?" he asked.

"Kate?" Helena called into the phone. "Kate?"

"What's going on?" Mike asked.

"I don't know. I was talking to Kate, and Nick was missing and..." Helena was frazzled and nervous, along with an achy downward pulling in the middle of her chest. Something was very wrong.

Mike Mason took the phone. "Kate, it's your dad, honey…" His nerves made him speak in almost a yell into the phone. He could hear the men and Kate's voice rise and fall. "Get the car ready!" he told his wife.

He was listening intently, trying to hear what they were saying, when there was a sudden "Hello?" from an unfamiliar male voice on the other end of the line.

Mike straightened up instinctively. "Who is this?" he demanded to know.

"This is Sergeant Forester, sir. I'm with the Blackwater Canyon Police Department."

Mike Mason leaned back on the kitchen table. "The police?" he said numbly. "Yes, sir, perhaps you'd better come. Your daughter is not doing well. Her husband, Nick, was in an accident."

"Nick? Where did they take him? How is he doing?"

"I'm sorry, sir. You should come to see her. I'm afraid he's passed away."

It was a suffocating feeling. The night had crept in and seemed to wrap around Kate's throat and slowly tighten. Her mother was staying with her for now and perhaps longer. She did not want to think about moving out of the house she once shared with Nick or the future for her baby, now fatherless. It happened so instantly and fluidly.

Kate couldn't sleep and stayed up late staring up at the moon, that mysterious orb that fascinated her. It glowed alive, and in some strange way, she figured it must be breathing, for it was there night after night, year after year. That night made her think of intangible things, things that fade away. Like the platinum of the moon and how it disperses into the daylight. After having been so formidable the night before, it was at the mercy of the sun and its dynamism. And at daybreak, its brilliance wanes. Kate felt just like that, as if she were at the mercy of life's unexpected twists and turns, and now, that power of trust, love, and everything she held dear had been drained from her. Her eyes felt swollen and heavy. Crying did not ease the feeling.

She must have fallen asleep sitting up in her bed, and towards the morning, she was jolted by a sharp, inner pain that made her whole body shudder. Suddenly, she couldn't straighten up, and she was doubled over in pain. "Mom!" The yell came out as a hoarse whisper. "Mom!" She tried again, and this time, it belted out in a short sound like a car horn blowing.

Her mother, who was barely waking up, heard the sound and rushed to her room. Kate was sitting on the bed, covered in blood.

The day whizzed by as if everything and everyone had been riding on a playground roundabout. And the strongest kid in class was vigorously pushing it round and round. When the spinning finally stopped, Kate was in a hospital bed with her mother and father by her side.

"What happened?" she asked weakly.

Her mother's anguished face said it all. "You, uh, you lost the baby, honey," she said, softly.

Kate's eyes were wide and lined in red. She wanted to burst out crying, but the pain was too deep. Helena wrapped her arms around her girl and cradled her, and after a while, Kate let go and wept bitterly.

Helena tended to Kate for the next few days at home. She would get up early in the day and cook breakfast for the three of them while Kate slept. "Go get the beach house ready, Mike," she said softly one morning, pouring the brown brew into his cup. "I'm going back, and I'm going to take Kate with us. She needs to leave here," she said.

Mike nodded, but before he could speak, Kate appeared at the kitchen door. "No," she said dryly. "I appreciate it, Mom. But I'm staying here," she said.

"But Kate, wouldn't you rather go to the beach house and..." Helena tried convincing her, but Kate had made up her mind.

"And what, Mom? There's nothing there for me anymore." Kate looked at the floor, then back up. "I think the two of you should go and take some time for yourselves. I know this has been hard on all of us."

Mike and Helena wouldn't have any of it. They wanted to stay there with their hurting child, but in the end, Kate won out, and they left for their home in Woodrose.

The first winter alone was hard on Kate, but she didn't let on to her parents. When they would telephone, she would tell them she was doing fine, but the truth was behind the undrawn curtains. Kate began to write letters she would never send. It sometimes eased her pain a little and sometimes made it worse, but she felt impelled to talk to Flynn even though he was gone. One night, she noticed a book lying half under her bed, and she picked it up to read it.

IT WAS AROUND midnight, and the coolness of the night crept in through her open bedroom window. Kate began to read a poem at first to herself; then, without noticing, she began to form the words with her lips, and her voice spilled out softly into the room.

DAYS GONE BY

To think of him
It still makes me cry
Although the feelings inside
Have found a way to hide

It's the memories, you know.
That won't let it die.
It's the feeling he awoke.
That won't say goodbye.

And no, there will never be another
With such brilliant eyes
Or another tender smile
That fills my soul with light
Another man to touch my heart
The way he did that summer night…

Kate paused a moment, and she shut her eyes tight, and tried to hold back the tears that were forming, and then she continued to read.

To reach that love, that place in time
To take him there is a dream of mine
Beyond the stars to a place that hides
Where the glitter of the stars
Can't compete with his eyes
And our love, like the luminaries
Will never die
Yes, this love is still just as strong
But I'm not surprised
For the days gone by
Don't seem like a long, long time

Kate slowly closed the book. She buried her face in her hands and wept, first angrily, then bitterly, until she finally resigned and dropped back on her bed. She was limp, hearing the soft murmuring of the trees outside her window as their leaves rustled to the rhythm of the wind. It sounded much like an ocean wave, she thought, much like the ocean back at Woodrose when the waves would rise and fall and be followed by a sudden surge, then ripples in the waters. How she wished to be back there now with Flynn.

The years moved on, and Kate spent her time with her dog, Bear, and he became her confidant. She would talk with him as if he were human, and at times, he almost acted as if he were, and she found peaceful happiness watching him and his antics.

The spring's pale golden light marked the end of winter, the first buds of her Peace Tea Roses appeared, and Kate's spirits lifted.

She and Bear would wake up early and walk in the fields near her home, and she'd stop and sit on a rock to watch the horizon turn from dark gray to a blush peach at dawn. As spring neared summer, around mid-morning, Kate could see from her kitchen window the soft coral of the sky deepen to a burnished gold like a sheer silk scarf that adorned the fields.

Each year, Kate's roses grew more abundant and more beautiful. Her prized ones were tall and broad, with dense cupped six-inch blooms of primrose-yellow with soft rose shadings. Every morning of every passing summer, she would work in her garden.

She had been more than content to swap her Hermès gloves for a stout pair of gauntlets and her silk dresses for trousers. And her heart finally had a home. She kept it locked in a fortress in a place that was hidden in the deepest part of her. After the first years dragged on, the latter ones whizzed by so fast she couldn't keep track of them. And she didn't want to.

CHAPTER 45
THE MYSTERIOUS NOTE

It was in the winter of 1979 that the forecast was given. There hadn't been a storm as the one predicted for Blackwater Canyon. Not since the cyclone in Woodrose so many years before. And when she awoke that morning and slipped on her robe to go outside and fetch the newspaper, she could already feel heaviness in the air.

The paper had been left near the curb. And Kate walked down the path that led to her home to retrieve it. Kate didn't mind walking the few steps, and she also remembered that she hadn't picked up her mail the night before, so Kate got that too while she was there. She tucked the newspaper under her arm, and with her hands free, she plucked a couple of envelopes out of the mailbox. Then carefully closed the door of the box and followed the path back to the house. Inside, Bear was sniffing his bowl and nudging it so that it moved noisily across the kitchen floor.

"Oh, Bear!" she said softly under her breath. "You're hungry already? Well, I suppose we'll have breakfast together," she told him.

Bear had grown old by Kate's side, and his vision had dimmed. Kate could not think of the day he would no longer be with her. To ease her anxiety, her father had given her a cat she named Ella. The Siamese kitten had no problem growing up alongside Bear, and they kept each other company.

That morning, the cat had curled its tail around her legs. Ella sauntered about in the kitchen like a queen. Kate smiled and stroked her fur. She understood her language; she, too, needed to be fed.

The pet food was kept in an overhead cupboard, and she reached for the cans, opened them, and plopped the wet food in their own dishes. Bear wasted no time munching on it, and he tore at it as if he hadn't eaten in a couple of days, instead of hours.

Kate poured herself a cup of coffee and sat down. She thought of calling to see how her father was doing. He had been diagnosed with pneumonia and had spent some time in the hospital. But just yesterday had been allowed to go home. She would call right after breakfast, she thought, and she sipped on her coffee and picked up the envelopes from yesterday's mail.

She sifted through them… a bill from the Gas Co., an advertisement for a new furniture store that was opening nearby, and a personal one addressed to Kate Mason. Who would refer to her as Mason? She turned it over; there was no return address, but it was postmarked Woodrose Post Office.

Kate sat up straight and set her cup down. How strange. Who could know her address, who lived in Woodrose? Her hands shook slightly as she opened it, but she wasn't sure why. She retrieved the lined paper and unfolded it.

Immensely important:
Go to Kings Hospital in Manhattan, New York.
Look for room 145.
Gavyn

Kate's whole body was now shaking, and she couldn't control it. It was alien to feel this way since there was really no reason to, but there was something about hearing from someone connected so intimately with Flynn. Her eyes roved the words.

Kate's mind wouldn't stop reeling, almost to the point of getting an ache. She was confused; she felt excited to hear from Gavyn, but she was shocked to hear he was perhaps hurt and needed her for something. Of course, she would go!

There was something else inside the envelope, and when she peered inside, a plane ticket to New York was visible. Gavyn must need her help. She quickly got up and began to make plans to be there on the next morning's flight. Bear was sent to her mother's, and Ella was going to stay with a neighbor.

The next morning, the day had dawned with heavy rain. Kate awoke, dressed, and waited for the taxi to the airport.

IT WAS 5:00 am in Manhattan when she arrived from California. She quickly got out of the taxi and walked into the hospital.

The halls were dim and quiet, with only the shuffling of nurses' shoes as they walked by her every now and then.

The fifth door on the right had the numbers 145 above it. Kate looked down the corridor as she placed her hand on the steel knob and turned it.

Inside, the room was cold and shadowy, and deathly quiet. Kate stepped into a depersonalized, blackened room. The only illumination was a stream of pale sunlight from a window near the bed. Her eyes jetted around the room nervously as she prepared herself for what she was about to see, and then they landed on the figure lying in bed.

She approached hesitantly, taking small, quiet steps; she didn't want to wake him. It took a moment for the image to process in her brain. The shadowed light reflected on the man's body sideways in slants across his face and hands.

His fingers were interlaced and resting on his stomach. Kate felt her body numb. She never expected to see what was before her. One of the fingers of his hand moved, and a flash emitted from it. She moved closer to look at what it was.

"Who's there?" the man asked quietly.

Kate was silent as she approached his bedside. There were long shadows from the trees outside the window that fell over the man on the bed. In the dimness, she could barely make out his face, but as she got closer, she realized that the facially scarred man was Flynn.

She instantly felt the strength go from her legs as she stood over him. Kate felt frozen and unable to move from the shock. Her breathing was coming shallow and irregular, but her heart beat steadily.

How could it be? Was she hallucinating? Gavyn and Flynn didn't look alike...but he was the one who contacted her... how could this be Flynn?

Kate trembled uncontrollably as she gently took his hand and cradled it in hers. The scars around his eyes were set from some time ago, and they ran jaggedly around his temples. She could see several thick old scars on the back of his hand and something shiny on his finger. It was the ring she hadn't seen in many years, Flynn's boxing championship ring.

The room was intensely quiet. But outside in the hallways, there was a variety of sounds. Nurses talked in undertones. Beeps and alarms floated in from somewhere outside the door. But all of it was wrapped in a sort of fog, like in a dream. Kate shakily brought his hand up to her lips, and she softly kissed it.

Flynn moved slightly, and she felt his hand tense up, but his eyes remained closed. Her eyes felt painful and raw as they filled with tears, but they did not run down her face. Her sight followed one of the lines from the top of the machine down to where it entered Flynn's arm. She gently smoothed the skin where the tip penetrated his flesh. She remembered how golden his skin shone in the summer sun. Now his skin looked thin, pale, and void of life.

"Flynn," she spoke softly through tears. She was desperate to hear him speak.

Flynn moaned a little as if waking from a month-long sleep, and then his lashes flitted. Kate pulled a chair next to his bed. She sat down and rested her elbows on the mattress's edge to be close to his face. "Flynn, it's me," she said gently.

She didn't recognize her own frail-sounding voice. After a moment of silence, she wasn't sure if Flynn could hear her, so she took his face and kissed it. Her lips stayed on his skin; it was Flynn's face she had just kissed! The realization came to her suddenly. The significance of that overwhelmed her. His mouth parted slightly, and the name Kate escaped along with his breath.

Kate's lips trembled as they formed a smile, and tears ran freely down her cheeks. His story was in the scars. Some of them looked thick, long, and jagged, one above his left eyebrow and two directly above his lids. They told of a blast like that of dynamite. Because of the zigzag pattern of the lines. And told of the time when it must have occurred because of their thickness.

Flynn suddenly grasped her hand and wrapped his fingers around it tightly. He peered into the darkness, but not at her.

"Is it you? But how?" he asked, with his voice in a trembling whisper.

"Yes, baby, it's me," replied Kate, and her voice betrayed her with a crack.

Flynn struggled to sit up, and his face suddenly beamed in the darkness. Kate kissed his hand again, and he smiled. They both laughed shakily and softly. The strength of her love came flooding back as if the solid ice that had encased the two of them was shattered, and time had never moved on from the last time she saw him.

Flynn cleared his throat. "It's dark in here. Come closer," he said, and she pressed her wet cheek against his lips.

"Don't cry, Kate. Please, don't cry," he whispered.

His eyes were misty, full of backed-up years of sorrow. He swallowed, and the inside of his throat felt like sandpaper. "How did you find me?" he asked.

Kate shook her head. "I got your note," she said, gathering strength and composure in her voice.

"Note?" Flynn sounded confused. Then he settled into the thought quickly, "It was Gavyn," he said. "Gavyn sent you the note on where to find me! I could kill him and hug him at the same time!" he laughed, but it sounded strained.

"It doesn't matter how, love. Yes, think it must have been your brother." Kate looked down, smiling big through tears. Then she looked back at him and sighed. "Come with me," she whispered softly in his ear.

His hands were shaking, and he reached for her face. "I can't believe you're here."

"Yes, all you had to do was call me, and I would have been here. I don't know why you didn't. I think I'll never understand why you kept us apart. But it doesn't matter now. I'll always be here. "

The corners of Flynn's mouth turned downward. "I know it's hard to understand, but you can't see the whole picture right now, and funny, I should say it that way," he said. "Maybe you won't want to be here after I tell you..."

"...Flynn," Kate interrupted. "I meant what I said. Nothing will come between us again," she insisted.

A silence fell. Then suddenly, Flynn's voice sounded like before. "First of all... I love it when you talk like that." He smiled weakly, and Kate laughed shakily and unexpectedly. "But what I need to tell you is..." he paused, "it's that I'm blind," Flynn stated.

Kate's eyebrows raised, but the rest of her expression remained aglow with love. She once again traced the scars above his eyes slowly with her forefinger. "I thought there might be something wrong with your eyes when I saw these," she said softly.

"It's gotten progressively worse. At first, I could see some, but now I only see shadows."

Kate glanced around the hospital room, then back at him. "Is that why you're here?" she asked.

"Yeah," he said, and the corner of his mouth gathered to the side. "A specialist says he can operate and bring some vision back…maybe all."

"Is it a dangerous operation?" she asked.

"Not really."

"Then why do you frown at it?"

"There's been a ton of doctors and promises year after year..." his voice trailed off. "This new guy now apparently thinks he can do some kind of groundbreaking operation to help. I said yes, but I'm skeptical."

Kate breathed in slowly and long, then out, and her eyes rested on his face. "You know, they say half the battle is having faith that things will have a good outcome and in God."

Flynn's mouth was downcast and hardly moved when he said, "I don't think he likes me too much."

Kate laughed softly. "Stop already!"

"Ok," he said, elated to have her near and holding her hand tightly.

CHAPTER 46
FROM DARKNESS COMES LIGHT

The night shadows were on the move as the moonlight washed over the hospital courtyard outside. The clouds were separating and dispersing into mist as they prepared for the arrival of the morning sun.

Kate had closed her eyes for what seemed a moment. When she was awoken by a nurse walking by the room with a cart. "I must have fallen asleep," she said groggily. "It was a long flight."

She made an effort to sit up, but Flynn took her hand and brought it to him. "Is it morning?" he asked.

"Yes," she said, looking at the white light filtering in through the blinds of the window.

Flynn swallowed hard and began to speak in a mutter. "I had a dream last night." He paused a moment. "I heard about your husband…Gavyn told me you got married," he said. His eyes became fixed in front of him, though on nothing.

"Yes, I married Nick, …but he died in a car accident years ago," Kate said quietly.

There was a pause again.

Flynn spoke softly into the darkness. "Must have been difficult. Did you love him?"

"Yes," she answered. "It was difficult, and while I did love Nick, I wasn't in love with him. He was there when I thought you had died." Kate took his face in her hands gently. "Why did Gavyn lie to me like that? she asked.

"It wasn't Gavyn's idea. It was mine." He closed his eyes. His voice became a gentle whisper. "He didn't want to do it, in fact."

"Why in the world would you ever do that to me? It was devastating!" Kate's eyes filled with tears.

"Because I was severely injured, Kate. Because I love you, and I didn't want you to have to be a nurse to me instead of my wife!" His voice was tense as it propelled into the darkened room.

There was a pause, and Kate spoke softly. "I will be your nurse, I will be your friend, I will be anything you need or want me to be because, Flynn, that's what it is to love."

It grew quiet, and a gentle silence filled the room like a warm, soft blanket. They both somehow felt comfort in releasing the bottled-up emotions they had kept in for so long, and now the reasons why they had kept them no longer mattered.

Kate's voice radiated into the room as delicately as the ethereal blush of a sunrise over the hills. "The day I thought you had died was the worst of my life. I was inconsolable," she paused. "My mother didn't know what to do with me." Her lips formed a weak smile at the memory. "I thought I would go insane, and I cried until I had no strength left in me, Flynn."

In her mind's eye, she could see herself that distressful night. Kate fought hard not to give in to the tears again, but the memory made them flow. This time, however, she felt strangely happy, happy to be crying at what was now, after finding Flynn alive, only a distant memory.

She smiled, staring out, envisioning the event. "That night, I lay on my bed, staring up at the ceiling, when suddenly a calm came over me. I was thinking of something I had read some time ago, and it brought me peace," she said. Kate suddenly felt the same mellifluous feeling as that night. But this time, it was a quiet joy. All the harshness of the years had melted away in a moment, just being with Flynn again.

Flynn smoothed her hair back gently. "I wish I could have been there to comfort you," he said.

"It's alright now. It's all in the past."

Flynn followed the length of her hair with his hand. "Your hair is so long now."

Kate smiled. "Yep, and unfortunately, there is now a little bit of salt sprinkled about," she said.

"I like salt," he said. "Kate, I spent all these years alone because no one else was comparable to you." He caressed her face, slowly remembering every curve in her features, the arch in her brow, and the prominence of her cheekbones.

There was a faraway sound of a speaker calling a doctor's name out in the corridors, and that was the only indication of where they presently were. Still, in their minds, it was as if they were back in Woodrose. A peaceful quiet filled the room. Flynn looked fixedly in front of him. As if he could see the doors to the closet that were directly opposite the bed.

"All of the things that happened back in Woodrose," Kate began to say. "Your dad and his endless desire to achieve greatness through you and Gavyn at whatever cost, and my dad's greed, such a regretful trait for an otherwise wonderful father, and all of those needful things came full circle. It was just like I read that night…nothing was gained from their toiling under the sun. All of the bickerings, scheming, lying, and all of the hurtful things that took place back in Woodrose. It was all for nothing."

Flynn pulled her down and held her tight. She smiled, and her eyes became wistful. "Come with me, Flynn. Let's go away just as we planned so many years ago. Remember when we'd dream of traveling out to sea?"

"Yes!" he said, beaming.

"The waiting is over, and the heartaches are in the past." Kate moved her head to glance at his face, then placed her cheek over his heart again. "Besides, you promised me, remember?" she asked.

"Yes, I do remember my love. That day by the ocean, I can see it vividly in my mind," he said. In the dim room, they emitted brightness from the memory. Bright as the sun that shone on the pier that day.

She held his face in her hands and kissed his lips gently. Her hair had the fragrance of lavender, and Flynn smiled at the memory of the hills. Kate gazed into the luminescent beauty of his eyes, and they were the color of heaven.

www.ingramcontent.com/pod-product-compliance
Lightning Source LLC
Chambersburg PA
CBHW060349260626
47160CB00006B/2248